THE
LAWNMOWER
CELEBRITY

Ben Hatch

INDIGO

First published in Great Britain in 2000
by Victor Gollancz
An imprint of Orion Books Ltd
Orion House, 5 Upper St Martin's Lane,
London WC2H 9EA

ISBN 0575 06833 7

Typeset at The Spartan Press Ltd,
Lymington, Hants
Printed and bound by Clays Ltd, St Ives plc

For Mum

FEBRUARY

Thursday, 11 February

We sat watching *Have I Got News For You*, Dad in his armchair, one hand held up to his head to block out the sight of me on the sofa like I was an eyesore. 'You do realise Broadcasting House was evacuated while they went over it with a robotic sensor, don't you? That the Humphrys interview was cancelled, Nicky Campbell's phone-in was late, and that the Prime Minister nearly missed a meeting with Gerhard Schröder?'

'You do realise the only reason the van wasn't actually blown up in a controlled explosion was that I happened to recognise the number plate on the memo during a Director-ate Heads meeting – a meeting attended by the *DG*? How did you get my swipe card? How dare you use my car-park space without asking. You are a selfish little prat, do you know that?'

How was I to know Tony Blair was coming into BH to give an interview? How was I to know security had been stepped up because of the Iraq thing? How was I to know they checked every number plate off against a list of BBC employees' cars? How was I to know Mum's old ironing van wasn't on this list? And Dad normally parks in Television Centre – I didn't even know he'd be in the building.

Dad spoke quietly, emphasising every word. 'You used my car-park swipe card – that you stole – to drive a white van – a van favoured by terrorists – through an armed cordon, to park in a spot surrounded by police tape – a spot specially reserved for the Prime Minister of this country. You are un-fucking-believable. I hate you tonight.'

Description of Dad: he is quite fat and very short. He has blue watery eyes, and quite a long nose, and he's balding rapidly. Dad's ultimate ambition is to be Director General of the BBC, although he won't admit it, and for me to get a job in the City so I have enough money to leave home.

Before we went to bed there was a documentary about artificial intelligence that made matters worse. Some scientist at a Reading Cybernetics lab reckoned there could be a robot with a cat-sized brain by the year 2010, but that a shortage of government funds would probably thwart the aping of the human neural brain network for a lot longer. It tallied with my theory that robots should be doing all the work in this day and age, and Dad had another go at me when I commented on this.

'It's the age of leisure. The technology's there. We split the atom, invented a particle accelerator, but we can't invent a machine to be a recruitment consultant. It *is* absurd, Dad.'

'You. Are. Not. Going. To. Lose. This. Job,' said Dad, without looking at me, and then, as if the two things were connected, he brought up the fact I hadn't bought the new work shoes he gave me £50 for the other day. 'That money's not to be pissed up the wall, do you hear me?'

'I'm getting them on Saturday – calm down. And I'm not talking about losing my job. I'm just expressing a point of view. I'm talking about robots,' I said.

'You. Are. *Not*. To. Lose. This. Job,' Dad just repeated.

Mr Gatley, from the London Writing School, is going to send me a piece of his own writing, and he came up with a good analogy in his letter today about my writer's block. He told me I wasn't allowing my imagination off its leash.

'If I get writer's block,' he said, 'I think about my imagination and actually picture it as a large panting dog. In my head I pat my imagination on the back and tell it to go fetch. I've been a professional writer for twenty five years and I've never ceased to be amazed at what it brings back.'

Mr Gatley also corrected my spelling for ameliorate and told me to use fewer semi-colons. For some reason; I love; semi-colons.

Friday, 12 February

Sarah and her fiancé Rob came over to cook roast beef today. Normally the conversational weight is distributed equally on these occasions with Sarah initiating topics for discussion like a TV anchorwoman: 'How's your writing course coming along, Jay?' . . . 'How's school, Charlie?' . . . 'I read that article on you, Dad, in the *Sunday Times* – any news from the board on the appointment?' It used to be good fun dropping irresponsible bombshells at these mealtimes, but because of the van thing nobody asked me anything today. I was ostracised, and had to eat my parsnips silently, listening to Sarah's boring nuptial arrangements, and Dad name-dropping about which famous people he sat next to at which BBC dinner.

Charlie's been scratching his elbows again and keeps getting 'urges' to do things that he thinks will prevent bad luck. It was today's main theme. Charlie's urges started with touching wood, but now he has to peer round corners before he gets to them, he slaps lamp-posts and telegraph poles, and sometimes, if he's really worried, he gets other people to join in, too. Yesterday, for instance, he made me do twenty-five keepy-uppies with the sponge ball to stop a fatal accident involving Grandad that he wouldn't discuss.

I tried to be positive after Charlie'd left the table to feed Greeny-Slowy, his new pet turtle. I said I thought Charlie's scabs looked better, and he hadn't scratched once through pudding.

'He was in the pads on Thursday,' said Dad, glaring at me. Charlie wears special elbow pads when his scratching gets really bad. 'And on Monday when Angela picked him up he had so many urges they were late for school. Now that's not fair on Angela . . . And, Jay, exactly why did you buy Charlie that turtle? Because he wanted it, or to annoy me? It was to annoy me, wasn't it? Well, it *has* annoyed me. I've got the Home Secretary coming to dinner any day and I

5

wanted everything to be nice and now the whole living room stinks like a reptile house. Well done!'

Before Sarah left she read me an article on New York novelist Jay McInerney which pissed me off as well. She'd saved it specially. 'The young *Jay*, said Sarah emphasising our common name, and smiling at Dad, 'who would later become the Brat Pack leader of a new literary scene, couldn't settle into a job. He was a misfit, permanently the outsider, drawn to writing through failure.' Sarah looked up at me. 'Misfit, failure. It's *you* my little brother,' she said laughing. Sarah never misses a chance to belittle me, which will be a shame for her when my autobiography comes out.

The reason I've started a diary is so that researchers will be able to piece together my early life when I'm famous. It will help them get their facts straight when deciding what exactly my character motivations were and stop them having to rely on potentially corrupting sources, such as Big Al, from Big Al's Golden Delicious Doner Kebabs, and Dad, who thinks I'm a loafer. My ultimate ambition is to write a great novel, which will make me a major authentic voice for a generation.

'*In a world where popular culture moves at something like the speed of light, it's rare to find someone quick enough to feel its pulse. Jay Golden not only places a finger on the jugular, but appears to understand the beat.*' This is what it'll say on the back of the dust jacket, next to a picture of me looking moody in corduroy.

I went to Debbie's Riverside Café in Chesham to work on it tonight. The main character in my novel will be called Wiggie, I've decided. He'll be an eighteen-year-old delinquent in a bobble-hat from a broken home on the Hivings Hill council estate in Bellingdon, and I will record the drama of our age through his sad, bloodshot eyes.

I tried to write the first chapter with this in mind but got nowhere. I think I'm finding it hard to shake off the influence of J. D. Salinger. Wiggie keeps slipping into jarring Americanisms and telling everyone they're goddamn phoneys, or that he had to walk fifteen gorgeous blocks with the rain coming down like a bastard. This is not at all how people speak from the farming community of Bellingdon.

Saturday, 13 February

High point of the week: Gemma and I went to buy the new work shoes. I didn't mean to waste Dad's £50, but there was a very grouchy assistant there who got on my nerves, and Gemma encouraged me by laughing. It started when she gave me some suedes to try on, but they were too small, so I asked for an eight. When she brought these back huffing and puffing like I'd asked her to go to the moon for me, even though they were a perfect fit, I said they were too small for a joke. After this I just kept sending her back for bigger and bigger pairs so that eventually I had on these shoes that were, no kidding, flapping about like a clown's shoes. You could get a whole fist round the back! The assistant kept saying, 'Aren't they a bit big?' and looking over and trying to catch the other assistant's eye.

But I kept walking around, squeezing the toe, saying, 'No, no – they're still tight. They're still *pinching*.'

Gemma had to leave the shop, she was laughing so much. But I kept a straight face all the way up to a Sasquatch-size fourteen. I fell into a rack of handbags at one point because I could hardly stand up. I bought them in the end because I felt guilty. The shoebox was the size of a coffin.

Still feeling skittish afterwards, we borrowed Dad's BBC contacts book and phoned Paul Daniels. Getting told to fuck off by celebrities has become a hobby of ours. So far Gemma's been shouted at by: John Inman, Carla Lane, Rod Steiger, Penelope Keith, Geoffrey Boycott, John Humphrys and Noel Edmonds. And I've been sworn at by: Anthea Turner, Tom Conti, Jonathan Ross, Bobby Davro (twice) and Ian Botham.

When Daniels answered tonight I pretended to be a South African reporter. I said I'd heard Daniels was being prosecuted for animal cruelty for pulling rabbits out of hats by their ears. There'd been a picture of him doing this on the cover of the *Radio Times*.

'Y've dameged de ears ov rabbets, Mr Daniels,' I said. 'We're running de story to-morra in de *Soud African Toimes*. Wortev you to say for yoursilf?'

I handed the receiver to Gemma so she could hear the reaction. Daniels fell for it completely and started jabbering about how he always carefully cupped rabbits' bottoms when he pulled them out of hats.

'Cuppin' de bottoms of animols – dat sounds like an evan more serios chorge, Mr Daniels,' I shouted, and Daniels hung up a confused and frightened conjuror.

Although we're having a laugh, I'm actually a bit worried about the Gemma situation at the moment. I'm not sure whether the state of limbo between us is the result of strong feelings for her I can't cope with, or whether I'm concerned the situation's spiraling out of control and secretly want to stop it. For instance, when I went over the other day I felt under pressure. Either directly ('I like people who make me laugh.') or indirectly through slanted stories ('Mark isn't interesting, I go for interesting people'), Gemma implied she fancied me. I fancy Gemma, but I'm worried we're incompatible. I have an interest in world literature and want to write a great novel. She drops her aitches and watches Blockbusters.

Another letter from my one-to-one tutor Mr Gatley today. I was skeptical about the London Writing School at the beginning. But from Mr Gatley's swirly handwriting and coffee-stained letters, you can tell he isn't doing his job for money, but because he loves it. He might come out with strange stuff about panting dogs and show off about how long he's been a professional writer, but it's nice to have someone take a genuine interest. He obviously respects me as a fellow writer too because he did include a piece of his own writing. It was from *Book Monthly* magazine and a metaphor about how true writers live outside society beyond the stockade like wild, sharp-clawed animals glaring in. Mr Gatley clearly has a thing about animal analogies and it made me laugh. Mr Gatley comes across as about as sharp-clawed as La La.

Sunday, 14 February

When I showed Dad the shoes today he bit his lip and challenged me to a game of double-patience. I thought he might have mellowed but it was his usual trick. He waited until the aces were out, then took advantage of his captive audience to give me the benefit of his wisdom. Apparently, there's now going to be an article about the car-park incident in the *New Statesman*.

'Number one: if you'd told me you wanted to use my car-park space, I'd have said yes, but you had to be sneaky, didn't you? You had to do it behind my back, and as a result it's going to be in a magazine that thousands of people will read. Number two: the shoes. That's £50 of my money – not your money – you've wasted. Sometimes I wonder if you do these things on purpose, old son. Do you?' I said the shoes had felt quite snug in the shop and I'd take them back unless he thought I'd grow into them. 'Do you do them to see how far you can push me until I crack? Because I warn you, I am *close* to cracking,' said Dad.

When I went to my room later there was an ominous letter on my pillow. It was on Dad's Maurice Golden, Controller of BBC2 headed notepaper (always a bad sign) and was basically sound-bites from earlier.

Dear Jay,
Never mind that you embarrassed me in a meeting with the DG, who is at this very moment deciding whether to give me an important new job. Never mind that the Prime

Minister of this country AND the Chancellor of Germany were inconvenienced. Never mind that 5000 people were forced to leave BH for fifteen minutes. Never mind you bought Charlie a turtle when I expressly told you no pets. Never mind the bloody shoes. That is over as far as I am concerned. But, my son, you are about to start a new job. That does concern me. It's a good job. It's your fifth job in as many months. You've done well to get it. I know you think robots should do all the work. The fact is they don't. People do. Get that into your head and try to make this opportunity count.

Lots of love, your silly old man.

P. S. Do you know anything about my contacts book being moved?

Sarah phoned before I went to bed and had a word with me. 'Jay, you're not going to lose this job, are you? Promise you're not. Dad was so pleased when you got it and he's got enough trouble with Charlie, and with the anniversary coming up.' I said of course I wasn't going to lose the job, and Sarah relaxed and said she thought it was ironic that someone who'd lost his last four jobs was about to start work as a recruitment consultant, a job that was all about finding other people jobs. Their constant sniping gets to me at times

I like Gemma, but she's doing something sweet that slightly irritates me. In preparation for the transition from friend to girlfriend she's begun asking solicitous questions about 'My Life,' forcing me to pretend to care more about things than I do. Tonight she said, 'Good luck,' meaning for Monday and my new job. And, as girlfriends are supposedly supportive, instead of laughing like normal at my irresponsible attitude, she disagreed when I said I'd probably end up getting sacked again. Overall though I would still like Gemma to become my girlfriend. Her skin is the colour of a pistachio nut shell and I would like to stroke it.

Description of Gemma: three inches shorter than me,

about five foot five, short black hair, blue eyes, a slim figure and a small birthmark on her face that I pretend makes her look like a giant panda. Gemma wants to get back into Sheffield University to study psychology (she flunked classics there last year). Her ultimate ambition is to track down a serial killer using psychological profiling.

Monday, 15 February

I started at Montons today. A brief synopsis of my colleagues: Pam Vince, the area manager, is loud and ambitious; she has a witch-like profile, and when she talks her forearms rotate as if they're attached to her elbows by ball-bearings; I don't like her. Bridget Wrights, the office manager: efficient; unfunny; sits next to me; I don't like her. Caroline Jones: a fat-faced girl who answers the phone too enthusiastically; the sort of girl who talks about her flat, her boyfriend and other girls' hair; I don't like her. Linda Park: prissy, athletically long-backed fool, whose personality's so wet you could grow cress on it; I don't like her either.

Montons is a recruitment consultancy for the building industry. I work on the Construction Temporary section and am known as 'Jay on Construction Temp'.

Today I after-cared the temps, mostly Irishmen, who've already been placed in jobs by Montons. I did this by phoning them and saying, 'So, Mr O'Leary, how's everything going down there?' (Down there, refers to the building site they're on.) To which they reply, 'Fine, fine, tank you.'

When I got home I tried to bond with Dad – two workers home from a hard day's graft looking to put their feet up and unwind in front of the box. I kicked off my shoes, massaged my socked feet like they do on Lean Cuisine adverts, sighed deeply, and said something Dad often says, 'Ooof. Aye-yi-yi, I'm tired. That was a tough one.'

Dad thought I was taking the piss though. '*Tired*,' he said. 'I've just worked a fifteen-hour day. You don't know what work is. Get up at 6 a.m., feed and dress a young child for school, chair a board of management meeting, arrange for same child to be picked up from school, make dinner, wash up, read a fifty-page task-force report on BBC Charter renewal, *then* tell me you're tired.'

'Do I have to?' I said. 'I've already told you I'm tired.'

Wrote him a reply on Montons stationery when he told me to belt up and get out of his sight, which I left on *his* pillow.

Dear Dad,

Just because I think in this day and age robots should be doing all the work doesn't mean I'm going to get sacked deliberately. I just think it's odd that we can put a man on the moon but can't invent a robot to do the job of recruitment consultants. Keeping Irish hod carriers in work is surely not as difficult as breaking out of the earth's gravitational field and splashing down a multi-tonned probe on an oxygen-less planet more than 300,000 miles away.

Yours sincerely, Jay Golden Construction Temps.

P.S. I don't know anything about your contacts book.

7 p.m.

Charlie wants to be a famous writer as well now, so, copying me, he is carrying a notebook with him everywhere. He showed it to me this evening. Instead of jotting down descriptions and snippets of conversation for the purpose of adding realism to a fictional narrative, he records things like this: 'Had Captain Crunch for breakfast, Mr Watson our geography teacher is a silly head and I want a pair of San Marino football boots for my birthday and the Turtle videos I saw on cable TV, and a dozen Beanie Babies.'

He got me in trouble tonight and Dad's banned *Teenage Mutant Ninja Turtle* enactments in the house. Charlie dented a lampshade jumping out of the way of my plasmarising Technodrome. When we play *Turtles* Charlie is Donatello and wears a blue mask cut out of a bath flannel. I am Be Bop, Lord Krang's evil Rhino henchman, and wear a toilet roll over my nose.

Dad told me he was pleased I enjoyed playing with Charlie, that was important, but wanted to know why I couldn't be more of a positive influence. He suggested this was partly why Charlie's failing at school.

'You're his older brother. The little lad looks up to you. Try to be a role-model. By all means have fun. I'm not stopping that. But try to be a better influence. And when I'm talking to you, do try to take it seriously. *Please* . . . take that loo roll off your nose.'

Description of Charlie: six year old, short for his age and has blond hair and blue eyes like me. When he's at home he wears a Man United kit and when he's at school he wears a tank-top that says 'Hello' on the front and 'Goodbye' on the back. Charlie's ultimate ambitions are to be bionic, to play for Man United and to fight with the Teenage Mutant Ninja Turtles against Lord Krang and his evil warthog henchman.

10 p.m.

I went round to Sean's to get out of Dad's way, but he was in the middle of a row with *his* dad. Sean's made a papier-mâché model of the Middle East on the kitchen table so he can follow the likely battleground if there's another gulf war, and he had apparently got some sand in the butter dish making Saudi Arabia.

'It wasn't even fucking sand,' said Sean. We were in his bedroom. The ceiling between his bedroom and the lounge is very thin and Sean shouted the next bit for his dad's benefit. 'It was some of Mum's fucking hen food.' Sean's mum keeps hens and Sean always blames them for everything because he thinks she loves them more than him. She probably does. Sean's mum is weird.

Tuesday, 16 February

Louise, my specialist, came over from head office today to teach me what construction workers do on building sites apart from wolf whistle and let their bums hang out of their jeans, and I learned what a theodolite was. Apparently, most of my job will involve cold-calling building contractors. Louise reeled off a sales quote about it. 'Sales is about listening, Jay. You've got two ears and one mouth. Remember to use them in that proportion.' The parroted wisdom annoyed me. I felt like saying to her, 'Louise, you've got no brain and one mouth, remember to use them in *that* proportion.'

In the *Current Men Working* book you're supposed to add 'after-care' details to build rapport for the next call. The stiff who'd run the section before had written things like 'Mr O'Shaunessy supports Crystal Palace' and 'Mr Malone is looking for civils projects.' It's very phoney and I've decided to add stupid things instead. Today after phoning Mr O'Neil at Bratwart Rogers, I wrote next to his name in the comments section: 'Was looking forward to the weekend when he would be experimenting with evil and drinking babies' blood on an altar of human bones. Needs a new time sheet.'

9 p.m.

A few cards arrived for Dad today to mark what would have been his and Mum's wedding anniversary tomorrow. Mum died last April and it must have been on Dad's mind because he dropped off in his armchair tonight and started talking about her in his sleep.

'She had a better day today,' he said. 'She slept well. Dr Maitland was more upbeat too, didn't you think?'

It took me a moment to realise he was talking about Mum and dreaming she was still alive. When I told Dad what he'd said later, he became emotional and gave me a hug. It's been so long since he's done this, and was such a surprise, I flinched.

'We start at different ends of the spectrum, but we meet in the middle because we love each other. You are impossible, my son, but I love you,' he said, as he clasped my head.

The thing Sarah misses most about Mum is ringing her up to tell her things. She says she's always thinking of little things she wants to say, picking up the phone, then realising Mum isn't there any more. The thing I miss most about Mum is that she always realised there were two sides to an argument. She never went off the deep end like Dad and always stuck up for me over tidying-up and odd-jobs. In fact, if I was Saddam Hussein and was threatening to start the second Gulf War, she'd probably have told Dad that at my age youngsters did things like this, only afterwards having a quiet word: 'Jay, I don't want to be a nag, and I'm not going to tell Dad, but I do think you should dismantle your chemical weapons factories and let in the UN inspectors. It is not clever to threaten civilian populations with deadly biological nerve agents.'

We drank a toast to Mum in the garden at midnight.

'Happy anniversary. How do you think we're coping, darling?' said Dad, pointing his glass of Cointreau at the rose bushes where Mum's ashes were scattered. We stayed out for a while, Dad filling in Mum on Charlie's latest outrages and the developments with Sarah's wedding.

'I think your mother'd be happy knowing you were driving her ironing van,' he told me at one point. 'I never minded her taking in other people's ironing. She thought I did, didn't you, darling?' He gestured towards the bushes. 'She thought I was embarrassed because of my job; the wife of a channel controller taking in ironing. But I wasn't. It was what she wanted to do. She liked to feel useful, that she was contributing. I admired her for that. I only wish her eldest son was the same.'

He said he was worried about me. He said, 'If you only

knew the number of conversations your mother and I had about you . . . What's he going to do? Is he happy? Should we do this? Should we do that? You were . . . you *are* greatly loved, you know that, don't you?'

I said I did.

Then he suddenly changed tack and got annoyed with me, possibly because of the article that's appeared in the *New Statesman*. And possibly because earlier, when Charlie was doing his homework in front of the telly and Dad told him to do it in the dining room, Charlie refused and said in this day and age robots should be doing all the homework.

Mum died of cancer. I read some of my old diary about it tonight. June 1st, the day she was diagnosed.

1 June: The nurses looked at me nervously at the ward reception. That was the first clue, but I didn't think anything was wrong until the one called Donna stopped me in the corridor. 'I'm afraid your mum's just heard some bad news – there's a nurse in there with her now,' she said.

I asked what news and my heart started pounding.

'You'd better ask the nurse,' she said.

When I opened the door I saw Mum. She was crying in the bed. There were flowers all round the room. The nurse I was supposed to ask was holding her hand.

'Hello, darling,' said Mum, drying her eyes. I held her other hand and looked at the nurse. 'The biopsy, darling,' said Mum, bursting into tears. 'It was cancerous.'

The nurse started telling stories about people who'd beaten cancer and how it was all about being positive, while Mum cried. When Dad arrived we sat either side of Mum's bed and between moments of optimism Mum got hysterical. She gripped our hands so tightly sometimes her knuckles went white and the tendons in her wrists stood out like sticks of spaghetti.

'My dad's seventy-three. Grandad's *seventy-three* – it's not fair. Why me?' she shouted. 'Why *me*?'

I wanted to cry, but couldn't because Dad was watching and I knew he was being brave for Mum and that I had to be brave for him. Between sobs Mum said all she'd wanted was to set Charlie, Sarah and me on our way.

'Now I'll have to give up the ironing. I wanted to give the kids a good head start,' she said to Dad.

Dad hugged her and I couldn't see Mum's face any more, but she carried on gripping my hand tightly and I thought, She's doing this so I don't feel left out. She can't see me, but she wants me to feel as important as Dad. I squeezed her hand back as hard as I could, and cried because I didn't want any of it to be true, because I hated seeing Mum like that, and because it'd never occurred to me she'd been ironing seven days a week, seven hours a day, for the last God knows how many years, just to give me, Sarah and Charlie a good head start.

Dad tried to reassure her. He spoke in an even voice. He said she'd live to be seventy-three, just like Grandad. It was his come-on-don't-be-silly voice. He nodded at me and I said the same thing in the same voice, and Mum looked from Dad to me, like she was trying to catch us out.

'You've got everything to live for,' said Dad. 'People only die of cancer when they've got nothing. You've got the garden and this one here.' He cuffed my head.

'It's true, Mum,' I said, drying my eyes.

'Yes, yes, you're right,' said Mum, sniffing back the tears. 'I'm sorry. It's because I've just heard. It's the shock. God, I don't know what I'd do without you two. Come here. It will be all right. I know it will. It has to be.'

But, of course, it wasn't. Looking back on it, she didn't have a chance. The doctors knew, but they didn't tell us because it's all about easy stages, not giving up hope.

'It's a hiatus hernia.' *Thank you, Doctor, we can deal with that*. A week later: 'No, sorry, it's a giant benign gastric ulcer.' *Thank you, Doctor, that's not as bad as it could be*. A month later: 'No, I'm afraid it's cancer, but it hasn't spread.' *Thank God it hasn't spread, Doctor*. Three months later: 'It *has* spread, but we think we've cut it all out.' *Thank God you've cut it all out, Doctor.* Then, a month after this: 'Oh dear, we haven't cut it all out. Sorry, she's got six months to live, but don't worry there'll be no pain.' *Thank God, she won't be in pain, Doctor.* Then she dies and they say she looks peaceful. *Yes, thank you, Doctor, doesn't she look fucking peaceful?*

Description of Mum: quite thin; long blond hair she wore in plaits; warm blue eyes; slightly wonky teeth; and the nicest person I've ever known. What's funny is Mum believed she *wasn't* that nice; that's how nice she was. She had a thing about the phone, for instance. We nicknamed her the Postman for it, because of that film, *The Postman Always Rings Twice.* Mum would always ring twice. You'd have a perfectly normal conversation with her but the minute you put down the phone she'd ring back. You knew not to do anything like get back in the bath or restart the video because she always rang back. On the second call she'd be paranoid she'd said something to upset you on the first call, even though she never had: 'When I said I wasn't going to cook a roast on Sunday, I didn't mean I didn't want you there, darling. It's just I haven't got a joint in. We can have a roast if you want. I'll get a joint in.'

That's one of the things that breaks my heart, Mum ringing back like that; when I imagine what Mum's face must've looked like between those calls. 'Shall I ring him about that joint? Did he think I didn't want him there?'

Wednesday, 17 February

Stood in on an applicant interview with Linda today. We have to pre-interview every applicant because Montons is proud of its professionalism. Linda was registering Mr Payne, a supposed site agent.

'Working inside don't agree with me sensa hoomer. Call me want you want, I'm not interested in fancy job titles – they don't agree with me sensa hoomer.'

It was quite funny – nothing seemed to agree with Mr

Payne's sensa hoomer, and after he'd gone, Linda said, 'You have to watch people like that. He's completely unqualified – basically he's a chippie. You must check applicants' qualifications. That might have made us look unprofessional in front of the client.'

In the afternoon I got told off for having an untidy desk. There's a Tidiest Branch competition this month and Bridget wants Harrow to win it. When Bridget was out of the room I told Linda I thought this was pathetic, and that having a tidy desk didn't agree with my sensa hoomer. Linda puffed out her cheeks, and said, 'I don't mind *your* desk being untidy, Jay, but can you stop it from spilling over into mine. I lost two QS applications this morning.'

I don't seem to be connecting with anyone at Montons. They all told me how well respected Montons was in the building industry today, as if I cared. And nobody gets my jokes.

9 p.m.

I phoned Sean tonight. He was in the middle of a row with his parents about moving to Scotland. They're moving when Sean's dad retires in April and Sean's worried he'll have nowhere to live if he doesn't follow them there.

'Does your dad get stroppy about the slightest thing, like this silly bag of a mum of mine?' asked Sean. 'Does your dad follow you around like a lost sheep the whole time, nagging you because he's got nothing better to do now that he's retiring to a Scottish potting shed?'

I heard Sean's mum in the background asking who he was showing off to in her screechy, playfully angry voice that their house-full of dogs always mistakes for real anger and starts barking at.

'Mum, go and feed the dogs. Go on, feed fucking Seffie or shave your hairy legs.'

'Is that you, Jay? Who are you talking to? Is that *you*, Jay? Sean, stop showing off to Jay. Jay, tell Sean he'll never get a girlfriend in Scotland if he doesn't wipe his bottom. There were skid-marks in his pants this morning.'

I heard Mrs F laughing.

'Hang on a sec,' said Sean, with strained patience and the phone went down with a clunk. There was a little scuffle, shouting, more barking, the slam of a door and a loud banging.

Then Sean came back on. 'I've locked the bag outside,' he said. Then he lowered his voice, and in the tone he uses when he knows I'm going to laugh at what he's about to say, he said, 'Jay-boy, when you wank over a porno, when do you come? When do you . . . like . . . come? Do you come when the bloke in the film comes or at some other point? Isn't it a bit dodgy coming when the bloke comes? Isn't that like you're turned on by the fact he's come, the bloke?'

'Jay-boy,' he said, after I'd reassured him he wasn't gay, 'the silly bag scalded them in a boil wash – they weren't skid marks. OK?'

Thursday, 18 February

Three jobs were 'phoned in' today, one of which I managed to fill: I got Mr John Graham a job as a general foreman at Norwest Holst. Bridget congratulated me, Linda asked whether it has given me a buzz and I received a bottle of white wine for getting my first 'starter'.

I tried to stay aloof from the fray, but was quite cocky later. When I sat in on Caroline's applicant interview with Mr Sheridan I made Caroline seem the junior by nodding and saying, 'That's right, Caroline,' all the time. She had a word with me about it afterwards. Apparently, it had adversely affected applicant-control.

Gemma came over tonight and we phoned Paul Daniels again. We wanted to make out the rabbit story was spreading round the globe like a major news event.

'It Niki Nakaroni from Tokyo *Delly Mail*,' I said. 'Is 'at Mitter Danls?'

'It is,' said Daniels suspiciously.

'Mitter Danls, you cormit cwimes of sexal naychah wi' bunny wabbits. May pepwl Japan big fan Poor Danls, not so big fan now, 'cos may pepwl Japan orso big fan o' bunny wabbits.'

'Oh, for God's sake!' said Daniels. 'Haven't you got anything better to report on?' And he hung up.

The celebrity I'd most like to be told to fuck off by would have to be Les Dennis. That's my ultimate. He'd have to be really angry, though. He'd really have to mean it. Unfortunately, Dad hasn't got Les Dennis's home number. He's got his agent's. I've been told to fuck off by his agent. But it's not quite the same. Gemma's ultimate, for a reason she has never satisfactorily explained, is Nerys Hughes.

I like making Gemma laugh. It happened three times tonight. She does it without making any noise. Her lips remain closed, and she vibrates from the waist up like a tuning fork. I wonder when, and if, we will start to go out with each other. It snowed tonight and it was quite tempting to push Gemma over in it, but I couldn't pluck up the courage. Pushing someone over in a snowdrift is a girlfriendy–boyfriendy thing to do and if she'd pulled me down with her or stuffed snow down the back of my jumper, it would have sealed it and we might have kissed. But what if she'd just stared up at me or complained I'd soaked her new chenille jumper which you're not supposed to tumble-dry?

I don't think that would've happened, though, because when I told her about the mysterious late Valentine's card I got today Gemma gave me quite a sexy glance. I think it was a cue for us to have a snog, but for some reason I couldn't return the look because I suddenly felt awkward and ugly. Gemma looked so pretty in her tight red jumper that my fingers felt thick and clumsy like giant pork sausages and I had to look away. It was like the moment before Beauty kisses the Beast in the fairy tale, except the Beast suddenly realises he's not God's gift and pulls away saying, 'Hey, that the time? Look, I'd better go, I'm due for a claw-clipping at two.'

Gemma wasn't surprised about Sean possibly being gay. Apparently, he once pressed his groin into her sister's boyfriend's knee when he was sat on a bar stool in the Ellie.

Friday, 19 February

Went for a drink with Caroline and Bridget after work. Caroline has conversations as if she's still cold-calling – relaying information, getting her message across, not listening to your reply, talking like you're not in the same room. I can see how this happens. When I phoned Sean the other night it felt like I was bullshitting too, being over-friendly. And the other day getting off the tube, when a woman asked me for the time and I wasn't wearing a watch, I actually found myself apologising, and pointing her towards somebody who I thought was wearing a watch. I almost thanked her for her enquiry.

Bridget took it on herself to fill me in on the Montons social scene when we got to the pub. It's apparently quite lively, but 'you've got to go looking for it,' and I got invited to a Construction social next Wednesday night. When Bridget loosened up she was even worse. She told me she'd once got so drunk she'd fallen asleep on the train home, and had woken up in Pinner. Why is it everyone has this same story to trot out to show how mad it is where they work? It's very depressing and it's made me think about resigning.

I wrote to Mr Gatley and thanked him for his recent letters. I like to think of Mr Gatley as an eccentric, good-natured old man of letters, who's thrilled to have spotted genuine talent and whose ultimate ambition is to fan this flame by taking me under his musty wing. Sometimes I can almost picture the scene each week when my manuscript plops on the mat. Mr Gatley hobbles into the breakfast room on his quadruped sticks to tell his wife he's heard from that young writer again.

His wife looks up from her egg, a benevolent gleam in her eye: 'Why don't you send him something of yours, dear. I think he would enjoy it. That article you wrote for *Book Monthly*, perhaps. The one I liked: sharp-clawed animals. Or was it huge panting dog on a lead? One of your animal analogies, anyway.'

When I'm a famous novelist I'll invite Mr Gatley to my book launch at the Intercontinental. Everyone'll be fawning all over me – famous people, publishers – and Mr Gatley will start thinking he's out of his depth. But right before he's about to get his coat and walk humbly away, I'll shout out his name and Mr Gatley will be dragged to the front, and I'll put my arm around him and say, 'Here he is. You want to know who I owe it all to. I'll tell you – I owe it all to this man here.' And Mr Gatley will start to cry.

8 p.m.

I wish Dad was more like Mr Gatley. He had a go at me when I mentioned resigning to become a sharp-clawed animal tonight.

'It breaks my heart seeing you waste your life,' said Dad. 'The world's a tough place, much tougher than in my day. You've got to forget this book fantasy and make a spurt while you're young. I'm worried you're getting left behind, my son. And you still haven't explained why you bought that turtle. The whole house reeks, Jay. What are you going to do about it?'

I told Dad I'd bought Charlie the real thing to knock out his *Teenage Mutant Ninja Turtle* obsession. I said it was recognised aversion therapy. 'It's like making someone smoke a whole packet of cigarettes in one go so they're sick,' I said.

Dad still didn't believe me, though, and said he wanted the tank out in the garage before the Home Secretary came round or there'd be trouble.

Saturday, 20 February

Gemma and I drove to the Captain Cook Memorial in Chalfont St Giles today. We put mattresses on the metal floor of the van, played drinking games and swapped confessions. The drinking game consisted of choosing a subject – say, European countries – and then taking it in turns to name, after two hand-claps for rhythm, as many as possible. Whoever failed to come up with one had to drink extravagantly from their can and reveal something. I confessed I used to fancy Gemma in the sixth form and wanted to be a famous novelist who wore bottle-green, and Gemma admitted to having recurring sexual dreams about Rutger Hauer. She fancies Rutger Hauer because he is powerful and deceptively evil.

When we got back the rivalry continued, and we competed at Mastermind at Gemma's. At one point we had a funny disagreement over an answer on Louis XIV, the Sun King, so I got out Dad's BBC contacts book and phoned Magnus Magnusson for a ruling. Mrs Magnusson answered.

'Would you get Magnus for me?' I said.

'Who is this?' said Mrs Magnusson.

'I'm sorry to bother you, but we've had a dispute here about a question on the General Knowledge round of Mrs Blenkinsop. She's the dowdy librarian from the fourth quarter-final in the Winchester Room, Bristol, and I wonder if Magnus would clear it up for us?'

'I don't really think—'

'It is important – we're tied at three-all. If Magnus could just give a ruling.'

'Why don't you phone the BBC?'

'I think it would be better coming from Magnus himself.'

'I'm sorry, he's busy.'

'Perhaps if I left a number.'

In the end Mrs Magnusson arbitrated herself and said she thought I was right, although Gemma refused to accept the verdict because she said Mrs Magnusson probably just wanted me off the phone.

Gemma's mum is an ex-history teacher and we had a conversation about the Napoleonic Wars tonight as we watched the news about Iraq still refusing to allow in U.N. weapons inspectors. Not the normal Tom, Dick or Harry you get round here, hey, Mrs Draycote? She also asked me about my novel and I used the word ameliorate, which caught her eye.

I told Gemma about Mum tonight as well. I didn't mean to. We were in the back of the van and one moment talking about Sean's papier mâché model of the Middle East – he's extended it into North Africa in case Turkey gets sucked in – then the next it all came out. Gemma was pleased I'd spoken about it. She didn't say anything, but at the end she stared at me with tears in her eyes, and her lips trembling. 'Oh, Jay!' she said, rolling closer to me, so we were side by side in the back of the van on our stomachs like sardines.

20 September: I was in the bath at Sarah's when Rob came to the door with the news. Rob used a voice I'd never heard before. 'Jay, your mum's on the phone,' he said.

The first thing I thought was something had happened to Charlie. Then to Dad. Mum'd been told she was in the clear. She'd had her whole stomach removed after they'd discovered the cancer, and Dr Maitland said he'd got everything. Mum was in remission.

'What is it?' I asked.

'It's some bad news,' he said.

Mum was in tears. 'You know I told you my legs had swollen,' she said. 'Well, I didn't tell you, but now my stomach's swollen, too. I've seen the doctor and he thinks it might be back.' There was a pause. 'The cancer.'

Dr Maitland had said the cancer spreading to the liver might explain the swelling. Mum said they'd taken tests but the results wouldn't be known until Dr Maitland returned on Tuesday.

'Just a week away from the all-clear and I feel so well,' said Mum, sobbing. 'I was planting bulbs this morning.'

I tried to sound optimistic. I told her the doctor's lack of urgency was a good sign. I pointed out that she wasn't off her food, the first symptom of liver cancer, according to Rob.

'Yes, I suppose you're right,' she said, 'and I've got a nice bit of salmon for tea tonight.'

'You'll be all right, Mum,' I told her. 'On Tuesday we'll have a party when they give you the good news, think of it that way. Think of us all on the phone to you afterwards.'

'Yes,' said Mum, warmly. 'It will be all right. It has to be. I'm not popping my clogs just yet.'

I felt a bit funny after I'd told Gemma about it, but not too bad. Normally I avoid talking about Mum – I get a lump in my throat that's embarrassing and I don't like the looks people give you, and those questions: 'How old was she?' 'How's your dad?' 'Was it *very* hard for Charlie?' People only ask these questions to show how knowledgeable they are about death and it gets on my nerves. It makes me want to laugh in their faces. That's another reason I don't like talking about Mum, because this happened once. I laughed in the face of Mr Twain, the funeral director. It was the sight of him walking down our drive in his ridiculous frock coat that did it. 'No prizes for guessing who that is!' I said to Sarah, and even though it wasn't that funny, I couldn't stop myself laughing. Dad had to tell me to pull myself together ('*I need you right now*').

Sarah went home after the funeral, Charlie returned to school, and for a week Dad and I just watched every video in the house. We watched *Bridge over the River Kwai, Kelly's Heroes, The Dambusters, D-Day, The Godfather Part I, The Godfather Part II, Papillon, The Great Escape,*

Lawrence of Arabia, *The Robe*, *Ben-Hur*, *Casablanca*, five Woody Allens and three Steve Martins.

I enjoyed the week in a strange way, watching telly with Dad, our lives frozen solid.

There was one brilliant line in *Spartacus*, which we watched three times. Laurence Olivier is Crassus, a Roman senator who turns up at this country villa unexpectedly and demands to see a gladiatorial fight to the death. Peter Ustinov is the owner of the villa and he isn't happy that they're going to fight to the death, because he thinks it will create bad feeling between the gladiators. It turns out he's right, because it sparks a massive slave revolt led by Spartacus. Anyway, that's irrelevant. The important bit is Laurence Olivier saying, in his clipped actory voice, 'Sulla – to the infamy of his name and utter damnation of his line.' He said this because Sulla had entered the gates of Rome with an army, which you weren't supposed to do, apparently. Dad and I just kept repeating it for days, trying to imitate how he'd said it so perfectly. Dad said it was one way; I said it was another.

'Sul-la – to the infamy of his name.'

'No, it's "Sull-a – to the in-famy of his name".'

'What about, "Sulla – to the infam-y of his name"?'

Over and over we said it.

Sunday, 21 February

Dad's thinking about sending Charlie to boarding school. It came out during today's family roast. 'Have a look at these?' said Dad, throwing some school prospectuses across the table after the pudding. Sarah gave me a sidelong glance to show she already knew about it and was worried about my reaction. There was another note waiting on my pillow afterwards as well. I wish Dad would stop treating my pillow like a bulletin board.

Dear Jay,

I have mentioned this to your sister, so I am saying the same to you – I am serious about Charlie. Something must be done about him. I know you'll think I am some kind of ogre. I'm not. I want what's best for him, just like I'm sure you do, and I am afraid this may have to mean a new home setting. His school work is suffering, you've seen his elbows, and the context here in this house has a great deal to do with this. I think we as a family should think (and at this stage it is just a thought) about boarding school.

Dad's appointment as head of BBC Charter renewal was confirmed too. The Director General phoned to congratulate him personally and Dad was so pleased he went round the house bowling imaginary leg-breaks. I was still annoyed about the prospectuses, though, so, to get Dad back, I criticised the second episode of a BBC costume drama when it came on. Dad's very protective of the BBC, or the Beeb as he calls it, and the drama was one he commissioned.

'Riiiight, you're doing your anti-everything bit again, are you?' said Dad, taking the bait.

'No, I just think the programme's crap, that's all,' I said.

'I see,' said Dad. 'Well, six million people, including me, disagree with you, my old son, what does that tell you?'

I said it meant six million people, including him, were wrong, and Dad shook his head and strode off to make himself a drink.

He came back, head down, in the flat-footed way he walks when he wants you to know how weary you're making him, but then in the middle of the room he thought of a way to get me back, and stopped dead in his tracks like he'd seen a rattlesnake on the carpet. 'I thought I asked you to vacuum in here,' he said.

'I didn't have time,' I said.

He said, 'Well you've got time now.'

'In a minute.'

'Not in a minute. *Now*, please!'

I walked to the Hoover cupboard. 'Just because you're losing the argument about the costume drama,' I muttered.

'You could always get a robot to do it for you,' Dad muttered back.

I phoned Sarah before I went to bed. If he does send Charlie away, I've decided never to speak to Dad again. Sarah told me to wait and see what happened – it probably wouldn't come to anything. She said I knew what Dad was like for going off the deep end, and anyway she was going to try to persuade him to get Charlie to see a psychiatrist friend of Rob's.

I also told her about the row I'd just had with Dad, hoping for some support, but Sarah laid into me. 'Jay, it isn't Dad who's being unreasonable, it's you. He works a fifteen-hour day, and what do you do to help? You nearly get Mum's van blown up, pick fights with him, threaten to resign, then you buy Charlie a pet turtle that makes the house smell. I know you think robots should be doing all the work, but it isn't robots who are doing all the work, is it? It's Dad.'

Dad is always the priority just because he works a fifteen-hour day. I'm sick of it. It's like when I asked to borrow his laptop the other day and he refused. 'Last time you clogged the mouse with Marmite, and left dirty coffee cups in my study,' he said.

When I think of other people's dads it depresses me. Everyone else's dad is interested in their children's ambitions. My dad's only interested in his own. A tiny speck of Marmite in his mouse. How petty! Imagine Shakespeare's dad behaving like this. Where would world literature be then? 'Yes, I know, William, I want you to finish *The Tempest*, too, but I'll not have you dripping venison fat over my blotter, I simply won't.'

10 p.m.

I went round to Sean's this evening. His dad had called him a poof as a joke because he'd asked for French mustard, and Sean had blushed and was now worried why. 'The thing is, I don't know why I blushed. I mean, I don't know whether I blushed because I thought, Wouldn't it be terrible if I blush now and my dad thinks I'm gay? or whether I blushed because' – Sean chuckled – 'deep down I really am gay.'

'You're thinking too much about it,' I said.

'What's worse, he noticed and came upstairs later and sat on the end of the bed and apologised, like I really *was* a poof,' said Sean.

'Maybe if you didn't think about it the whole time.'

'He said if I ever wanted to talk to him about absolutely anything, he was always there.' Sean inhaled on his cigarette and gave me a bug-eyed grin. 'The trouble is,' he said, stroking his chin and wincing nervously, 'I don't know whether to go and tell him I'm not, because if I'm wrong and he didn't mean what I think he meant and I go barging in and say, "Oh, hi, Dad, it's all right, I'm not gay," then he really is going to think I'm gay, isn't he?'

'What else could he have meant, and what does it matter what your dad thinks.'

'Maybe he thinks I'm just shy or something. "Is this what all this is about?" That's what he said. Maybe he was talking generally about me blushing. Perhaps he thinks being shy is holding me back, stopping me reaching my full potential, getting a job and stuff.'

Sean's mum came upstairs with two cups of tea. 'It stinks in here, Sean,' she said, opening his bedroom window. Sean called her a bag. 'Don't be so rude,' she said, vehemently with one breath, then immediately bantery with the next: 'It's all right for him – he's used to it, Jay. *He* can't smell it. We can though, can't we? Honestly, he's worse than the hens.'

'I do know', said Sean, lowering his voice when she'd gone, 'when blokes are handsome. I can tell when' – he sipped his tea – 'they're handsome.'

'Yes, but are you thinking like a bloke thinking like a girl thinking, That bloke's attractive. Or are you thinking' – I took a swig of my own tea – 'he's attractive yourself?'

'I dunno,' said Sean, grimacing, 'I dunno.'

After this we talked about the Middle East. Sean's definitely obsessing about the Gulf. He knew nothing about military hardware three weeks ago, but now, as if it's the most natural thing in the world, standing over his model tonight just before I left, he said, 'Of course, airfield denial weapons are successors to the bombs developed during the Six-day War – two below-wing pods carrying thirty-kilo payload segments of sub-munitions. And as for the F15E Stealth Bomber, the Pratt-Whitney F100–100 turbofan engines, well, they're simply the best in the business.'

We've agreed to go out and test his homosexuality at the Orchard on Tuesday night. Mark got off with three girls last month in the Orchard and reckons there must be something wrong with you if you can't pull there.

When I got home I finished *The Cruel Sea* by Nicholas Monserrat. A gigantic novel, on a gigantic theme. Against the backdrop of the Atlantic War, Monserrat gives us real characters, characters we admire, characters we cry for. The human element is its focus – through the lives and deaths of wardroom officers we see the war. The dreaded U-boats hunting in wolf-like packs. Lockhart and Ericson drinking pink gin in Gibraltar after the sinking of *Compose Rose*, Lockhart agreeing to stay on as first lieutenant on the *Saltash* seeing out the war with Captain Ericson. Men in oily water choking to death, men dying well, and men dying badly. Went to bed thinking deeply about World War II.

Monday, 22 February

Half of me thinks Dad's serious about boarding school, and half of me thinks it's an idle threat. When I was nine I stole stamps from the Hepworth Approval Company. They sent me booklets of stamps in the post and I was supposed to take out the ones I wanted and then send back the money for them. Only what I did was change all the stamp numbers and all the prices in the booklet and nick all the valuable ones.

I'll never forget the day Dad took the call. I had to do it in his name because I was too young, and at first they thought he was the thief. 'Jaaay, I've got a man on the phone who says if I don't return an unmounted mint King Edward ten-shilling ultramarine then he's going to the police. What do you know about this?'

They didn't prosecute (I was too young), but that night Dad came into my bedroom and said I was going to boarding school in the morning. He may have been scaring me, which means he may be scaring Charlie now. Or he might have been serious but Mum talked him out of it.

I'd definitely never speak to him again if he sent Charlie away.

7 p.m.

I phoned Grandad tonight to wish him happy birthday and to talk about the war. Grandad was seventy-four today and knows people who were blown up. It must have been great living through the war. Life's so mundane these days. People who lived through the war always have interesting stories, even those who didn't fight and were just auxiliary bus drivers. Grandad loves reminiscing about the war and his strange-sounding comrades – Smudger, Stumpy Harris, people like that – and we spoke for about half an hour.

It bothers me that I'll have nothing to reminisce about when I'm a grandad. What are the major events I'll talk to my grandchildren about? 'Tell us again, Grandad, about when the EU banned the Cox's Pippin?' It's hardly the same.

Grandad also asked how the little 'un was, and I said Charlie was doing well at school. I didn't mention boarding school. Grandad was badly affected when Mum died. His voice goes weird whenever you mention her, or even if you say anything related to her, like Charlie getting urges and misbehaving.

Description of Grandad: he is very tall, has grey Brylcreemed hair, wears a suit the whole time and has a squashed nose that resembles a coconut pyramid after someone has sat on it.

10 p.m.

The Home Secretary, Jack Straw, and a few top BBC people came over tonight. They talked about the licence fee, the Gulf coverage and the BBC in the twenty-first century in the snooker room, so Dad could show off the pictures he has on the walls down there of him with his arm around celebrities.

Dad was very edgy – he always is when he's out to impress – and kept coming up to me when no one was looking and whispering crossly for me to do things, then being all nice and bantery when they were watching. '*Jay, take your bloody shoes upstairs* . . . And this is Jay, my eldest – handsome lad, isn't he? . . . *Jay, for God's sake find out how long Charlie's going to be in the bathroom – the Home Secretary wants a pee* . . . Yes, there *is* a funny smell. It's the turtle tank, the youngest's. Teenage Mutant Ninja Turtles! Ha, ha, ha. They drive us both mad, don't they, Jay? . . . *Jay, take that filthy turtle tank out to the garage this instant.*'

'What was all that about?' I asked, after they'd left. I was quite angry.

Dad was in the kitchen. He'd changed into his pyjamas. 'What was what about?' he said, pouring himself a drink. He made an 'ah' noise as the glass filled up. Dad likes his Cointreau before bed.

'Treating me like that,' I said.

'Like what? I've earned this tonight,' he said, and took his first swig. 'Ah – that's good.'

'Like I was some underling of yours at work. Like I was some junior producer.'

He walked into the living room, closing his eyes contemptuously as he passed me in the doorway. It was his wrestling-with-himself mode, look-how-patient-I'm-being mode. But he couldn't keep it up. He stopped halfway into the room, then came back, pointing his drink at my head like it was a rifle sight he was looking through.

'Don't,' he said.

'Don't what?' I said.

'Just *don't*,' he said.

'What?' I said, and in a very restrained, menacing voice, Dad said, 'You live in a nice house and have nice things. For this to carry on – and I am sure this is what you want, you don't seem to be making any hurried alternative living arrangements – things have to change around here.' He was speaking like I imagined he did in meetings: slowly, his chin jutting out aggressively with pauses at odd intervals. 'You knew important people were coming back tonight. I told you about it four days ago. I reminded you about it this morning. But does it make any difference? No.'

I asked what I was supposed to have done wrong this time. I hadn't brought up the robot conspiracy with the Home Secretary like he'd told me not to.

Dad did a sarcastic laugh, bent forward so he could get his face closer to mine. 'You agreed to take the tank out to the garage. You said you'd do it on Friday night. You promised you'd do it on Friday night. As a result, the house stank. You might not mind living in a pigsty, but I do. And so did my guests, clearly. You heard what Jack Straw said about the smell.'

Charlie must've heard Dad muttering about me on the landing, because he came into my room at midnight and said I could sleep on his top bunk if I ever got chucked out, but that I'd have to clear my stuff away because he had his work cut out as it was, putting his Beanie Babies away at bedtime.

Tuesday, 23 February

The Gulf situation hotted up today. Iraq's still refusing to allow in UN weapons inspectors and there's talk of another Gulf War if Saddam doesn't back down.

Sean phoned at 8 a.m. in the middle of flattening the military targets on his model that the news said had been destroyed in overnight air strikes. 'If he wants a slugfest, he'll get a slugfest. God, I love the smell of papier-mâché in the morning,' he shouted excitedly before informing me about the 500-m.p.h. thermal nuclear wind that would rip through the Chilterns following a direct 100-megaton neutron bomb attack on RAF Strike Command in High Wycombe. He acted even more weirdly before he hung up and said 'Jay, what comes first? Do you get a twangy voice which makes you realise you're gay? Or do you realise you're gay and then develop a twangy voice? And if you do develop a twangy voice, is this a natural twangy voice based on altered hormones, or is this twangy voice merely put on to attract other gay people with twangy voices. Jay, tell me honestly, no bullshitting, have I got a twangy voice?'

The prospect of global war distracted me at work, and I was told off by Bridget for forgetting to say, 'Hello, Montons,' with a smile in my voice. How are you supposed to put a smile in your voice when the skeletal riders of the Apocalypse have galloped into view? I told Bridget this, but she just raised her eyebrows and threatened to make me file time sheets if I answered back again. Bridget's so myopically professional the Apocalypse would only concern her if Montons were involved in the rebuild.

No placements again either. While I was canvassing this afternoon, witch-woman Pam came into the office and said she wanted three starters from me this week. She told me I couldn't live off my John Graham success for ever and wouldn't listen when I repeated what Bridget had said the other day about soaring house prices scaring off property developers who'd been burned in the last boom. Caroline discovered some of the funny remarks I'd made in the comments section of the *Current Men Working* book as well, and everybody said I was mad. They devalue everything. There must be a benchmark. Not everybody can be mad. One per cent is a fair proportion. The rest must be stupid, forgetful or have an out-of-date train timetable.

2 a.m.

Went to the Orchard nightclub with Sean for his gay test. It was a bit of a disaster. The only two girls not scared off by Sean's monologues on the Tomahawk missile guidance system were from Bradford and weren't impressed at all when I lied and told them Sean was a bit-part actor who'd appeared on *The Bill*.

'So how much do yer get for appearin' on *Peak Practice*, then?' Sean's one asked menacingly.

My one was a secretary who worked for (drum roll) four directors. She was keen to stress how important her role was and how the directors all insisted on using her rather than hiring somebody else to share the workload, because she was so good.

I tried to steer the conversation back to Sean. 'And he was in *Superman IV*,' I said, pointing at Sean.

My one loved this. 'Did you 'ear tha'?' she shouted to her friend. 'He were in *Superman IV*.'

Sean's girl looked at him admiringly. 'Were yer?' she said.

Sean said modestly that he was only six at the time.

'It was the scene in the square outside the United Nations Building,' I said. 'I can't believe people only remember him for that film. He's done much better stuff.'

They both swarmed round Sean and he was doing quite well for about ten minutes until he suddenly ruined it by asking if they thought fundamentalist African nations might get sucked in if the U.N. began bombing Baghdad. I couldn't believe it. The girls looked at each other blankly. Sean must have realised something was wrong and it was slipping away because he glanced across at me desperately and said, 'Yeah, and Jay here was in a Knorr soup advert, weren't you, Jay?'

On the way home Sean made a pathetic apology. He said he was going to say I'd been in the recent James Bond, but for some reason it'd come out wrong. 'I had Knorr soup for tea,' he said, as if that explained it.

Phoned Henry 'Going For Gold' Kelly and went to bed: 'Henry I am a person who constantly rings up quiz-show hosts at inconvenient times with little or no regard for their privacy, what 'T' am I? Yes, that's right, a Telephone Pest – very well played Henry – you join Icelandic Magnus in this week's 'Going for Ex-directory Status' final.'

Wednesday, 24 February

Air strikes on Iraq were stepped up today. I don't really believe there will be a full-scale conflict, although, thinking more about it, Sean's right it would be great: swapping my *Current Men Working* book for the steering wheel of an MP7 tank-buster. That would give me something to reminisce about.

Sean says he will become an artillery officer if he gets called up. If I'm called up I will get a job with the Arab Bureau and work behind the front line, undermining the enemy like the late, great Lawrence of Arabia, stick-whipping my dromedary as – *hat-at-at* – I go in search of the Hashamite bedouins.

> 'Say, did you know T. E. Lawrence?'
> 'No but I shook his hand in Damascus.'
> 'It is written that no white man will take Aqaba.'
> 'Nothing is written until I write it.' Etc.

I found a note on my desk this morning when I got in. It said, 'You are not in school. Tidy this desk up now.' Bridget glanced over as I read it and gave me one of her stern looks. She brought it up again later: I'd lose vital messages and forget what I was doing if I didn't discipline myself to keep it clear. I told her a messy desk was a busy desk, and she said she was losing patience with me.

Linda's blind obedience and plaintive telephone manner are beginning to irritate me, too. She actually gets annoyed if I fail to ring back applicants. At first I thought this just good manners; I could understand it if it was that. But today I discovered it wasn't: Linda's concerned about the company's image. She even used those words, 'company image': 'It's Montons' image that'll suffer, Jay.' How do people get like this?

Construction social at London Wall after work. Claire was circular and probably selected her clothes size using *pi*; Rachel's idea of a wild night was trying other people's pizza toppings; and Simon was a worldly wise Mancunian. He asked relevant questions and used stock phrases for everything – 'I bummed-about abroad', 'I pen-pushed at Barclays'. He'd pigeon-holed every feeling, every action into two words and a hyphen. He was a right prat.

It was a shit evening and I missed Gemma. I think it's because of the way she holds things. I think this is what I like most about her. I watched her the other day making a lasagne. It's something to do with the way she clutches. Her thumbs bend backwards with the strength of her grip and her knuckles go white. But, once she has the item safely in her palm, she waves it around, whatever it be – pasta, a biro, her make-up bag – casually, almost as if to show how confident she is of not dropping it. Although Gemma's beautiful, she's clumsy and has no poise. I like this a lot.

What I'd really like to do is lend her a copy of *Catcher in the Rye*. I expect she'd get heavily influenced by it, and want to run away and live in a mud hut with me in Africa. It'd be great living in a mud hut with Gemma – we could make our own bread, keep a few chickens, and I could sit around a log fire just watching her pick up things, like mangoes.

I wrote her a letter when I got in. It's a military analogy based on the Gulf. It's about us both stepping into no man's land for a snog. It's sufficiently ambiguous to serve two purposes. First, it's witty enough to be construed as one of my 'little jokes' should Gemma feel alarmed, and, second, it's a sincere enquiry about her feelings that might help us cross the limbo bridge.

If I start going out with Gemma I doubt I'd want to be at the steering wheel of an MP7 tank-buster. I think I'd be content then.

8 p.m.

Dad's going to postpone the boarding-school issue until Charlie sees Rob's child psychologist mate, Dr Roberts, Sarah phoned up to tell me. Apparently, Dad took a lot of persuading, especially after tonight. Charlie's got to learn to keep his arms in when he's excited – it's like playing with a wind turbine. He swept a plate off the dresser playing *Teenage Mutant Ninja Turtles* this evening. I hid the broken plate under potato peelings in the outside bin, but Dad found it throwing out his Cointreau empties. Charlie made it worse, shouting, 'Humungus misery to the max,' instead of apologising. Turtle-speak's been banned in the house, as well as enactments, and Dad's making me pay for the plate. Humungus misery to the max is right – it costs twenty pounds.

Charlie quite likes the idea of seeing a shrink and we played patient–psychiatrist on his bed during his five-minute talk before lights out.

'So, Charlie – tell me about your childhood.'

'Well, Jay – I like football, the Turtles, stories about pirates and drawing.'

Thursday, 25 February

Today Martin, the temporary canvasser, here on placement, noticed my enthusiastic telephone manner and imitated my exuberant 'Hello, Montons'. I told him it was part of the job. You say, 'Hello, Montons,' differently each time you answer the phone, partly to sound interested, partly to keep fresh and partly because you're bored with the sound of your own voice. Sometimes I say, 'HelloMon-tons,' sometimes, 'Helllllo Montons,' and other times, 'HelloMontons,' all in one exclamation. Martin's quite a laugh and we experiment-ed with a few new ones in the afternoon, including a robotic, 'Hell-o-Mon-ton-sss,' which made Linda look up. I'm trying to keep in with Martin. He's setting up a comedy magazine with friends and might be looking for contributors, which would be a good boost to my writing career.

I went to Debbie's café after work. I like to think there's now an air of mystery surrounding me at Debbie's. My sudden appearance, my pages of notes, my cheeseburger loyalty, the fastidious way I insist on a pint of Coke with three lumps of ice must, I feel sure, have led to excited chatter behind the serving hatch about my identity.

To begin with, I merely ordered my meal. But lately, feeling my custom's earned me certain indulgences, I've started requesting certain off-menu touches. Today, I asked Debbie specifically for seven slices of cucumber to accom-pany my burger, following that up later with a request for the lighting to be dimmed over my table because of a 'glare.'

The waitresses do my bidding without grumbling, which makes me sure this spills out behind the scenes in swapped stories of my quirkiness. 'You'll never guess what? That man, from table four, now he wants the lights dimmed. Do you think he's a novelist? Or an actor? Or a millionaire?' Next time I'm planning to stipulate the precise width I'd like my cucumber to be sliced.

I didn't get much work done, but I did have some great fantasies. Following the end of this block and the triumph of my novel ('*Magnificent – it purred*' . . . '*Unputdown-able*' . . . '*Golden is a genius*'), I will give one interview to Lynn Barber. One interview at Quaglino's over seafood marinière and caramelised squid, then I will disappear into obscurity to becomea hermit like J. D. Salinger, leaving the world to argue over my novel's true import. The world's literary media will descend on my rural hideaway, but it won't do them any good. I will be shielded from their prying eyes by enormous remote-controlled gates, huge dogs and the fiercely protective locals, who, despite their slow wit, will know true genius when it overtakes them in a Ferrari GTB down a village B road.

The only people I will speak to when I am famous will be Charlie, Sean, Gemma, Sarah, Mr Gatley and Dad if he makes an appointment and promises to put a picture of me up in the snooker room with his arm around me.

11 p.m.

Nothing is written until I write it – *hat-at-at*! I think Gemma and I will end up going out with each other. I spent the evening at her house and it got quite intimate after I told her I'd posted her a letter. We sat on the floor of the back living room and asked each other questions from the board game Therapy. Therapy's a game designed so you don't have to think of conversations yourself – Waddingtons do it for you. 'So tell me on a rating scale of one to ten how charming you think you are.' . . . 'So tell me on a rating scale of one to ten how passionate you think you are.'

The cards gave us a good excuse to ask embarrassing questions without either of us drawing conclusions as to why we were asking them. After a while the questions weren't revealing enough, and, feeling a bit rash, I made up my own. 'So tell me on a rating scale of one to ten how much you fancy the person asking this question,' I said.

Gemma blushed with surprise. 'Does it say that?' she said, suspiciously.

I nodded.

'I've had this game two years and I've never—' said Gemma, and lunged forward to grab the card. I snatched it away and we fought over it – me holding one end, Gemma the other – in a way that often ends in a snog on films.

'Right! My turn,' said Gemma finally, slumping against the sofa leg, giving up the struggle and pretending to read from her set of cards. She sighed with exaggerated contentment. 'Jay, so tell me, on a rating scale of one to ten how incredibly worried you are about' – she grinned – 'what you've said in your letter.'

Gemma stood on the doorstep and watched me climb into the van. She was smiling. My heart felt weightless, like it'd been pumped full of helium.

'Nine,' she shouted, as I was about to pull away.

'What?' I said, winding down the window.

'On the scale of one to ten how much I fancy the person who asked the question,' said Gemma. She was shielding her eyes from my headlights with her clumsy, spatula-like arms. She looked gorgeous.

'Me too,' I said.

'What?' said Gemma, frowning.

'On the rating scale of one to ten how much I'm incredibly worried about what I said in my letter,' I said.

When Gemma's happy she's beautiful. Her face flushes and her dimples suck in so much it looks as though her cheeks have been pierced with an invisible arrow. Her asymmetrical face goes symmetrical when she smiles, too. Normally her nose and lip curl to the right. But they snap into position when she grins, like the legs of a balloon animal do when inflated.

Friday, 26 February

Bridget made a comment that does not bode well for my future. On checking my administration, she discovered I'd failed to keep my records of interviews up to date. 'Jay, you must keep all your admin current. What happens if we have a query to deal with when you're not around?' she said. What does she mean, 'not around'?

And I committed a serious blunder at 11.30. I telephoned Paul Arnold, a quantity surveyor, at Westville Developments, and left a message that Jay Golden from Montons had rung and that I might have a new job for him. I suddenly remembered our guarantee of discretion at work in the middle of this and my voice trailed off. 'No, no it's not Jay Golden from Montons – it's someone else, argh sorry, wrong number.'

I think I might've jeopardised Paul Arnold's prospects at Westville Developments, as well as my own at Montons. I've decided to keep quiet and wait for it to blow up in my face.

The office meeting after work went badly, too. Relaying the minutes of Wednesday's regional board meeting, one interesting fact emerged. In the monthly consultants' league table I was the second-least productive. The league covers the Home Counties and the entire Midlands.

Although I don't want to get sacked just yet (I still owe Dad three hundred pounds, which he keeps reminding me about), I can't stop committing sackable offences. Canvassing's so boring that I've started mailing out unprofessional rate guides instead. Rate guides contain prices for the various types of site staff Montons have on their books, from carpenters to quantity surveyors. Initially, on the compliments slips I wrote:

Dear Mr Client,
I enclose a copy of our current rate guide. If interested

please contact me on the number opposite.
　　Jay Golden Construction Temps
　P.S. I enclose a complimentary car sticker.

But then I started sending out:

Dear Mr Client,
Here is our current rate guide. Look after it. Owing to increasing stationery costs, you will never receive another. I repeat never.
　　Jay Golden Construction Temps.
　P.S. I enclose a complimentary car sticker.

Then:

Dear Mr Client,
Owing to increasing stationery costs, could you please return this month's rate guide to let someone else have a look. Montons appreciates your co-operation.
　　Jay Golden Construction Temps
　P.S. Could we have the car sticker back, too?

And finally:

Dear Client,
Rising stationery costs have forced Montons to the wall. Thank you for selfishly hogging our only rate guide, that was very helpful.
　　Jay Golden Construction Temps.
　P.S. Keep your filthy car sticker.

I tried the cucumber trick at Debbie's tonight. It worked brilliantly. There wasn't a word when I ordered them to be no more than one centimetre thick. And when the salad arrived I made a point of ostentatiously checking their dimensions by holding one to the light and closing one eye like a gem dealer.

I might befriend Debbie. It'd be quite cool to have a cockney friend when I'm famous. The crucial difference, though, would be that I'd never patronise Debbie like Dad's celebrity friends do to me. I'd talk to her on the same level, probably go to her daughter's wedding, and be just as interested in the problems she's having with her meat stockist as she would be in my literary career.

8 p.m.

The Gulf crisis seems to be over. The inspectors have gone in. I went round to Sean's to see how he was taking it. He was in the kitchen standing over his model, fingering the Baghdad–Amman railway sadly. I put an arm around his shoulder and reminded him there was still sporadic fighting in Kurdistan, but he brushed me off.

'Bollocks to international law – they should be nuking each other,' he said, knocking over a Basran desalination plant with a sweep of his hand.

I know how Sean feels. I thought the launching of biological weapons wasn't a question of if, but when. I thought Saddam Hussein had a nuclear bomb. I feel lost. Keeping my admin current seemed somehow more poignant when there was the prospect of Armageddon. I had got quite into the idea of starring as a latter-day Lawrence in an epic movie: me, atop a camel in Riyadh, my full kaffiyeh robes billowing in the wind behind me.

'Say, did you know Jay Golden?'
'No, but I shook his hand in Chartridge.'

When Sean calmed down I gave him another gay test. 'Right,' I said, spreading a copy of *Hello!* magazine, 'you've got to tell me to stop when you fancy someone. But you've got to be instinctive. Don't think about it or it won't work.'

I turned the pages over slowly, starting at the royal section. 'Princess Stephanie of Monaco,' I said, hovering for a moment. Sean shook his head and wasn't really paying attention. We got on to movie stars. After several pages of no reaction I got to Nick Nolte at home with his wife. 'Nick Nolte, Sean. Fancy Nick Nolte up your Suez Canal?' Sean smiled, but shook his head.

Nicole Kidman and Tom Cruise were next and Sean put his finger down on the page. 'I can see how girls would find him attractive,' he said grudgingly.

'Yes, but do you find him attractive?' I said.

Sean said he didn't know and fell into a depressive sulk about what he was going to do all day now there'd be no more hourly updates of the escalating crisis on *Sky News Digest*.

There are two types of people: veerers-towards and veerers-away-from. The latter are horrified by terrible examples of what they could become; the former are excited by images of what they'd like to be. Dad's a veerer-towards. I'm a veerer-away-from. Sean's a hideous manifestation of what I might become.

Saturday, 27 February

Sarah's now getting married in the Henry VII Chapel of Westminster Abbey. Dad announced it today over chicken curry (Sarah forgot to get a joint in so Dad had to cook). The wedding was going to be at the Church of Christ in Bellingdon, but Dad got talking to the dean of the Abbey, who does *Songs of Praise*, and he said Sarah could use the chapel.

Sarah's pleased, Gemma wants to visit the Abbey to gauge what to wear on the big day, and Dad was so excited he went around the house bowling imaginary leg-breaks, telling me, 'I was born in a two-up, two-down council house in Wakefield and now your sister's getting married in Westminster Abbey. That's what I love about this country.'

He still managed to have a row with me, though. I went to the toilet straight after lunch and he reckoned I'd done it to get out of the washing-up. When I came back down it was finished and he said, 'Very clever. Another job somebody has had to do for you. Well done.'

I told him I hadn't been trying to get out of the washing-up and that I'd just wanted the loo, and he told me it was time I started helping around the house. 'Charlie does more than you – and he's half your age,' he said.

He came up later when I was in my room working on my Wiggie novel. He said he knew Mum used to do everything without complaint, but he was not Mum and it was up to me to start chipping in. 'I'm serious,' he said. 'And when are you going to write me that cheque?'

I got a bit annoyed he'd brought up Mum like that, and told him I'd start helping around the house when he started cooking us something other than chicken curry for dinner. Dad crossed his arms and asked what was wrong with chicken curry, and I said nothing except that we'd eaten it nearly every night for two weeks and that he never did enough vegetables with it and that if he wasn't careful we'd all get bowing deformities from a lack of vitamin D.

Mum taught Dad how to cook about a dozen meals before she died. She took him through them all – fish-pies, stews, casseroles. She even wrote down recipes on Post-it Notes and pinned them to the fridge, but now Dad says they're lost.

'You could cook for yourself, of course,' he said, 'and perhaps even for the rest of us once in a while. But no, how silly of me, that would mean doing something for other people, wouldn't it?'

The whole thing made me feel down. When J. D. Salinger was my age he was already writing stories for *Esquire* magazine. He wrote sardonic articles for the Valley Forge military academy when he was just fifteen. What am I doing? You don't become the voice for a generation ringing building contractors from the Yellow Pages and getting shouted at for not rinsing pans.

Went to Debbie's to write my book and cheer myself up,

47

but she ended up shouting at me. She told me this wasn't the f-ing Ritz when I asked if I could have a quarter of a slice of processed cheese instead of a full slice in my burger. I made a veiled threat about eating at Sizzlin' Sausage in future, and I think we understood each other because she gave me extra chips and a free roll with butter.

10 p.m.

Even though Gemma flunked classics at Sheffield last year, she was very interesting about the ancient Greeks tonight. When Alexander the Great was my age he had Aristotle as a mentor. Gemma showed me an illustration of them in one of her old textbooks after we got back from playing on the pub quiz machine at the Ellie. In the drawing they're both studying an isosceles triangle Aristotle has drawn in the sand with a stick. It must've been great being Alexander the Great and having the most intelligent man in the world following you around with a twig. I'm not saying Dad's got a small brain, but if he didn't have a skull he could probably wear a clothes peg for a hat.

I had another run-in with him tonight. When Mum was alive she always stopped things getting out of hand. She'd hate seeing us fight so much she'd come up to me and persuade me to say sorry. She'd say Dad loved me and he was very sorry, too. Thinking about it, she probably said the same thing to Dad as well, because often we'd coincidentally bump into each other on the landing after a fight and make up. I'd assume Dad had come up to admit he was wrong and in a fit of magnanimity I'd say sorry first, and Dad would think I'd come out of my room to admit I was wrong and would, if not actually say sorry first (Dad never says sorry), imply he was sorry by giving me his sorry look.

(The reason we have fights in the first place is simple. It's because Dad's unreasonable and overbearing, and, unlike his minions at his work, I won't do what he says. I do

48

occasionally provoke him into petty rows. These are not proper fights, though, and are done for his own good and mine because it allows him to exercise his overbearing and unreasonable nature over trivial matters that are of little concern to me. For instance, that's why I refused to write him a cheque tonight to start paying back some of the money I owe him, and why sometimes I deliberately forget to write down money I've borrowed on the calendar where my debt is recorded. I do this for the good of the household. It's not the thieving Dad says it is.)

The argument tonight was over the Middle East. Dad said he was pleased the Gulf scare was over because overseeing the late night coverage on *Newsnight* had been a strain on him. I told him I was sad it was over, as I, like Sean, wanted it to escalate into a nuclear pan-Arab holy war because I was bored. 'I worry about you, my son,' said Dad. 'Your mother used to say you were the sensitive one – but she was wrong, wasn't she? You have the sensitivity of a gorilla.'

Thinking about it, when I'm a famous writer I might actually pay the most intelligent man in the world to follow me around with a twig. He'd be at my beck and call twenty-four hours a day to answer queries about science, religion, philosophy and everything else Dad knows nothing about. Gradually, as he comes to appreciate my enquiring mind, we might even become friends, me and the most intelligent man in the world. We'd stay up late drinking and arguing about highbrow topics, until one day I'd probably correct him over some trigonometry question or something, and he'd nod sadly and say, 'I see my work is done.' I'd say, 'Nonsense, Old Man – I've still much to learn.' But in the morning I'd get up early for my Urdu lesson, he'd be gone and I'd be distraught, but then I'd find a note from him, maybe even *in* Urdu, saying, 'The pupil has become the master,' and I'd understand.

Probably pretty good for pub quiz machines, too, having the most intelligent man in the world around the whole time.

You get a lot of tricky square-root questions on the *Give us a Break* machine down at the Ellie.

11 p.m.

I'm going to read some more of my old diary, looking for inspiration for my Wiggie book.

23 September: It feels like my insides are being eaten away by worms. It's not a surface depression that can be washed away by a night's sleep and a reappraisal. It goes right to the core. Dr Maitland, the specialist, thinks the tumour's back. 'Could it be anything else?' Mum asked. Dr Maitland didn't think so and Mum was admitted to the Chiltern Hospital. Her legs and stomach were aspirated to reduce the swelling and we went to see her in the afternoon.

We sat on chairs around the bed. Charlie watched in amazement as pink fluid with bits like half-eaten prawns flowed from Mum's stomach through a plastic tube into a bag on the floor. We were told to make sure the fluid in the bag didn't exceed half a litre. Charlie made it his job keeping an eye on it ('It's two-fifty' . . . 'It's three hundred' . . . 'Wow, did you see that big bit, Jay?').

We talked about mundane things mostly, but every time we came back to the cancer, Mum was indignant the tumour hadn't returned because she said she still felt well.

Outside, in the hospital grounds, Charlie and Sarah still inside with Mum, Dad leaned over a stone wall next to the car park, looked away from me across the adjacent field of hay, and told me more than likely the cancer had reached Mum's liver and that that meant 'there's very little chance, my son'.

We talked about it that night when Sarah was putting Charlie to bed. Dad was matter-of-fact and filled me in on practicalities: how Sarah and I had to stagger our visits to the hospital so they increased when things got nasty at the end.

'How nasty will it get?' I asked.

'Very nasty,' said Dad. He said Mum effectively had six months to live. 'She's going to undergo chemotherapy but Maitland isn't optimistic and says apart from this there's very little they can do.'

I phoned Grandad and told him the news. He didn't know what to say. And when I put down the phone I was nearly in tears. It's OK when you talk about the facts, but as soon as you're shown sympathy it gets to you.

I can't imagine the house without my mum in it: ironing in the kitchen; padding about in her yellow dressing-gown; trying to get me to eat a tomato.

It's weird – you get told the facts of life, but never the facts of death. Maybe you should. Maybe your dad should call you into his study when you're about five and give it to you straight: 'Now you might have heard a bit about this in the playground, old son, and I don't want to take up too much of your time, and for you to get too upset. But I think you're old enough to know. At some future point – it's different for everyone – you'll have an accident or catch a disease and your heart'll stop beating, your brain'll be starved of oxygen and you'll die. And there's no heaven or reincarnation or anything afterwards, you simply get burned in a wooden box to a pile of ashes or buried in the ground and eaten by maggots until there's nothing left of you. There, there, here's a handkerchief, now run along and play – it's a lovely day outside.'

Sunday, 28 February

In Gemma's reply to my letter she said I was cowardly and proud and just as scared of rejection as she was. She hand-delivered it today and it concluded with the word 'Battle-stations'. I read it in front of her and afterwards we discussed having a snog. We talked about it theoretically and agreed it would be hard to break down the friendship barrier.

In the afternoon we visited Westminster Abbey, and I

nearly burst into tears in the transept. Never mind Sarah getting married there, it is written, I'll be *buried* there. Gemma asked what was wrong so I told her.

'Kiss me,' I said, 'for when I am a ghost of a famous novelist buried between these walls I will remember thee.'

Gemma replied quite loudly, causing some tourists to look around, 'Don't talk out of your arse.'

If I do become a famous writer and they want to bury me in Westminster Abbey, I'd like a place near the west entrance – admission to this section's free. That way more people'll be able to visit my last resting place. I wouldn't mind a spot between David Lloyd George and Ramsay MacDonald. I walked over this area a couple of times and each time a prophetic chill went down my spine, although Gemma said it was probably a draught.

Gemma's mum's given me a picture of Napoleon. It's of Napoleon looking dejected just before his exile to the island of Elba. I gave a talk on Napoleon for my mock English GCSE. He's my hero because he came from nowhere, was mad enough to think he had a destiny, single-minded enough to work towards it and lucky enough to achieve it. The gift seemed significant, too, and I made a big point of saying thanks. There's no way Gemma's mum would give me a picture of Napoleon if she didn't think Gemma and I were about to start going out with each other, and there's no way she could know we're about to start going out with each other unless Gemma's said something.

10 p.m.

There is nothing quite like reading in the bath. If I could, I would live in the bath. I would put wheels on the bottom, motorise it and whirr around like Stephen Hawking. Finished *Books and Bookmen* after three hot-water top-ups and Dad knocked on the door and said if I filled it too full it would leak down into the kitchen if I got up suddenly. I told him in that case I would not get up suddenly. Dad must realise I am eighteen and have an answer for everything.

Books and Bookmen has made me realise something. I must get on with my novel and fulfil my own destiny. The book was recommended by Mr Gatley and depressed me slightly. Coleridge wrote 'Kubla Khan' after a vivid bit of REM sleep and Robert Louis Stevenson was always waking up and scribbling things down he remembered from his sleep. All I seem to dream about is getting three starters and a forward for next week. I don't think it's fair. Called Richard Whiteley a grinning popinjay on the 'phone and went to bed.

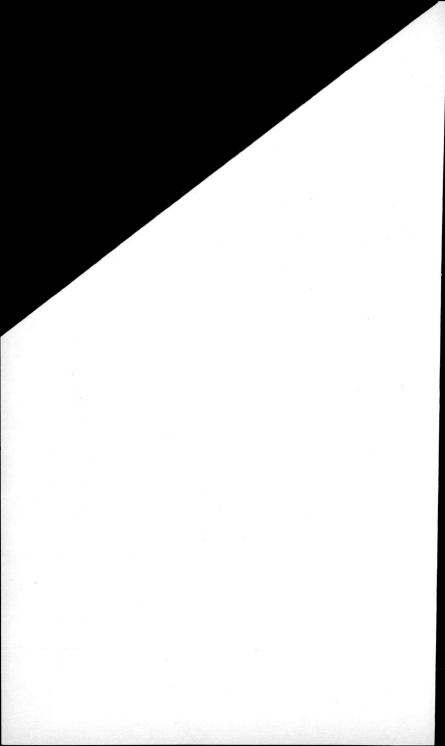

Monday, 1 March

More fruitless canvassing in the morning and there was a meeting at the Victoria branch at 3 p.m. It was a Results Progress meeting chaired by Pam Vince. Each branch had to relate its performance. This performance was measured in terms of men working and average weekly starters. It was very embarrassing. My figures came after John Bits-and-Pieces Wilson's from Watford. He had fifty men working and a five-starter-a-week average. With the weight of an area manager's stare upon me, I mumbled that I had ten to eleven men working. I knew I had ten, but for some reason thought that ten to eleven sounded more acceptable.

'You should know how many men working you have, Jay. How many starters are you getting in Harrow?' asked Pam.

I looked around the room, hoping to catch Bridget's eye, but her head was down. 'One,' I said.

'One per week?' said Pam Vince, picking up her pen to write it down.

'No, one all-told,' I said. For some reason I said 'all-told' in a slightly silly voice.

Pam put down her pen and didn't write the figure in her book as she had done for the others. There was an oppressive silence and everybody looked at their notes, including me.

'I've been here about a month, which works out at a quarter of a starter per week,' I felt like saying, to put it into recordable form.

For the rest of the meeting I sat dumbly sucking the strong mints that were passed around. I didn't take any of the Bourbon biscuits (I didn't think I deserved them, or rather I didn't think they thought I should think I deserved them) and Bridget answered all the questions directed my way, taking a dutiful manager's responsibility for me.

Bridget came up to me afterwards. We were having a drink in the boardroom. 'Well, that went pretty well,' I said brightly, but she didn't laugh.

'I took you on, Jay. Pam Vince wanted someone else. Were you trying to make me look stupid?'

8 p.m.

Dad got roasted by someone in the audience of his Charter renewal 'Meet the Public' forum tonight, and he came home in a bad mood. There was no bread left in the bread-bin and he wanted a sandwich, the hot-water tank was empty and he wanted a bath, I was watching the football and he wanted to watch *Dispatches*, I sat around all day doing 'eff-all' while he worked his socks off, and so on. He went even more ballistic when I hinted about being sacked again.

'You go on about it enough, but how many pages of this great book have you actually written?' he asked. 'I mean actually *written*.'

'Not counting notes?'

'Not counting fucking notes.'

'Three,' I said. 'But I haven't done it for a while and I've had a block and—'

'Three!' He laughed nastily. 'Let's get this straight, then. I've been working a fifteen-hour day for the last year, I've been busting a gut, and in that time you've written *three* pages.' He did his laugh again, shook his head and took a large swig of his drink. 'And are they good pages? These three pages?'

'They're OK.'

'They're *OK*,' he said, sarcastically.

'Well, the first page is quite good and the second isn't bad. And I've worked out some of the plot. I've got loads of ideas. I've been having a break to let it gel. It's—'

'We all have ideas. I'm interested in what you've *actually* done. I want to know just how stupid I've been. Indulge me. In the time it's taken me to reorganise a whole department, allocate a multi-million-pound budget and oversee three documentary series – one about the entire history of democracy in the Western world – you have written one "quite good" page. In your opinion.'

'It hasn't taken a year. I've had jobs as well.'

'Which you've lost.'

'Yes, which I've lost. But I've still had them. I've still had to go to work. And, anyway, you can't just toss a book off. It took J. D. Salinger ten years to write *Catcher in the Rye*. Tolstoy didn't write *War and Peace* in an—'

'*Ten years!*'

'Yeah . . . I'm not saying it's going to take *me* ten years. It's not going—'

'*Ten years!*'

'I was just making a point—'

'Which is what I am doing too, Jay. You're not stupid, you must know how ridiculous you sound. I can see it in your face. Three pages in one year. Come on. It's time to end this nonsense.'

Holden Caulfield wanted to be the catcher in the rye. It's metaphorical. The metaphor was lots of children playing in a field of tall rye on a cliff. Holden Caulfield was on the cliff's edge. His job was to stop innocent kids toppling over the edge into the phoney adult world. That's what his book's about. When I got sacked from Video Plus last year Dad told me to stop trying to be a catcher in the rye. He thought that's why I kept getting sacked.

'Jump off the cliff,' he said, 'it's a softer landing than you think. And anyway, aren't you embarrassed about being the oldest kid in the rye? You're twice their size – shouldn't you be playing adult games at the foot of the cliff with people your own age?'

'What, like Scattegories?' I asked, for a joke, but I understand what he means now. Most of my friends have got jobs and he wants me to be the same. He doesn't like the idea of my becoming a writer. Parents don't like their kids taking risks: they have minds like Endsleigh.

11 p.m.

First snog with Gemma in the back of the van. My fingers felt slightly sausagey, but not too bad; chipolatas, maybe. It was very embarrassing at first. We'd had a few drinks, but there was an incestuous barrier to cross. We couldn't stop laughing and had to have a tiny peck on the lips before we went fully ahead with it.

'How did that feel?'

'OK. You?'

'OK.'

It was very enjoyable in the end, though. I think I might be falling in love with Gemma. She's exerting an unsettling pull over me – I want to be with her the whole time, especially when it's dark. Other things I like about Gemma: she doesn't take anything seriously; her strong character means she can return, without bitterness, my good-natured insults, and her sense of humour means her ripostes are funny; plus, she hasn't got a job and doesn't intend to get one; and she thinks the start of my Wiggie novel is good. I showed her it tonight.

Tuesday, 2 March

The pressure's mounting. Bridget asked this morning whether I'd been logging my calls and I've heard this is often a prelude to dismissal, an unsatisfactory number deemed a legitimate excuse for the sack.

'I haven't been doing it because it's a waste of time. You spend all your time logging calls instead of actually making calls,' I told Bridget.

'Do it from now on, Jay,' she said. 'Pam wants it done.'

I will predict my own sacking. It'll be when Pam Vince

returns from holiday. I don't get harassed about starters any more and nobody's checking my current admin.

What I'd like to do is go out in a blaze of glory, do something that will leave an indelible smirch on the company name. Perhaps I could place myself in a job. When one is phoned in I could describe myself to the client, go down for the interview pretending I'm the site engineer I've just spoken so highly of, and get the job. It would reflect very badly on the company: 'Montons staff have begun placing *themselves* in the jobs they're supposed to be filling, they're so desperate.' I could just imagine Bridget's face when she finally unravelled that one.

8 p.m.

Perhaps I should base my book in London. Would the social rebel of our time really come from a dormitory town in the Home Counties? Holden Caulfield lived in New York and was at the centre of the metropolitan thrum. Wiggie is from a small town without a Marks & Spencers. I think it matters.

Mr Gatley thinks I should try to write on subjects I know more about. He wrote today and said this might be the problem with my Wiggie novel: 'I don't know you, but you certainly don't sound like someone who has ram-raided Dixons.' I'm a bit annoyed. One moment Mr Gatley says imagination is a large panting dog he wants off its leash, the next he wants me to write about what I know. I wish he'd make up his mind. And anyway, how can I write about what I know? I don't know anything.

All the writers in *Books and Bookmen* seem to have done much more interesting things than me with their lives, which has started to worry me as well. Lermontov, who wrote Russia's first psychological novel, was killed fighting in a duel at the age of twenty-seven. I'd like to die in a duel.

Went to the Limelight nightclub and I had my relationship with Gemma baptised – 'werheys', most notably from Mark and Kate. Sean looked shocked and disgruntled that it was official, and kept talking about old boyfriends of Gemma's, Rutger Hauer or other blokes he thought she fancied, then putting his hand in front of his mouth, giggling and saying, 'Oh dear, I'm sorry, Jay, I probably shouldn't be talking about Paul/Rod/Rutger, should I?'

I'd brought Dad's contacts book and when Gemma and I got bored of listening to Sean winding us up, we used the foyer call-box to phone famous people. I couldn't get through to Zsa-Zsa Gabor, but eventually got hold of Zoë Ball. Gemma told her where we were and asked her to join us, but somebody opened the main door right at that moment and the burst of M-People drowned out what Zoë Ball said. I don't think she was very happy, though. It was after 1 a.m. and she does the *Breakfast Show*.

Gemma and I went home early, and we spent about an hour in the van playing backgammon and discussing the sort of nightclub we'd like to set up if we had the money. We agreed our nightclub would be called Boffins, the letter B in the title made into a pair of round spectacles, and it wouldn't have a dress code on the door, but an intelligence code. Never mind a shirt with a collar, you'd need a certain IQ to get in, which would be tested on the door by Tefal-headed bouncers asking questions about trigonometry. It would be great: all the dumbos in their Next shirts loitering resentfully outside, scoffing chips, urinating up alleyways. *('Sorry sir – the answer's cosine 45. Perhaps another night.')*

Kissing Gemma puts me in a lethargic mood. All I want to do is more of the same. Gemma often laughs at things when I'm like this. I pretend to laugh back or it would make it uncomfortable – girls hate it if you stare at them too much – but I'd really just like to carry on snogging and staring into her eyes.

Wednesday, 3 March

Bridget was out all afternoon on a client visit and when Linda was at lunch, Martin, the temporary canvasser, and I took the opportunity to fuck around. We sent out a few unprofessional rate guides, tried to do the best cow impression answering the phone 'Hello, Moooo-ntons,' and eventually Clive Hart, the managing director, phoned. Clive Hart asked whether Bridget was around. I told him I didn't know, but that I'd put him through to somebody who might know, and put him through to Martin. He asked Martin whether Bridget was around and Martin told him he didn't know, but that he'd put him through to someone who might know, and put Clive Hart back on to me. Clive Hart asked whether Bridget was there again. He was already starting to sound impatient. I told him I didn't know and Clive Hart said, 'I've just spoken to you, haven't I?' I said I didn't think so. 'Hold the line, I'll just put you through to somebody who might know,' I said, putting him back to Martin. Clive Hart asked whether Bridget was in the office and again Martin told him he didn't know. Clive Hart asked if he'd just spoken to Martin and Martin said no, he'd just walked in the door.

'I've just spoken to four people now – what's going on down there? Get your act together, Harrow,' said Clive Hart, and Martin hung up in an embarrassed flurry. It was the first laugh I've had at Montons and it hurt my stomach. Linda came in on the end of it and when she saw me laughing accused me of being 'very unprofessional this afternoon', which made me laugh even more. I really should get out of this place. Lermontov wouldn't have put up with Montons. Lermontov would have resigned weeks ago.

Martin and his friends have apparently now got some office space for their comedy magazine. He told me this when we went for a drink after work. He said they'd been working on the concept and reckon the magazine's going to be modelled on *Viz*, although they haven't thought of a title yet. Martin said he thought I was funny as a person, but wanted to know if I could be funny in print as well. I said I was even funnier in print, and reminded him of the unprofessional rate guides I'd sent out. It's exciting: he wants us to meet up in a few days' time and for me to bring along some ideas.

I didn't mention this to Dad tonight. I'm not going to tell anyone until my first article's been commissioned. I'll be very cool. After it's been published I'll bide my time. I'll wait until Dad has a go at me for being lazy. He'll be laying into me, going on about what a busy day he's had and I'll suddenly say that today had been quite busy for me, too. Dad will scoff at this. I'll let him scoff for a long time but I won't back down about how busy I've been. Finally, after about an hour of scoffing, Dad'll ask what I've *actually* done in a sarcastic voice. At this point I will fling over a copy of the magazine, open at my article, and say, incredibly off-handedly, 'Oh yeah, I forgot to tell you, Dad – they're calling me the new Willy Rushton.'

9 p.m.

Charlie had to give Dad a note from school today. The note was from Mr Watson. It said Charlie'd got into trouble for kicking a little girl in the head, but that Charlie was aware being a Ninja Turtle at school was wrong and was very sorry. Dad was angry and sent him to bed early without any chicken curry.

'Could *I* get out of chicken curry if I kicked a little girl in the head?' I asked, and Dad said it wasn't funny and made a veiled threat about boarding school again. Charlie's seeing Dr Roberts this week at his home in Hemel. Rob's taking him over.

I can't believe Dad's serious about boarding school. I know exactly what would happen if Charlie did go: he would come back just as emotionally retarded as Dad is. He would grow stiff and distant and wouldn't be able to hug loved ones without feeling compromised or unless he'd drunk a vat of wine. That's the only time Dad drops his guard. People who go to boarding school are all the same. They all acquire born-to-rule toffee-nosed manners and hang around in floppy-haired cliques. A couple of people Gemma knows are like that. They put on an act of pretending they don't think they're superior because they went to a better school, but the act is deliberately not that great so everyone knows they really *are* superior.

I talked to Gemma about Charlie tonight and she said he sounded quite a character. He is quite a character. He's much cleverer than I was at his age. Charlie's already a good reader, and if you leave the room to get something during a film you can rely on him, even if it's quite complicated, to fill you in on the plot: 'Michael found the Godfather alone in the hospital that was supposed to be guarded by the police but wasn't, and he realised it was a set-up and Salazzo was behind it and now he's called Sonny and everything's going to be all right, although I don't trust Gambini.'

I'd like Gemma to meet Charlie. She'd like him, and he'd like her. The trouble is I don't want Gemma to meet Dad. Dad's always embarrassing when I bring girls round. He gets all suspicious I'm up to something in my room and keeps coming up on the pretext of one thing or another to check on me. The last girl I went out with was called Sophie and she came round once with both her legs in plaster. She'd had an operation to correct something to do with her feet and Dad even came up then. He didn't like the fact she was lying on my bed. She couldn't do much else with her legs in plaster, but Dad still made her sit on the floor, and then, of course, he helpfully brought up his all-world jigsaw for us to do, and sat down with us for half an hour doing Greenland.

Sophie dumped me eventually. I've been dumped three times in all, and I've dumped two girls myself. Sophie gave me the most amazing excuse I've ever heard when she dumped me: it wasn't that she didn't like me, but that her mother had told her she'd have a brain tumour if Sophie carried on going out with me. Her exact words were 'It's a choice between you and my mum, you're my boyfriend, but I'm stuck with my mum for life.' I never get on well with other people's parents. Gemma's parents are quite nice to me at the moment, but it's always the same, and it'll happen again: what a nice boy, what a funny boy, let's give him a picture of Napoleon; what a nasty boy, what a selfish boy, let's threaten a brain tumour.

Thursday, 4 March

Made the sort of unprofessional mistake that two weeks ago I might have worried about. I sent Mr Peris, an unintelligible Indian plasterer, down to the London Borough of Harrow to be interviewed for a senior quantity surveyor's position.

Bridget called me into one of the interview rooms when I got back from lunch. I knew it was going to be about Mr Peris because his CV was strewn over my desk. Bridget had been hunting for it in my drawers.

'Mr Peris,' she said as we sat down.

'Mr Peris,' I repeated. 'Who went for an interview today,' I said, trying to sound on the ball. 'How did he . . . er . . . get on?'

'Not very . . . er . . . well.' Bridget grimaced ironically.

'Oh, why's that?' I tried to look surprised.

'Well, Jay, he knew nothing whatsoever about quantity surveying for a start – which isn't surprising seeing as though he's actually a plasterer. The client's furious – it's the first time they've used us and he says frankly it's the last and frankly I don't blame him. I'm very disappointed, Jay.'

Martin's been dismissed. Bridget couldn't abide his sarcastic attitude, and is blaming him for the incident with Clive Hart. We're still meeting up in a few days' time to discuss the comedy magazine. I've written some things already. One sketch is particularly funny: it's about a character called Berty Bathtime, who has baths in unlikely situations. I even had a dream about it last night. Martin and I were raising a toast to celebrate the magazine crashing through the 1 million circulation mark. 'To wit,' said Martin, raising his glass. 'Towoo,' I replied. It's a boost to be able to make jokes in your sleep, even if they are only ones about owls.

10 p.m.

Gemma came round to our house for the first time and met Charlie tonight. They got on well, but Dad was annoying – he made out we had a better relationship than we do by not nagging once and pretending not to mind missing *Newsnight* so we could watch a Billy Crystal comedy-romance. I think Gemma was a bit disappointed: 'You made out he was a complete ogre. He was actually very nice,' she said. Dad . . . will he never cease to find new ways to undermine me? He could at least've been drunk.

Gemma brought her Tarot cards over and gave me an enlightening reading. Apparently, I'm three-quarters through my life-cycle and give joy to women. My career will be in the creative arts (naturally), although I must be prepared for a lot of disappointment, and I'll be married only once and have three children, all boys. I'm also to be wary of an authoritative person preoccupied with other people's opinions – probably Gemma's dad, Gemma thinks – and I'll shortly go through a trying period of arguments, with Gemma, according to Gemma, which I must endure to reap future benefits. I also have a niggling health worry, which I should be careful about.

Sean cropped up as well – he's heading for certain ruin. He'll fall in love and it'll cost him everything. It all seemed pretty accurate, especially the bit about Sean. I've always thought he was doomed.

When I got back from dropping her off tonight Dad joked that he might soon be hearing more wedding bells. I can imagine marrying Gemma, that's the funny thing. When Sarah goes on about her wedding, I even have daydreams about it: Dad's best-man speech, Charlie doing a reading, Sarah in tears, me thanking Gemma's parents for never threatening a brain tumour.

It's slightly unnerving – I'm doing everything I once thought corny. I can't help myself. Gemma and I ask what each other is thinking, kiss when we meet and part, have long silences that don't feel uncomfortable and if we're not careful we'll be eating at Pizza Hut soon.

I half wish I hadn't told Gemma about Mum, though. She keeps wanting me to talk more about it. As part of her attempt to get back into Sheffield to do psychology Gemma's read a book on bereavement and has got it into her head that I haven't grieved properly. There are stages you have to go through, apparently – anger, denial, understanding, or whatever – and she thinks talking about it will help. I don't agree. Last time we talked about it I got my terrible recurring nightmare: I'm in a hospital and there is an old man, Dad, I think, but who is Mum in spirit. This old man is being violently sick into a bowl. Great jets of orange spew shoot from his mouth almost continuously and his wrinkled fingers delve into the bowl to retrieve morsels of the undigested food he's brought up. He pops these back into his mouth and swallows them between spasms. Meanwhile, a nurse whispers in my ear, 'He needs the protein.' Mum didn't die of cancer. Officially she died of malnutrition. The cancer got to her liver and she couldn't eat.

Friday, 5 March

I wanted to spend the day with Gemma, so I phoned in sick this morning. A swollen uvula. The perfect ailment –

obscure, serious-sounding and totally impossible to refute without a doctorate in medicine, and at least five years on an ear, nose and throat ward.

Bridget asked if it was psychosomatic, bearing in mind Mr Peris. And Dad overheard me and shouted, 'The only thing swollen about you is your opinion of yourself.'

But it was worth it. I went to the cinema with Gemma in the afternoon and on the way back, when we got to the Amersham Hill roundabout, she pushed my indicator up into the turning-left position and gave me a funny look. I went left like she wanted and at the next roundabout she flicked it down and gave me the same look so I went right. This went on until I'd turned into a dead-end dirt road in Aston Clinton. At the end of it was a five-bar gate leading to a farmer's field. When I reached it, Gemma climbed into the back, took off her top and beckoned me in with a crooked finger. I put on the brake, turned off the van headlights, covered the back window with a sleeping bag and we had sex for the first time. It was very enjoyable. It lasted about fifteen minutes. I think Gemma had an orgasm. Either that or she rolled over on to one of her shoes.

11 p.m.

Sean phoned up with some of his pathetic coincidences this evening. He used to do this after he failed all his A levels and it's a bad sign.

'Another one for you, Jay-boy,' he said. That's always how he introduces them: 'Couple for you today, Jay-boy' . . . 'Just the one, today, Jay-boy.' 'I was feeding blummin' Seffie,' said Sean, 'and I noticed blummin' DIXY written on the bottom of the blummin' tin.' Whenever Sean talks about coincidences he gets excited, loses his eloquence and says blummin' all the time. 'Dixey is what Mum wants to call the house in Scotland. And I'd been to Dix-ons that morning to get a new plug for the kettle. Blummin' weird. Why do you think they keep happening to me?'

I said it was probably because he had special powers. Gemma thinks Sean might be schizophrenic and that I should take him to see someone, but the real trouble is Sean just spends so long in his bedroom doing nothing.

Tonight Sean told me he was planning to spend the next two years reading the entire online *Encyclopaedia Britannica*. He's still being funny about Gemma though. He came out with his parting speech this evening, the one he always comes out with whenever I have a girlfriend: 'I suppose we had some good times.' And he even asked at one point if Gemma and I were getting married. A number of coincidences had apparently pointed to it.

'I.e. us spending a lot of time together, you mean?' I asked and Sean said not just that, but that he'd found a metal blummin' ring outside in the Jobcentre car park and had watched *Morse* the other night and in one scene Morse's Jag drove past St Mary's Church in blummin' Chesham.

Saturday, 6 March

Charlie kicked up a fuss about chicken curry today. Sarah was late coming round because of a wedding rehearsal, so we missed our Saturday roast again. We've had chicken curry three days in a row; the meat was particularly stringy and Charlie couldn't stand it any longer and threw his plate on the floor using some pointed Turtle-speak to condemn it. I told Dad that Charlie was right – it was time we had something else. And it threatened to turn into the scene in prison dramas when disaffected inmates turn over canteen tables and start a riot, until Dad took the heat out of the situation by promising Viennetta for pud.

It was nerve-racking in the afternoon waiting for Charlie to return. Sarah and Rob took him for his informal consultation at Dr Roberts's house. Dad and I paced around the garden, while Dad told me that I knew, didn't I, that something had to be done.

'He's getting worse, my son. Did you know he's been trying to get out of lessons at school by pretending to have hay fever? He's running wild. You're the closest person to him – surely you can see this can't go on. Why don't you try to have a word with him?'

When Sarah got back she asked me how Dad was before she'd even tell me about Charlie. Apparently, Dad's been moaning about how long I'm spending in the bath. He thinks I'm to blame for the bill we just got for emptying the cesspit. I told Sarah I didn't spend any longer in the bath than normal, and it was just that Dad wasn't used to dealing with the bills. He hasn't paid a bill himself for twenty years – Mum did all that – so he's bound to think they're all high.

'Why can't you read in your bedroom like normal people?' asked Sarah. 'Reading for two hours in there, that's what does it.'

'I suppose we'll have to start having basin washes like the Railway Children to save money now will we?' I said.

Sarah told me not to be stupid. I said I wasn't being stupid. It's not my fault we live out in the sticks and can't get on main drainage. The bath is the flash-point between Dad and me. It's like Alsace-Lorraine between France and Germany.

Before she left, Sarah said I should brace myself, because she thinks it's likely Charlie's going to boarding school. 'Dad's up at the crack of dawn dropping Charlie at Angela's for school. You forget he's got to be mother and father now, Jay. He's got to cook, tidy the house and do all the things she used to do – pay the bills, shop, all the rest of it. He just can't cope. We've got to look after him. I hated the idea to start with, but I can't see there's any other option. We won't know until Dad gets the report, but I think Dr Roberts agrees.'

I felt depressed at the Charlie situation when I went to bed and dragged my duvet across the hall and climbed into my old top bunk in his room. I tried to have a chat with Charlie about school, and his urges and what might happen. But halfway through, down the crack between the mattress and the wall, I noticed him wiping something on the wall. 'Hey . . . I saw that. You're not wiping your bogies on the wall, are you?'

Charlie said no, but when I lifted up the top of the mattress and peered through the slats, I caught him wiping one into a red square he'd crayoned on to the wallpaper. He was making a bogie fresco.

'Does Dad know you're doing that?' I asked. He didn't answer. He was too busy picking. 'Hey you, Michaelangel-bogie – does Dad know you're doing that?'

'No,' said Charlie, and pointed nonchalantly further down the wall, where there was another one, completed.

'Charlie, you do know Dad's deciding whether to send you to boarding school right now. He's just decorated this room. And what's this about pretending to have hay fever?'

Charlie looked at me defensively. He was depositing another scraping carefully in the corner of the square. His tongue was in his cheek from the concentration.

'Charlie, you're going to have to clear that up. Or at least cover it with something. You don't want to go to boarding school, do you?'

Sat on the bed cross-legged, he was now trimming the bogie with his fingernail so it didn't overlap the crayon line. I had to admire his neatness.

'Charlie,' I said, 'Dad'll kill you if he finds that. That's brand-new wallpaper. Why are you pretending to have hay fever?'

'I've had three nosebleeds,' said Charlie proudly. 'Two for that one, and one for this one.'

'Charlie, I'm talking to you.'

'You have to wipe them before they're dry.'

'*Charlie!*'

'They snap when they get dry and they don't stick.'

'Charlie, promise me you'll clear that up in the morning. Promise me?'

72

'All right,' he said tiredly.

'Charlie,' I said, because I thought he was falling asleep and I wanted to ask him something.

'What? I'm not doing it.'

'Charlie, when do you think about Mum? Is it more at home, or more when you're at school? Dad thinks it's more at home. Charlie?'

Charlie banged his head on the pillow three times, counting them out, then said in a sing-song voice, 'I think about Mum sometimes at home, sometimes at school, but she's with God and the angels and Grandma and she's not coming back . . . *silly head*.' Then he switched off the light.

Sunday, 7 March

I watched a film at Gemma's this morning about an English toff called Charles, who one day just suddenly jacked in his job, sold his house, left his wife and went to live in a mud hut in Africa because he was sick of the West. This Charles fell in love with a beautiful black laundrywoman called Boban, who'd lost a leg in a landmine accident. It was a funny film, although it wasn't supposed to be, and Gemma and I cracked up all the way through. They met at a waterhole when Boban showed Charles the best way to rinse out long-johns. And pretty soon he was spending his whole time giving her romantic piggy-back rides and singing nursery rhymes to the little children of the village, who they both kind of adopted.

It was the corniest film I've ever seen, but the stupid thing is that it got to me. A disabled woman, some wattle and daub, a few nursery rhymes – it's more attractive than pretending to worry about starters and forwards. I'd marry a woman called Boban with *no* legs if it meant I never had to pretend to worry about a starter or forward again. I reckon I've got another week before I'm fired.

After we'd had sex Gemma and I decided to go around pretending to be Charles and Boban. I copied Charles's accent, strapped Gemma's leg up with a belt and gave her a piggy-back ride around Chesham park until she got cramp. Afterwards we returned to the van and cut a pack of cards to decide whether to go right or left at each junction, then whether to do a particular dare or not.

In the Sarrat Garden Centre we cut the pack to decide whether we would climb into the back of the van and have a snog. Halfway through the snog the car-park attendant banged on the back window and asked what we thought we were doing. I hate that – people asking what you think you're doing, as if it's going to be any different from what you *are* doing, so I put on my Charles voice and told him we were waiting for our chauffeur, who was inside buying bulbs. The man was confused by this and didn't know what to say.

'My wife Boban has one leg,' I told him. 'We met at a waterhole. I've been giving her piggy-back rides all morning and now I'm tired and need to lie down.'

The man looked in the back of the van, saw Gemma's belted-up leg, and said something apologetic about a shed having been stolen the week before from the garden centre. When he walked away we both cracked up.

Afterwards back at Gemma's she let me read her diary, or rather wasn't too annoyed when I stole it and locked myself in the bathroom to read it. It was very revealing and I learned that she's in love with me. Gemma was very embarrassed about it and I spent the rest of the night trying to force her to say it out loud. Gemma's had other boyfriends but claims she's never said it, let alone felt it before, so I'm quite honoured. We worked up to it gradually because she was too proud to concede it immediately. Initially I got Gemma to repeat the phrase, 'A mother cat loves her kittens,' before saying 'love' on its own, and finally in the sentence, 'I love you, Jay.'

It's invigorating that we're going out properly. We've

started having tremendous fights about who'll do little things. We're battling for supremacy in the relationship and keep joking about who's 'The Boss'. When we played backgammon tonight, for instance, I refused to set up her counters for the next game when she went to the toilet, only doing my own. In turn Gemma refused to make me a cup of tea when she made one for herself. It's all meant good-naturedly and adds healthy spice to the relationship.

9 p.m.

I tried to have another word with Charlie tonight. He was doing his teeth. When Charlie does his teeth he always makes sure he gets lather all over his face so he can wipe it off with the toothbrush blade and pretend he's shaving with a cut-throat razor. You're not supposed to talk to him when he's using his toothbrush blade. He could easily cut himself if you did.

'Charlie, what's all this about hay fever? You haven't got hay fever,' I said when he'd finished.

'Yes, I have,' he said. He was looking in the mirror, massaging his chin to make sure he'd got everything, which made me laugh.

'Charlie, I know you haven't got hay fever.'

'I've got hay fever,' he said again. He picked up a towel to wipe his face and then, quick as a flash, he turned his back on me, fiddled with his face for a moment, turned back to face me and sneezed three times in my face. 'See!' he said.

'How did you do that?' I asked.

This time he didn't turn his back. 'If you put your finger up your nose,' said Charlie, putting his finger back up his nose, 'you get hay fever. Colin Higgins told me.' Charlie's face contorted, he yanked out his finger, and sneezed again. 'Colin Higgins has had hay fever for two years.'

Gemma's coming to Charlie's birthday party on Friday to try to have a word with him. I hope this doesn't affect him too much because I quite like Charlie misbehaving. I don't want him to grow up to be a ram-raider like Wiggie or anything, but a little misbehaving shows he's got imagination. There's nothing worse than a kid with no imagination. There are a couple of them in Charlie's class: it's like they've already had their personalities knocked out of them, and you know they're going to end up as the sort of adults who'll tell people, 'It's the company image that'll suffer.'

Monday, 8 March

Bridget asked me in for a quick word as soon as I arrived this morning. I followed her into one of the interview rooms. I expected the conversation to be about Mr Peris, but Bridget took me by surprise.

'A little bird tells me you've been doing foolish things with the rate guides,' she said.

I didn't know the correct response, so I said, 'You've got a lot of little birds working for you,' thinking this particular little bird must have been Linda.

'No, only one,' said Bridget, confirming my suspicion. 'It doesn't matter anyway. I am remarkably perceptive, Jay. I can tell when somebody begins to slacken off.'

I stiffened, conscious of looking flaccid in the chair, and Bridget paused, waiting for me to incriminate myself with a nod or a smile. It seemed rude not to oblige.

'You don't want to believe everything you hear,' I said mysteriously. I thought for a second about going into a resignation speech. Then it occurred to me I might make a case of it all being a deliberate ruse designed to entrap Linda, feeding her misinformation to test her loyalty and self-restraint. 'People often say things they don't mean.'

But Bridget anticipated me. 'I've got one you sent to AMKA Builders. I know the MD,' she said.

I couldn't suppress a small laugh and our eyes met, mine conveying good-natured admission, hers good-natured triumph.

'If it was only this it might be . . .' Bridget sighed. 'There's the comments in the *Current Men Working* book, Mr Arnold, Mr Peris, your punctuality, there's your performance and . . . Jay, I'm going to ask you what you think I should do. What would you do – be honest – if you were me?'

'I'd sack me,' I said.

We talked quite pleasantly afterwards. Bridget said she thought we could've been great friends. I wondered about the 'great', we shook hands and I left, wondering whether it should've been a kiss.

Dad asked what I was doing back so early. I'd forgotten he was working from home. His arms were folded uncompromisingly. I told him I'd resigned to embark on a five-year course of self-education and went upstairs to read a Maupassant novel and Dad shouted 'Loafer' after me.

I thought I'd got off lightly at the time, but later when we were watching the football highlights I made the foolish mistake of trying to have a conversation with him. All I said was something about lazy players like David Ginola being the best because they let donkeys do the hard work to give themselves time to be creative. Dad must've thought I was referring to our relationship and my book, and was labelling him a donkey, because he flew into a rage. He started shaking his head like he had a wasp in his ear. I couldn't work out what was going on at first – what I'd said had been so innocuous – and I was about to suggest pouring some boiling water down his earhole to dislodge it when he came towards me thrashing his head about like Rick Parfitt during 'Rockin' all over the World'.

'You're eighteen – *eighteen*! And you have the mind of a child. Can't you see you're giving me a heart attack? Do you want to kill me?' Charlie was more responsible than I was. I was never going to get anywhere with my attitude. When was I going to start paying rent? Did I want to end up a tramp, sleeping on a park bench? Did I know how upset Mum'd got about my messy room? Had I seen the bruises she'd got slipping over on pieces of A4 paper I'd left on the floor? This wasn't the attitude of someone who was serious about work. I was a bright boy, but I had to get myself sorted. It was time I got myself sorted.

It was all a bit annoying because I'd had to keep glancing his way and ended up missing a fine left-foot shot from Arsenal's French midfielder Patrick Vieira.

Travelling up on the Metropolitan Line, complaining about signal failures at Chalfont Latimer. Going to Construction socials to get your face known, eating chicken tikka-flavoured crisps. There must be more to life than this. I want to be a famous writer. That's all I want to be. I want to live outside society beyond the stockade like a wild, sharp-clawed animal glaring in.

'I see,' said Dad, when I mentioned this to him. 'And who's going to finance this existence "beyond the stockade"? Me, I suppose?'

I told him I'd become a thief to finance myself if I had to. Dad said I was one of those already, and reminded me about the last five-pound tube fare I'd borrowed, but hadn't noted down on the calendar.

Charlie heard the racket and came in to ask what was going on. Dad didn't say anything. Charlie looked at me and I said, 'It's nothing, Charlie,' and Dad turned round and said, 'Yes, that's right – it's nothing. Your brother's lost another job. It's nothing to him. Quite important to me. Quite important to his father who shall soon be hairless.'

Dad came up to me later when Charlie had gone. I thought he'd come up for round two, but instead he dropped his own bombshell. I think the timing gave him a certain satisfaction. 'You might as well know, I've heard from Dr Roberts,' he said.

Dr Roberts's letter was lying open on the kitchen table. He'd written that he thought Charlie's urges were 'a way of trying to control an uncontrollable world', and were perfectly explicable bearing in mind what had happened to Mum. There was a lot of psycho-babble about displacement.

Then the killer paragraph – Dr Roberts thought a new setting 'could well be useful'.

2 a.m.

Pushing the van indicator upwards has now become a code for 'Let's have sex'. I did it going down Chesham's new one-way system on our way back from the pub, even though there were no turn-offs in sight. Gemma understood immediately.

It's odd – in the past I've always treated women's breasts carefully, as if I were handling a fragile kitten, stroking lovingly and resisting the urge to throttle them by squeezing violently. With Gemma, it's different. She's a passionate woman and in the thick of the action loses herself totally, allowing me carte blanche over all her important areas. Now I pummel and knead, yank and twist and behave towards them, generally, much as a nifty housewife would in a dough-rolling contest. We had sex four times tonight – my record in a twenty-four-hour period. Gemma says sex with me gives her a whoosh. It gives me a whoosh, too.

She tried to cheer me up about Charlie afterwards. She said he wouldn't have to go until the school year started in September and he might be better by then. She also thinks I've got an irrational grudge against boarding school. She said one of her best friends on her old classics course, Rod, had gone to boarding school and he'd come out all right.

28 September: It's amazing how resilient human beings can be. You imagine when something tragic happens you'll crack up. But your life carries on almost as normal. Instead of worrying about unimportant things – your writing, that you're slightly overweight and haven't got a girlfriend – you worry about a very important thing instead.

It's almost as if your brain only has so much space in it. However bad things get, you can't go beyond your worry capacity. It's like Dad's laptop – you can't borrow worry space from other functions, can't dip into Word or Agenda. You still eat when hungry, drink when thirsty.

I visited Mum in the hospital today. It's less than a week since we heard the news and already she's a lot worse. Her muscles have wasted because she hasn't been moving and when her lunch arrived I had to cut up her crispy duck because she hadn't the leverage in bed. Later she got trapped wind, which the peppermint water wouldn't shift. She was in agony with it and one of the nurses and I had to half lift her out of bed to try to dislodge it. The whole thing nearly made me cry and I had to kiss the top of her forehead to stop myself. Mum's suddenly like an old lady – light and weak like a badly made DIY table you get frightened will break when you pick it up.

Dad and I took Charlie to McDonald's tonight for a Happy Meal as a treat and because Dad can't cook anything. There was an elderly lady with a walking stick in the no-smoking section who'd obviously just met her son there and the whole spectacle got to me. The elderly lady's eyesight was bad and her son had to read the menu board out for her, and I thought: I'd like my mum to grow old. I'd like to have to read the menu board out for her.

Dad says I should look on the whole thing philosophically. The family's been very lucky and Dad, Mum, Sarah, Charlie and I have lived nearly 130 years between us without a major disaster, and this is just a hand we're due.

Reading my old diary – that's another idea of Gemma's I'm not sure about. If I can't talk about it, she reckons I should read about it. It's pretty tough, though. It just seems so absurd that Mum's not around any more. Sometimes I almost don't believe it. She's just shopping at Hivings Hill and will be back any minute with a basket of ironing under her arm, I think. There is so much around that reminds me of her: a lot of her clothes are still hanging in the wardrobe, the dowel rod fastened to the beam in the kitchen she used to hang her ironing on is still there, a couple of her coats are still in the cloakroom and there's even one of her driving gloves in the back of the van I haven't the heart to throw away. It's like Mum's left a thin film of herself over everything and I fantasise sometimes that if I could gather together all this and mould it like Plasticine I might be able to recreate her.

Tuesday, 9 March

Dad practically made out he'd caught me lifting the Crown Jewels when he came home early and saw me watching *Countdown* this afternoon.

'It must be pretty tough being a sharp-clawed animal,' he said. 'All those hours toiling away at your book. I really admire your motivation, old son. I understand completely now why you can't hold down a job and haven't time to help around the house.'

I told him I was taking a screen break, which I was – I'd just been writing a funny article for Martin's comedy magazine – and Dad said, 'Well here's another,' and switched off the telly.

To show him what he'd reduced me to, I went down to Chesham's McDonald's. They didn't have any managerial positions, but the boss, obviously impressed by my two months' experience at Big Al's Golden Delicious Doner Kebabs, said they were short of part-timers and I could start in the kitchen on Thursday. When I told Dad I would be frying Big Macs for a living and asked if he was happy now he said, 'I see, another dossy job to get your father back. Very clever, very grown up, my son, but it's not going to change my mind. He is going and that's the end of it. Here's a cloth, now go and wipe that filth off Charlie's bedroom wall.'

Dad spent the rest of the night pacing up and down, regurgitating the BBC Charter renewal speech he's giving to the National Heritage Secretary next week: 'Across the whole waterfront from news and current affairs, light entertainment, schools' programmes, music and income-generation the BBC provides a unique and unrivalled service for a licence fee that still works out at less than thirty pence a day. The public think it's good value for money. We think it's good value for money, *blah, blah, blah*.'

I tried to bring up Mum at one point. I wanted to tell him that she would never have sent Charlie to boarding school if he'd been the one who'd died, but Dad just steered the conversation round to his work. 'Bless her, your mother was never impressed by titles. She probably wouldn't even have known who the National Heritage Secretary was. I remember when she met my friend the Chief Rabbi *blah blah blah* . . .'

That's something else that annoys me. Dad can't bear anyone else talking about Mum. It's all right if he does, but if you do it he shouts you down. All our memories of Mum have to conform to his picture of her, which is inconsistent anyway and which he only summons up to justify things he does for which people might think badly of him. At the moment he's going on about the fact that he might get a knighthood if the BBC Charter's renewed. He says he wants it for Mum, that she would've been tickled pink with the idea of being Lady Bel and that's the reason it's important to him. But Mum wouldn't have cared less, because, as Dad said himself, she wasn't impressed with titles at all. This shouldn't annoy me as much as it does.

11 p.m.

I like Debbie's café but I think it might be part of the problem. It's just too noisy. How can anyone write great fiction when Debbie's bellowing, 'Two teas, one with, one without,' and 'Whose is the sausage, chips and beans?' at the top of her voice?

When Hemingway was in the Café Closerie des Lilas he was mixing with literary figures like Ezra Pound, talking about the essence of prose and the latest exhibition at the Louvre, not Eddie Stobart lorry drivers talking about the tits on page three and how many Flo put away for Chelsea on Saturday.

The comedy magazine modelled on *Viz* is a non-starter, too. I met Martin tonight and I don't like his attitude. He seems convinced his material's funnier than mine. He doesn't say so, but I know he's thinking it because of how silent he goes when I read it out.

'Berty Bathtime – he has baths all the time in unlikely places,' I say.

Silence.

'You know, when he's stressed, or under pressure, that's when he has them.'

Silence.

He reckons I should try to be more satirical. 'What you've done is fine – but it's a little whimsical for us,' he said.

I asked how all the plans were coming along, as if the overall picture of the comedy magazine was more important than this tiny setback, and Martin said they were negotiating the ground rent, but that he'd just thought of a great title for the magazine.

'What's that?' I asked.

'We're going to call it *Shite*,' he said.

I told him that was a good idea, because although it was obviously anti-establishment, the 'e' on the end made it less rude than 'shit', and more likely to be acceptable at WH Smiths. 'It's short, self-mocking and also quite a matey title. I like it,' I said.

It was only when I got home and thought to myself, Hang on a sec, they're not going to call a magazine 'Shite', that I realised Martin had probably been making some satirical reference to my Berty Bathtime material that I'd been too whimsical to spot. Martin is a cunt.

Wednesday, 10 March

Sarah came round tonight to drop off Charlie's birthday present (he's seven on Friday) and I told her about Dad being an ogre. But Sarah just said Dad was only being tough on me because he was worried about me. 'He doesn't approve of McDonald's. He sees it as just the next one,' said Sarah, "video shop, barman, kebab man, recruitment consultant, McDonald's. He thinks you're being lazy, delaying the inevitable – and he's got a point. For instance, Jay, I don't think he was very pleased when he came home from work yesterday and caught you watching *Countdown* in your pyjamas."

Although I have seven UCCA points and know the chemical symbol for iron, there's a good reason why I'm working at McDonald's. 'I'm doing it to gain an insight into hardship,' I told Sarah. It's true – if I want to write a great novel, I must know what it's like to suffer. Everyone in *Books and Bookmen* suffered. Tolstoy suffered: he wrote *War and Peace* after witnessing men drop like flies in the Crimean War. J. D. Salinger suffered: he wrote *Catcher in the Rye* after a string of dangerous jobs on Icelandic trawlers.

'The nearest I come to suffering is waiting for the immersion to heat up for a bath,' I said. '*Delayed Bath*, by Jay Golden, a gritty story of life under Economy Seven heating. It's annoying, but there's not a book in it, Sare.'

Sarah said Dad wasn't trying to stop me doing what I wanted. 'He's pleased about your correspondence course. Why do you think he paid for it? He wants you to succeed. We all do. Dad just wants you to meet him halfway. You mentioned the bath, so let's take the bath. He's annoyed you spent two hours in there yesterday. You're annoyed he banged on the door and nagged you to get out. Why don't you spend an hour in there next time? You're supposed to be the intelligent one. Why is it always me who has to point out a compromise? And you've got to stop fighting over Charlie. It isn't doing anyone, including Charlie, any good. Maybe if you were more of a role-model none of this would have happened. Have you thought about that?'

I felt a bit guilty after this and tried to involve Dad in my writing so he'd see how serious I was about it and change his mind about Charlie. We were all watching TV, and I told him the problem I was having getting the characters in my book to actually do anything, and how they always seemed more at home sitting about talking. I wish I hadn't bothered, though.

'Don't tell me your characters are even lazier than you,' said Dad, and he and Sarah laughed.

9 p.m.

I phoned Sean this evening, but Mrs F butted in on the extension.

'Is that Jay?' she said to Sean. Then, to me in a wheedling voice, 'Jay, have you two had a row?'

Sean told her to shut up.

'Where've you been, Jay?' she said.

I said I'd been busy.

'Busy with your new girlfriend,' said Mrs F, giggling.

'Muuuum,' said Sean.

'He misses you. He doesn't want to move to Scotland with us, Jay.'

'Fucking hell, Mum,' said Sean.

'Well you do miss him and it's true, you don't want to come. He's been a right pain, Jay,' said Mrs F. 'First that silly model I had to climb over to get to the fridge and have you heard the latest?'

'Right!' Sean slammed down the phone, and went to get her off the extension.

'Have you heard about this silly encyclopedia business?' said Mrs F. 'We used to think he'd be an officer in the army like his Grandad, Jay. We don't mind he isn't, but I am so ashamed dropping him at that Benefits Agency, all those dossers. Geoff's going to have a word with him tonight, aren't you, Geoff? We've offered to pay for his retakes, but he doesn't want to know. I just hope he's different in Scotland, Jay. I hope he meets a nice girl like you have. If he's going to stay in his room all day studying, why doesn't he study something worthwhile? Why doesn't he retake his A levels and get a decent qualification? Has he mentioned anything to you about the encyclopedia, Jay?'

Suddenly there was a commotion as Sean got to the phone. Mrs F's voice went higher. '*Sean!* . . . Put that down! That's not funny,' she said, laughing. 'Geoff, tell Sean to put that down. *Geoff!* Jay, Sean's got a poker.' Mrs F couldn't stop herself laughing and it made me laugh, too. 'Sean, don't be silly! *Sean!* The handle's loose. You'll . . . *Ouch!* That's sharp! *Sean!* That's sharp . . . *Ouch!* . . . You're getting soot on my . . . *Stop it!*' There was another scramble, followed by giggling from both of them and finally the phone went dead. I waited by the phone expecting Sean to ring back but when it was clear he wasn't going to, I went round to his house with Gemma and we took him out for a drink. Sean was very odd throughout, probably because Gemma was there, and kept scratching his neck, not listening to what we said. He kept either insisting he hadn't ever done anything gay, even though we didn't say he had, or just reeled off facts he'd learned from the *Encyclopaedia Britannica* about the acacia plant.

Thursday, 11 March

First day at McDonald's. I'm now having serious doubts about suffering. All employees wear a badge. The badges define your standing in the restaurant. The more stars on them, the greater this is. Chris, my trainer, has four. It means he's competent on the ovens, toasters and in the lobby area, and that he has 'a good personality'.

A person can order about anybody with fewer stars than them. Because I have none, I can't order about anybody, but can be ordered about by everyone. This is depressing, especially when the bins need emptying. Dad was as unsupportive as ever. When I complained good-naturedly about this over chicken curry tonight, he got aggressively smug: 'Yeah, welcome to the real world. Not very nice is it, my son?'

I was annoyed and pretended I thought he was talking about the chicken curry. 'No, you're right, Dad, it's disgusting as ever,' I said and Dad tried to get me back by ordering me to vacuum the porch. He reckoned I'd walked some mud in. I hadn't. Charlie had. So I refused. 'Nature abhors a vacuum. And so do I,' I said, and went up to my bedroom to read a Strindberg play.

11 p.m.

I had another battling-for-supremacy-in-the-relationship row with Gemma that nearly got out of hand. I can't help sparking them off. We were at my house and she made a remark about Rod, this guy from Sheffield University who I think she used to fancy, which I found offensive. She stubbornly refused to apologise for it, saying she'd done nothing wrong. In the end, to make a point and increase the likelihood of her apologising in future, and so avoiding further such situations, I threatened to take her home as a punishment.

We got to Hivings Hill before she said she was sorry. However, on the way back to my house, everything seemingly resolved, Gemma called the whole thing stupid. I slowed down to intimidate her and asked menacingly, 'Who's stupid?'

'You are,' she said, in a last-ditch show of defiance. Naturally I swung the van round, headed for her house again and demanded another apology. Later, after it had all been satisfactorily resolved, Gemma tried to convince me that she had, shortly after the incident, implied she was sorry by rubbing my foot with her own foot while we sat apart on the sofa.

I think we can safely assume I am now the boss and she won't be going to Sheffield.

Friday, 12 March

Nightmare day! I kept cooking quarter-pounder buns in the wrong toaster. I put relish on the plain burgers, dropped meat on the floor and couldn't remember what dressings went with which burger. After about two hours Jane said to Eddie, the manager, 'I've got an idea – he can put his counter shirt on and mop the lobby.' She said it right in front of me as if I wasn't there and I had to do this for the next five hours. At the end of the shift, Chris, my trainer, said, 'So what do yer think of it?'

I said, 'It's a laff, isn't it?' very sarcastically.

'Yeah, you can 'ave a laff 'ere. It's all right, McDonald's is,' he said, adding it wouldn't have been nearly as much fun if Maria had been the floor manager. 'Eddie's all right. He doesn't mind yer having a laff.'

What constituted a 'laff' was the two slack hours between 1.30 and 3.30 p.m. when Jane, Chris and Eddie hid behind the Wheelie-bins and re-enacted *The Good, the Bad and the Ugly*, squirting Germicide disinfectant at each other in a cowboy-style shoot-out.

I didn't join in: first because Germicide disinfectant can cause skin irritation; and second, because there were only three bottles of Germicide, and nobody lent me one as I'm a Yellow Badge.

Some of Charlie's friends came over for his birthday this evening. For his present I gave him a bionic panel I made out of silver foil and bottle tops in McDonald's today. He can attach it to his forearm and imitate Lee Majors from the *Six Million Dollar Man*, another retro hero that he took to after

I bought the whole of the first series (plus the pilot movie) for a fiver from Blockbusters' remainder bin. Gemma gave him a light-sabre, Dad bought him a thermostat for his turtle tank and Sarah gave him the new Man United kit. I felt a bit tight making his present, but I couldn't afford the San Marino football boots he was after and Dad wouldn't lend me any more money.

The bottle tops are dials that control Charlie's bionic functions: I have given him bionic drinking (Colgate mouthwash bottle top), bionic running (Germolene) and bionic penalty-taking (Domestos). Charlie does the second two in slow motion, like Lee Majors, but for some reason he bionic-drinks super-fast.

Charlie came with Gemma and me when I took two of his friends home after the party, and Gemma tried to have a word with him about being better behaved. Charlie nodded at everything she said but I don't think he understood because he started fiddling with the air cooler on the dashboard and when I told him to stop, he said, 'Jay, it's an urge – park next to Martin's Newsagents and buy me a lolly. Or Gemma will be run over by a lorry.'

11.30 p.m.

Another thing I like about Gemma is her chin. It's very flat and blends very well with her lips, which are always rough and chapped like pebble-dash. I still don't comment openly on her dimples. They're so obviously endearing that her former boyfriends must have gone on about them. I don't like to bracket myself with them, even in a matter as trivial as dimples.

It was great watching Gemma wrapping Charlie's present this evening. It almost made me cry – she looked so beautiful as she did it, and took so much care. She cut the wrapping paper into thin strips because she didn't want to waste paper, and folded them meticulously around the handle. When I wrap things I do it in a slap-dash way. I can't help thinking that what's inside is what's important. I'm wrong – you should judge a present by its cover. It's how you tell somebody cares. Anybody can buy something expensive, but they'll only wrap it nicely if they care. I handed pieces of Sellotape to her as she did it, looking at her reverently. Every time she took a bit off my finger she looked at me. She wasn't interested in my reverential expression, though; she just carried on wrapping. She put everything into it. I've never seen anyone care so much about wrapping. The present was for Charlie, but although she likes Charlie, she wasn't wrapping it for him – she was wrapping it for me, trying to do a nice job for me. It puts things in perspective when someone spends that much time wrapping. I've got to try to stop having these battling-for-supremacy arguments with her.

What will happen if Gemma gets her place at Sheffield? She'll have to do a pre-fresher course because she mucked up the first year doing classics, and this starts in April. I asked her tonight whether she'd go if she was accepted. My directness took her by surprise and she was non-committal and said there was no way they'd readmit her after she flunked last time. I said yes, but what if they did, and she held my hand and said, 'They won't, Jay – and, anyway, one of us has got to get a career, haven't they?' She was staring at my Go Large McDonald's badge when she said it. I wonder if Gemma disrespects me because I work with fast food. She called me McRomeo the other day.

Saturday, 13 March

We were all shown the new McDonald's staff-induction video today. Boxer Frank Bruno was in it. Bob Prescott, the company president, led him around the restaurant, pointing out McDonald's was a people-focused, environmentally friendly employer, and at the end there was a close-up of Frank savouring a Bacon McDouble Cheeseburger, saying,

'What a team, know whatamean!' while sticking up his thumbs.

I tried to make a joke about this when Chris refused to give me the last Germicide spray-can to join in the afternoon shoot-out. 'What a team, know whatamean!' I said, wittily sticking my thumbs *down*.

Chris didn't get it. He just shouted, 'Everyone! Jay's Lee Van Cleef,' and I got squirted in the eye and then carpet-bombed with desiccated onions.

9.30 p.m.

'He's been sticking his finger up his nose,' I told Dad tonight. 'He thinks it's hay fever if you sneeze and he's promised not to do it again.'

Dad thanked me for having a word with him and I casually brought up boarding school. I asked if it'd make a difference if Charlie started behaving. But, silly me, I didn't know Dad's rescheduling changes to BBC2 had been criticised in the papers.

'I've got enough to think about right now,' said Dad, and flung over a copy of the *Daily Mail*. There was a story on page five about a campaign to stop the moving of *Newsnight* and under a picture of him the caption: 'BBC boss, Maurice Golden, the most unpopular Controller for thirty years'.

'It ain't the sort of personal publicity the head of BBC Charter renewal really wants right now,' he said.

That was weird, I said, buttering him up and trying a new approach, because Gemma's mum really liked the new slot for *Food and Drink*, and someone at McDonald's had only been saying the other day what a tired format *Newsnight* had. 'I don't mean Charlie shouldn't go, Dad,' I said. 'I've thought about it. I agree, he should go, you're right. But why can't he be a day boy? I could pick him up from school if I did the early shift. And if he got a place in, say, Harrow, I'm sure Sarah wouldn't mind dropping him off.'

'I've made my decision, Jay,' he said, holding up his hand

like a cop directing traffic. 'So unless you've got any more dubious testimonials' – he looked at me impatiently – 'can we drop it? I've been on my feet all day and I. Am. *Very*. Tired.'

It annoyed me that he wouldn't even talk about it and, to get him back, when *Have I Got News For You* came on I criticised the new opening titles. Dad must have had a few drinks before he got home, because even though I'd hardly said anything, he suddenly started laying into me. He gave me the 'Is-that-what-you-want?' Charter renewal speech I'd heard him use on the Nine O'Clock News last week: 'The whole BBC down the Labour Exchange, is that what you want? One of the most respected institutions in this country, probably *the* most respected institution in the country, on the scrap-heap? Is that what you want? The end of schools' programmes. The end of the World Service. The end of *Panorama*. A global force for democracy disbanded. Is that what you want? You're as bad as the bloody Labour Party.' He did an exasperated shudder.

'So what, the BBC's going to fold, and global democracy's threatened, just because I don't like the new *Have I Got News For You* titles?' I said, and Dad called me a supercilious cretin and had to go for a walk round Cholesbury Common to cool down.

11 p.m.

Gemma and I spent the night down our dirt road in Aston Clinton, and out of the blue she said she didn't want to have any more battling-for-supremacy-in-the-relationship rows. I could be the boss if I wanted. 'The truth is, I don't mind being steam-rollered,' she said, 'I like doing things for you – that's what makes me happy.' I have been steamrollering her, it's true. I think I'm doing it because I feel insecure that she might be going away. She asks what I want to eat and pays for it with her dad's money. She lets me choose the videos we watch, and what we do in the evenings. I feel like Emperor Nero. She'll be dangling grapes in my mouth next, and it's difficult not to take advantage. In company sometimes it's very embarrassing, especially if it's her dad. I keep thinking he'll turn around and say, 'How dare you treat my daughter like that? Put that bunch of grapes down, Gemma. He can feed himself!'

Sunday, 14 March

Worked the 7 a.m. to 1 p.m. shift in the kitchen. For every oven, fryer or toaster there's a buzzer, which goes off when what's in them has been cooked. It's different for each one and it's very disorientating. The toaster for the buns has a gruff, staccato *narr*-sound like a factory hooter. The oven for the burgers is a sonic bleep. The McRib marinater is like a doorbell and for the fryer it's a dull metallic knocking noise. Jane says I will get used to them all, but I doubt it, and I was moved back to mop duty this morning after accidentally putting a gherkin in a McChicken Sandwich. The serious way they treat mistakes makes me laugh. 'Watch your gherkins,' Jane said when I was mopping.

'Yeah, sorry. I'd just done a Big Mac and wasn't thinking,' I said.

'You shouldn't have been asked to do a McChicken Sandwich,' said Jane confidentially. 'Not in your first month.'

7 p.m.

Dad confiscated the bionic panel tonight and left Charlie in tears. He was very slow undressing for his bath and keeps getting hiccoughs from drinking his Ribena too quickly. I protested, but Dad was adamant. 'This can't go on. My day's busy enough as it is without having to wait half an hour for the Six Million Dollar Man to take off his bloody vest,' he said.

We had another row about it afterwards. I asked Dad how much his boarding-school decision was down to what's best for Charlie, and how much was down to the fact he was now head of this BBC task-force on Charter renewal and was too busy to be a proper dad.

Dad stared at me and said he couldn't believe I had to ask that question. He'd obviously been thinking about it, though, because he came up later, stood in my bedroom doorway, and asked me how much I was thinking of Charlie's education and how much I was thinking of myself. 'He's removed from all the bad associations,' he said, bending down one finger at a time, glaring at me. 'He gets a good education, he's with professional people with more time to spend with him, he gets a resident child psychologist, the sports facilities are excellent and' – he stared at me hatefully – 'he doesn't have you around as an example of how not to do . . . practically everything.'

10 p.m.

I phoned Sean tonight, but he wouldn't take the call. His mum said Sean had told her to tell me he was too busy reading about the Bosporus.

I got a rejection from the *Bucks Star* for my funny article on baths today as well. Ms Angela Turner, the editor, told me I wasn't 'writing for *The Times*'. I'd left in synergy, a word of over two syllables, which would apparently fox readers. It's repugnant having to write down for the hoi polloi. I feel like Robert DeNiro in *Raging Bull* having to take a dive to appease fight promoters. And Mr Gatley has written saying he cannot be my tutor any more as well. He wanted to pass me on to somebody else – he's having to pack it in for health reasons – but I've written back to tell him not to bother. It wouldn't be the same without Mr Gatley's animal analogies.

It's disheartening. You hear the tales of thwarted writers and you think, Not me. Straight to the top. Straight to the book launch. Yet here I am in the middle of the night listening to the Eels, staring out of my bedroom window. Perseverance is misunderstood. It's a myth. Nobody embarks on a task expecting to be knocked back. They anticipate instant success. If they envisaged failure, they wouldn't bother. To succeed, you don't need perseverance, just a good selective memory to forget what the *Bucks Star* have said about your funny article about baths.

I've just reread the start of my Wiggie novel too. What happens to my writing during the night? It's like it goes off like milk left out of the fridge. Yesterday I was sure it was very funny yet deep, but tonight it didn't seem funny or deep at all. I miss Mum tonight. I want her to be downstairs in her yellow dressing-gown knitting on the sofa. I want to be able to go up to her and tell her I'm in a mess. I want to put my arms around her and watch her stick her tongue in her cheek the way she did when she was concentrating or feeling strongly about something. I want someone to tell me it's going to be all right in the end. That was always Mum's theory: it'll be all right in the end. Mum always liked what I wrote. Whenever I showed her anything she'd call over Dad after she'd read it as if what I'd done was so good it had shocked her. 'Have you seen this?' she'd say, and Dad would have to read it, too, and say something complimentary, even if he didn't want to.

Mum thought she was going to be OK in the end, too. She never gave up hope. Every new cocktail of drugs was going to lead to a dramatic recovery; any day the chemo would kick in or someone would devise a miracle cure. 'Oh, I'll be out by the weekend,' she told me the last time she went into hospital.

It would be great if I did become a writer. Mum would have loved that. According to *Books and Bookmen* Robert Louis Stevenson, John Keats, Albert Camus and the Brontë sisters all had TB. Their impending deaths inspired them. I read this before I went to bed. They worked harder, more intensely and more brilliantly because they knew they had little time. It's what drove their genius. Nobody tells you any of this when they line you up at school for your BCG. Maybe this is what it is – I've been inoculated against achievement.

4 November: Dad, Charlie and I went to the Rose 'n' Crown for lunch today. Mum didn't come. She's having difficulty walking because of the swelling in her legs and stomach, which has returned. 'My stomach's so huge I couldn't see my fanny in the bath last night,' she said, trying to sound upbeat. 'Why don't you bring me back a nice piece of melon?'

We weren't going to talk about Mum, but during the dessert one of her ironing customers, Mrs Morton, spotted us from the bar and came over to ask how she was. Mrs Morton is old and a bit senile and started telling us how her husband had died of throat cancer 'after a *looong* struggle'. She wanted to empathise with us, I think, but it was really inappropriate and upset Charlie. Nobody had mentioned anything to him about Mum dying.

'That *stupid* woman,' said Dad, staring after her as she walked away.

I squeezed Charlie's knee under the table, Dad and I told him it was going to be all right, and just as it looked like he would quieten down, Dad got all aggressive and leaned across the table, gripped Charlie's head very tightly and whispered crossly, 'Come on! Do yer want the Mrs Mortons of this world to see yer hurtin'? Nerrr,' he said, answering his question and slumping back in his chair. 'Of course, you don't.'

'Mum's not going to . . . die,' said Charlie, shocked back to tears by Dad's behaviour.

'Nobody's gerner die, kidder,' said Dad, and he slapped Charlie's cheeks playfully. 'Yer mother's tough as old boots . . . Now, are you going to eat that ice cream that I paid for and you said you wanted?'

In the driveway Dad stopped the car, turned around in his seat and said, 'It's important that you boys remember something. The

96

best medicine for yer mother is a positive attitude. Am I being understood? I don't want any negativity.' He looked at Charlie and did an exaggerated impression of Charlie's long face. Charlie laughed, but Dad looked back seriously. 'In a way it's down to you boys. I'm doing what I can, but it's you who will make the difference. Now, let's go in and tell her what a wonderful meal we've had. Charlie, have you still got that melon?'

Every time I read about Mum I have this mental image of crushing my emotions. It's like the bin-liners of rubbish that are hydraulically compressed in the compactor room at McDonald's. I'm making them smaller and smaller, packing them in tighter and tighter. They're nearly all bad memories, too: that time at the hospital the day before she died and I cut up her lamb because she didn't have the strength. The day after she died when Charlie watched me pour her lime juice, the only thing she could drink at the end, down the sink and said, '*Jaaay*, Mum's going to be mad with you when she gets back. She's just bought that from the shops.' I keep pressing them down, but sometimes I worry just how many I will be able to squeeze in before . . . I don't know, before I go mental, I suppose. Sometimes I almost want to go mental. I think I owe it to Mum to go mental. I always thought I'd go to pieces when she died – fling myself on the coffin or something, become a tramp and live drunkenly in Oxford Street doorways with a misty stare of incomprehension. Life has just carried on, though. When Holden Caulfield's brother died in *Catcher in the Rye* he cut his hand punching out every window in the garage. I didn't even do that. I didn't even bruise a knuckle. The worst I got – the most deranged – was the day after, when a vein in my forehead throbbed all day and I shouted at Charlie after standing on one of his Lego blocks in bare feet.

Monday, 15 March

Eddie treats staff like criminals in a good cop/bad cop scene, I noticed today. He told Chris off this morning for dropping a meat pattie on the floor, then later came up to him, playfully punched him in the belly and said, 'Sorry about earlier, mate – the bacon was burnin'.'

When Eddie told me off for leaving dirty footprints by the tills at closing time I tried the same tactic for a joke. But when I went to punch him playfully in the stomach Eddie pushed me aside and said, 'There's 'alf a dozen tables want clearin' away aht there, we wanta get away t'night, yer know.'

I forgot to put the 'Wet Floor Beware' board up later as well, and a customer slipped and banged his knee on one of the kiddie toadstool chairs.

Eddie called me into the office. 'Cam on, Jay, use yer 'ead – if you got a wet floor, yer put up yer board, duncha? And stop splashin' worta arand, will yer? Mop gently – it's like the River Thames aht there!'

I resisted the urge to tell him I had seven UCCA points and knew the chemical symbol for iron, and nodded respectfully.

10 p.m.

Dad suggested I ring his friend from the City about a job tonight when I complained about smelling of gherkins. Any sign of weakness and he's in there. 'You tried to write a book. That was very brave,' he said, changing his normal tactics. 'Not many people would take a chance like that and you deserve applause. But now it's time to be realistic. You're going to live to be seventy and you've got to find a way of making a living to support yourself. You aren't doing that at the moment. It's time you were. You have a business qualification – you've got to use what you've got. Ring him. It's not as if you like what you're doing now, and you *do* smell of gherkins. Come on, old son? I'll even ring him if you want.'

This is all very well . . . but punching numbers on a console? What sort of life is that for someone who's read half a dozen Penguin Classics and has three Woody Allen films in his top ten all-time movies? Fucking none, that's what. I told Dad I'd think about it if he thought about what I'd said the other night about Charlie being a day boy, and Dad tutted and told me to get out of his sight because I was putting him off his gammon rashers.

11.30 p.m.

Gemma and I didn't go into our normal dominance sparring tonight. We sat in front of the White Swan's log fire; it made a hypnotic hissing noise that was very soothing. Some kids came in at one point: the youngest had blond hair, like me, and whenever he did anything wrong, like upsetting his drink, Gemma said, 'I bet you were like that.' I knew she was imagining what it would be like to have children with me and before we left she asked whether I loved her. She said it very seriously. I said, 'Yes,' very seriously back. We both got upset after this for some reason. We parked outside Wycombe Six cinema and watched cars streaming along the M4 in the dark. Gemma cried because I told her to imagine getting a phone call in the morning to say I'd died in the night, and I cried because Mum will never meet Gemma and she would've really liked her, and because I started imagining Charlie growing up, failing at school and getting a job in Dolcis.

I phoned Sean tonight as well, but his mum said he wouldn't come to the phone again. Mrs F lowered her voice before I hung up and said she was glad I'd called, she'd been meaning to have a word with me. She put the phone down a second. I heard her close the kitchen door. When she came back she said she was worried about Sean.

'You mustn't say anything to him, you mustn't say I've

spoken to you – but well, the other day he said . . . he said he was going to become the Prime Minister,' she said.

There was a pause. I didn't say anything. I couldn't believe she was taking Sean seriously again. Sean's parents are a lot older than normal parents. Sean's dad is almost as old as granddad and Sean's mum is half-Spanish and must be almost sixty. They're pretty doddery and they believe everything he tells them, his mum especially.

'He said he was going into a chrysalis and would re-emerge as a beautiful butterfly,' said Mrs F. 'At least I think it was a butterfly.'

She shouted over to Sean's dad, 'Geoff, Geoff, come here – did Sean say he was re-emerging as a butterfly or as a moth?' I heard them arguing for a second and then Sean's dad came to the phone.

'Hello, Jay,' he said authoritatively.

'Doreen's told you we're worried about Sean. Yes – he's probably just being a menace like normal and it's not as if we haven't been here before – but what Sean said to me yesterday in the garage was that he'd reached the end of the pupae stage. That's all he said, he'd reached the end of the pupae stage. He said he was going to go into his bedroom where he would re-emerge at a later date as a moth. Although he told Doreen a butterfly.'

I loved the way it made a difference if it was a butterfly or a moth.

'He said he'd be reading the Encyclopaedia Britannica,' said Mr F, 'and wouldn't be coming out until he'd finished it. He seems to think he'll come out as Prime Minister, which is nonsense. Has he said anything to you about it, Jay? Or is it just another caper to get out of moving to Scotland with us?'

Tuesday, 16 March

I really hate McDonald's. I've started getting spots from the fat fryer and I was told off in the kitchen again today. It's always about such trivial things: forgetting to put up the 'Wet Floor Beware' board, dropping meat patties on the floor, leaving the freezer door open. Whenever I feel the weight of Eddie's or Chris's stare and sense I'm about to be rebuked I pop an ice-cube in my mouth. This is how I'm coping: noisily sucking an ice-cube conveys nonchalant impertinence.

'You gotta remember to mop the till area, Jay.' *Schlllllurp*. 'Did you leave those McKitchen wipes on the tills?' *Schlllllurp*. 'Take that fuckin' fing out of yer mouth.' *Schlllllurp*.

Ann, from Birmingham Human Resources, arrived in the afternoon and called me into the manager's office immediately for a quick word. Whenever anybody's about to tell you off, or sack you or probably even shoot you, they always ask for a 'quick word'.

'Roite, Jay,' she said. 'Oi've a few things to t'say t'yow.' She opened a black book on the desk in front of her. On a page marked. 'Member of staff: Jay Golden', she read out five points: 'Number one: yow didn't . . . Number two: your attitude seems . . . Number thray: it would be better if yow . . .' When she'd finished she said, ''Ave yer anything t'say?'

I asked her where she'd got her information from and she told me she knew a hell of a lot more than anybody 'give' her credit for: 'My job is managin' payple,' she said. 'I look avtah twelve restaurants, Jay – Oive got a hundred and fifty payple workin' for me. I know what 'appens in my restaurants.'

I let her go on for a while about her restaurants, nodded and pretended to have great respect for all she said, then I tried to defend myself. I labelled other members of staff informants and pleaded ignorance about the procedural complaints. Ann said that she didn't have informants. I said she did. Ann told me that I heard, but that I didn't listen.

Finally, as if conceding an unthinkable compromise, she

said, 'Jay, what I'll do's this. Yow show may an improvement in the lobby area, and genrally in the next two weeks' – she looked at me pityingly, like a benevolent owner about to give a bone to a spoiled dog – 'and Oi'll cross out all Oi've written.'

She expected me to burst into tears of relief. What I really wanted to say was 'OK, can I go? We're cutting into my lunch hour here.'

9 p.m.

Dad was in a bad mood again today because I refused to call back his friend Mr Griffiths from the City. Dad phoned him today and Mr Griffiths phoned back to speak to me, but I wasn't in.

'At least you're consistent,' said Dad. He was shuffling about in his seat like he was wiping his arse on the upholstery. From side to side he went. Eskimos have 101 words for snow; Dad's got 101 ways to show he's fucked off with me. 'At least you're inconsiderate with everybody.'

I didn't say anything, but I could see him out of the corner of my eye still practically giving his arse a friction-burn.

Charlie was lying in front of the fire on his boxing-glove bean-bag. I asked how his show-and-tell had gone. He'd done a show-and-tell in front of the class on Captain Bluebeard. He said it'd gone OK, but that his friend Colin Higgins had dried up with nerves halfway through his talk on Man United.

'If someone phones you, you phone them back,' said Dad without looking at me.

He was starting to sound like Linda at Montons, I thought. Any minute he'd probably accuse me of being unprofessional.

Charlie said it was his fault Colin had dried up in his talk because he'd had an 'urge' beforehand, but hadn't been able to carry it out because it was an urge to touch wood and there wasn't any wood around, and Mrs Willis would've been annoyed if he'd gone over to the pencil drawer in the middle of the lesson.

'I don't know where we went wrong with you,' said Dad. 'You don't know the first thing about common decency, do you? You don't know how to treat people. Perhaps it's a good job you're a dosser. Heaven forbid you ever become a manager. If I behaved like you . . . If I treated my department . . . How can everything we've ever taught you have washed straight over your head?'

Talking about urges gave Charlie another. 'It's about Rob and a screwdriver,' he said, explaining himself, as he got up to fetch a glass of Ribena.

'Elbows!' said Dad, as Charlie walked past.

'I wasn't,' said Charlie.

'You were,' said Dad.

'They're itchy,' said Charlie.

'Well, turn that fire down . . . I'm not surprised,' said Dad. 'Are you thick?' he said to me when Charlie was out of the room. 'Is that what it is? Are you thick?'

Gemma was very depressed tonight. We had sex and spent the night in the van but just before we went to sleep she became hysterical, started crying and told me how unhappy she was. All her sentences started, 'My life is . . .' and ended with swear-words. The more she talked, the more desperate she became. She said she obviously wasn't going to get on her course because she hadn't heard anything, and that she was jealous of me because she hadn't got any direction. I tried to cheer her up, and said they were probably just late in sending out the letters. And what did she mean? I had about as much direction as a burst balloon.

Gemma's dad is the boss of a confectionery multinational. When she'd fully recovered Gemma said she might ask him for a job there. She thinks I should persuade my dad to use his contacts to give me a leg up as well. 'He must know some famous writers,' she said. I said he did, but the trouble was

I'd probably phoned them all up already and been told to fuck off.

I'm starting to feel old. It's the lack of achievement. Alexander the Great was on his way to conquering the known world at my age. What've I done? Got a fucking McChicken Sandwich station competency badge at McDonald's.

Wednesday, 17 March

Spent the afternoon off helping Gemma fill out job applications. When Sarah and Rob came over for dinner I told them I was frustrated by my writing rejections, implying I couldn't hope to end up with a full-time writing job unless I was given a leg up somehow.

Dad missed the nepotism hint, though, and interrupted to say, 'Talent will out, my son,' in a stentorian voice, before signalling the end of the audience by reaching for a parsnip.

It irritated me and when I tried to say I didn't think he understood the way things worked in the literary world, he was angry at being interrupted, and added even more authoritatively: 'Somebody will see what you do if you do it well enough. I am a great believer in the talent system.' It was almost as if he was answering a question on *Points of View*.

When I told him later I'd decided to give up the writing course I expected him to be angry, but instead, and even more humiliatingly, he cuffed me playfully around the head and said, 'Maybe – just maybe – you're growing up, my son.' He doesn't believe I have any talent at all. He's obviously just been humouring me.

I think something's brewing about Charlie and boarding school. Nobody spoke about him during the meal, and afterwards Sarah and Dad disappeared for a private chat. It gets on my nerves the way Dad and Sarah are so buddy-

buddy. They're always deciding things, disappearing off for chats about Charlie and me and making proclamations about new household ways of doing things: 'From now on the Hoover will live in the cupboard under the stairs, instead of the utility room – do you hear me, boys?' . . . 'Now hear this, now hear this – there's now a hook for the dustpan and brush, so remember to hang them up.' It's like Pol Pot eradicating the past. They'll probably disinvent the calendar next and declare a new Year Zero in Bellingdon.

11 p.m.

I went out for a drink with Sean, Mark, Kate and Gemma at the Ellie tonight. It was Sean's official goodbye. He doesn't move to Dumfries for a while, but he reckoned it was the last time he'd be coming out because tomorrow he's going into his room to read the encyclopedia full time.

'You won't see me until I re-emerge as a beautiful butterfly who knows everything there is to know about everything,' he said, after Gemma had got the drinks in.

Mark asked how long the metamorphosis would last.

'Two years,' said Sean, stroking his chin. 'It'll take two years.'

'And you're going to stay in your bedroom all that time reading up on general knowledge?' said Kate, raising her eyebrows.

Sean said yes, then got angry trying to justify himself. 'I mean, do you know how a fridge works? I don't mean how you switch it on. How it *actually* works?' He looked disdainfully away from Mark and towards me for support.

I said he was right, none of us knew exactly how a fridge worked and it was probably something most world leaders ought to know.

He was pleased with this and leaned back grandly, more sure of himself. 'Plus I'm conditioning myself to need just four hours' sleep, like Boris Yeltsin.'

Gemma had a go at me for not taking it seriously

afterwards. She said I was his best mate and it was up to me to do something. I tried to tell her he wasn't serious, that it was all attention-seeking again, but Gemma was so adamant I almost started believing her. Can Sean really be going mad?

Dad was up when I got in, so to needlessly perturb him I told him what Sean was doing to panic him into thinking I might do the same. 'He has got a point, Dad – it is embarrassing not knowing how a fridge works.'

There's definitely something brewing with Charlie. Dad wasn't nearly as angry as he should've been.

11 November: Mum was watching *EastEnders*, knitting Charlie a jumper, when I arrived home. Her legs were propped up on the foot-rest. They looked like giant sausages because of the swelling. Dad was at a BBC do; Mum had had to turn down her first ironing job that morning, and she'd been too upset to go.

'At least I can still do something,' she said, lifting her elbows slightly to indicate the needles. 'Honestly, I feel so bloody useless.'

I went to make her a lime juice.

'I worry about Charlie, you know,' she said, taking the glass from me when I came back. 'How's he going to cope over the next few—' Because of her legs, she couldn't reach to put the glass down on the coffee table. 'Buggeration,' she said, looking around her. I took it from her and put it on the table. 'I mean, what's it going to be like for him over the next few years? What's it going to be like for—' Her chin started wobbling. Her hands, yellowed like marzipan from the jaundice, went up to her face and the knitting fell into her lap. 'Jay, I might not be here in a few years' time,' she said, and repeated in a frightened whisper, 'I might not be here.'

I sat on the sofa beside her, put my arm around her bony shoulders and told her she'd probably still be knitting Charlie the same jumper in ten years' time if she didn't get a move on.

Mum tried to smile, but the bottom of her mouth twitched and she put her head on my shoulder and started to cry. 'I still can't believe it,' she said in a muffled voice. 'It's like it's not happening, you know? I was in the garden today and I thought, It's just so unreal.'

I put on my formulaic voice and told her she had to be positive, she was starting the chemo soon and who knew what that would do?

'Yes, I know, I know, but it's so hard. One week away. I was one week from the all-clear.' She lifted up her head, breathed deeply and picked up her knitting. 'It's piss-making, that's what it is,' she said, suddenly defiant and OK again.

Thursday, 18 March

I can't believe it. Subject to references, they're allowing Charlie to start at Roxburgh in a couple of weeks. *A couple of weeks!* Normally you have to wait until the school year starts in September. The head waived the normal admission procedure, though, because of our 'special circumstances', supposedly meaning Mum (but really because Dad mobilised a few Old Roxies; the BBC's crawling with them).

Dad was very happy and went outside to read extracts from the school prospectus to the rose bushes. He said Mum would want to hear what some of the Old Roxies had to say about Charlie's new school. ' "I cannot imagine a more beautiful place to be educated. I would give almost anything to have my time again at Roxburgh." That's Sir Clive Dunley, OBE, artist and conservationist, Wren House, 1953–64. He hasn't done so bad, eh?' said Dad, shouting through the kitchen window at me. ' "A Roxburgh education teaches youngsters to think deeply, to think for themselves and to think about others." Paul Hetherington, chairman of TPF plc, Grenville House, 1959–71.'

Dad came up to me later and had another stab at the low-skilled work I'm doing. 'OBEs, directors, lords, MPs, chairmen of public companies, seven winners of the Victoria Cross . . . They don't get jobs down the McDonald's after this school, my son.'

It was my worst night yet at work. Some drunken girls said, 'Snaaazy,' in bored voices when I walked past them in my shiny black uniform trousers that have the pockets sewn up so you can't steal anything. A woman complained about the state of the lobby area in the Customer Comments box. Eddie was bad tempered because he thought we were losing the battle to win back the 'four-to-eights'. And I failed an OTC appraisal for my lobby area badge. I scored nought on 'Hustle Is Evident'. Even when there's nothing to do you're supposed to look busy in the lobby. I find this very difficult. It's pointless and degrading. Careering urgently towards a puddle of milk shake as if it's radioactive waste makes you look as if you really relish your job and can't wait for the next spillage.

I've been exaggerating Dad's faults up to now, but tonight his actions speak for themselves. Dad went to boarding school, and he says it didn't do him any harm. *Not much.* Spending his childhood at some ex-Victorian workhouse is probably why he's so uptight.

'He'll have the time of his life,' said Dad when I returned home from work and had a go at him. 'All those sports facilities, and the class ratios. He'll get much more individual attention. He needs that attention. You've seen what he's been like these last few months. I know how you feel about him. I know you like having him around. I do too. I love having him around, but—'

'*Having him around!* You make him sound like a dog,' I said.

Dad said he wasn't going to discuss it if I was going to shout at him, even though I wasn't shouting at him at all.

Charlie's taking it well and doesn't seem bothered. I think Dad's been brainwashing him about indoor five-a-side facilities, because that, and whether he'll be allowed to take Greeny-Slowy, is all he's going on about.

I hugged Gemma in despair tonight What are we going to do with our lives? We must find proper jobs and save up to become drop-outs. I would love to see the rest of the world. Bellingdon's so small. You visit a safari park and complain the animals haven't got enough room, but what about Jay

Golden? My natural habitat's the globe and here I am cooped up in South Bucks.

We sat on the sofa in her back living room and Gemma sighed and said she was now half hoping Sheffield would turn her down because she wouldn't be able to bear it without me. 'Come over 'ere and give me an 'ug,' she said. (Gemma drops her 'h's when she's feeling soppy.)

'I am over 'ere. Give *me* an 'ug,' I said. (I've started to now as well.)

'I'm very 'appy with my 'edge.' (Gemma's started calling me Hedge because she thinks I look like a hedgehog.)

'And I'm 'appy, with my Gem Gem.' (And I've started calling her Gem Gem because she looks like a giant panda.)

Friday, 19 March

Phoned in sick at McDonald's. I said I had a pain in my stomach. Eddie told me to get a doctor's note before I came back. 'If it's food poisoning, I don't want you contaminating the place,' he said. Dad asked what was wrong with me, and when I told him he must've been feeling guilty because he didn't have a go. 'Come on, my son,' he said, 'it's not the end of the world. You knew this was going to happen. Sooner's better than later. It *is* a very good school. Have a game of snooker with your old man. *I'm* still going to be around.'

I told him snooker was the gin of the twentieth century, it addled mind and body, and ought to be taxed. I came upstairs to abuse celebrities but couldn't think of anything witty to say so just phoned everybody from A to B in his contacts book and called each of them a cunt. Then I started to read *The Naked and the Dead* by Norman Mailer, which depressed me even more. It's a gritty story about life, death and human frailty in World War Two and was written when Mailer was twenty-three. *Twenty-fucking-three!* It's not fair – I want to pierce through the Jap Tokayu Line on a

South Pacific island and bond with hard-nosed comrades over raisin liquor in a rain-lashed bivouac worrying about whether my nerve will hold out under combat. I'm sick of McDonald's. There's no bonding, nobody is hard-nosed, and the grittiest thing I've had to do is scrape a dry gherkin off the lobby floor with my fingernail because it wouldn't shift with the mop.

I'm going to give Wiggie a job in McDonald's in my novel to get them back. I'm going to have him run amok during the lunchtime rush with an AK47 assault rifle, gunning down the fictional equivalents of my colleagues through the serving hatch in revenge for a rebuke about the erroneous application of McChicken Sandwich sauce to a Fillet-O-Fish.

But, then again, should I really be living my life vicariously through some retard with a bobble-hat? My life is going nowhere. Something has to be done.

10 p.m.

What is it with dads? Gemma's turns out to be as bad as mine. He kicked up an almighty fuss about a few pathetic drops of oil he found in his drive when I dropped Gemma off tonight. I couldn't believe it! He kept storming in and out of the kitchen with a bucket of soapy water telling Gemma and me 'It won't shift – it's oil!'

He didn't seem to care we were busy discussing becoming drop-outs. The first few times I ignored him, went 'hmm,' and looked towards the drive sympathetically – pointlessly in fact, because the kitchen door was closed. But the more he moaned about it the more difficult disinterest became. It seemed rude not to care about something he cared so much about, so to placate him I asked, 'How's it going?'

'It won't shift – it's bloody oil,' he replied, aggressively filling his bucket with more soapy water. He got through his bucket very quickly and was back in for another. As it'd only been seconds since I'd last asked how it was going and I didn't want to repeat myself, but thought I should do something, I smiled in a fatalistic way instead to convey I knew what he was going through.

Gemma's dad must've misconstrued my compassion because he strode straight past my tortured grin to the sink, turned the taps on more violently than was necessary and with his back to Gemma and me asked in a menacing tone, 'What's 'e grinning at?'

The knives are out for ex-lobby assistants. Gemma's dad's offered to buy her a new car if she gets into Sheffield as well.

Dad's just come into my room. He was still angry from earlier. He told me maybe if he'd sent me to boarding school I'd have a proper job now instead of working in Mc-Donald's. Had I thought about that? He said he blamed himself for spoiling me, and the way I'd turned out was his fault. He's right. Richard Branson's dad forbade books in the house when he was growing up. He was brought up to be a doer, not someone who reads what other people do. What's become of me is Dad's fault. If he hadn't given me *James and the Giant Peach* for my ninth birthday I'd probably be hot-air ballooning with Per Lindstrand by now with my own brand of cola.

11 p.m.

Borrowed Dad's contacts book and called every celebrity from C to D a cunt and went to bed.

Saturday, 20 March

Dad asked what the matter was with me tonight. 'You've been mooning about all evening,' he said.

I said I was bored with my life and was thinking of resigning. Dad was relieved it wasn't about Charlie and told me he pitied me, and later came to my room and tried to give me a new perspective on life. He told me all anybody could hope for was to be as good at their job as they possibly could be. Then he totally changed his outlook on McDonald's, as if he thought that was all I was good for after all. He said he used to go to this bar in Covent Garden when he was my age just to watch the cocktail waiters in action. He said their jobs were the same as mine, but that they were so good at it they made it an art form.

'There were two of them,' said Dad. 'One, two, three, they'd grab a bottle of vermouth, flick it over their heads, catch it behind their backs, spin it this way, that way, pour it out. Throwing ice-cubes, catching them in the glass simultaneously, not even looking up . . . The routine ended with them shouting "oucha" at the same moment. It was fantastic, my son.'

He said any job could be turned into an art form if you were really good at it. 'Become the best lobby assistant they've ever had,' he said. 'Then, when they promote you from there, be the best at that. Then the next job and the next one. Don't think about it – just do it. That's what I've done at the Beeb. People'll notice. They *do* notice. Talent will out – I've always said it. I said it to Peter Allen when he came to me for a job. He'd been rejected everywhere . . . Look at him now, presenting *Drive* on Five Live.'

Dad went straight from school to Oxford on a scholarship, then to the BBC. He's got no idea of what it's like at McDonald's. How the fuck can you turn being a lobby assistant into an art form? What does he expect me to do? Get some mop routine worked out ending in 'oucha'?

8 p.m.

Sarah popped in with Rob to discuss their wedding tonight. Sarah apparently wants the reception on the Thames barge to have a tangerine feel. I mentioned Charlie and she said there was nothing she could do. Then she asked whether Dad had said anything to me about a memorial party to

Mum, and what did I think about the idea? Apparently, he's planning one to coincide with the anniversary of her death in April. I said he hadn't mentioned it, and that I thought it was a shit idea. Sarah said she thought it might be nice, and that it would be 'a turning point for us all', and, anyway, she was sure he'd invite Mum's friends, too. 'Charlie'd probably come home for it,' she said, to black-mail me.

Mum hated Dad's celebrity parties, and I do, too. I always feel such a waster when a household name tries to make small-talk with me. 'I see! So you work in McDonald's. And what does that entail exactly?'

'Putting tartar sauce on the Fillet-O-Fish and mopping the lobby area.'

'Oh! Nice to talk to you, I must just have a word with Anna Ford over there.'

10 p.m.

Sean's up to C in the encyclopedia. He reckons he knows everything there is to know up to C. I phoned him tonight and tried to have a word with him about seeing someone, but he wouldn't listen. He just told me about the problems he was having sticking to the four hours' sleep regime. Even with Pro-Plus tablets he can't get by on anything less than seven. 'It'll be different,' he said, 'when I'm actually in power and have important things to think about, like Foreign Policy. There isn't quite the same incentive when you're reading about caterpillars.'

It was impossible to talk to him, which got on my nerves. I was in the middle of telling him about Charlie going to boarding school at one point when he interrupted me to regurgitate a fact he'd learned about how certain species of bamboo could grow more than three feet in a single day.

'What did I just say about Charlie?' I asked angrily, but he didn't take the hint.

'And did you know bamboo isn't actually classified as wood, but as a grass?' he said.

Sunday, 21 March

Oucha! Called into McDonald's and dropped off my uniform. I've resigned. I felt like an American cop handing in his shield when I returned my yellow badge to Eddie. So long, McTossers.

Dad flew into a predictable rage. Didn't anything he said get through to me? He said at the National Radio Awards he'd spoken to his good friend Michael Buerk. When Michael Buerk had asked how I was getting on at Big Al's Golden Delicious Doner Kebabs Dad had had to say I'd been through three jobs since then. 'I was embarrassed for you, boy. His kids are much younger and they've all got proper jobs.'

'I resigned for dignity's sake,' I said.

Dad laughed sarcastically. 'For dignity's sake!' he said. 'That's a whole new twist. The truth is you just don't want to work. I could think of a hundred and fifty reasons why I shouldn't go to work, why I shouldn't battle up to the Beeb every day, but I have to earn a living to pay the mortgage and feed you two. Everyone has to earn a living. The whole world's discovered this. You're a quarter of the way through your life – it's time you discovered this. I can't go on supporting you. I'm just a little fella, I'm only five foot two, I can't bear the burden.'

Went to the Ellie in Old Amersham with Gemma and told her what Dad had said about being five foot two and not being able to bear the burden any more, and we both laughed.

11 p.m.

Dad mentioned the memorial party when I arrived home. It's going to be for about a hundred or so of 'the usual crowd' (i.e. celebrities, and not Mum's friends at all), and Dad wanted to know my 'movements' because there would be a lot to arrange and he'd need me to make myself 'useful'. I asked Dad whether he was sure it was appropriate, and he completely misunderstood.

'It's not going to be black armbands and long faces,' he said. 'I'm going to wear my rainbow jumper.'

It led to another morbid session in the garden. 'Do you remember her operation? – God, that seems a lifetime ago,' he said, rubbing the back of his head and staring up at the moon.

That night has become part of the family folklore. It was a couple of weeks after she'd been diagnosed. Mum was in the Chiltern after having had her stomach removed to stop the cancer spreading. We were all sitting, fretting at home, waiting for Dr Maitland to call to let us know whether the operation had been successful.

'Maitland said he thought he'd got everything. Then we all phoned her up. Do you remember that? I don't think I'll ever forget that night,' said Dad. He laughed resentfully. 'She'd just come round from a six-hour operation, her whole stomach removed, and what was she doing? Yer mother was talking about going back to her bloody ironing. She was a bloody marvel that woman. And, my God, she worked hard for you kids.'

I shuffled closer and put my arm around him. Dad didn't respond, but I left it on his shoulder anyway. I felt guilty for laughing at him with Gemma and for resigning, and tried to tell him I'd been thinking about Mum, too, in Debbie's the other day, but he interrupted me.

'Now she's here.' He broke from my embrace. 'Ain't yer, me old darlin'?' He waved his Cointreau at the under-growth, spilling half the glass, then turned towards me. He closed his eyes, stuck out his chin and his eyelids flickered as he searched for the right words. 'Yer mother was my rock,' he said, with dignified patience. 'We were married for twenty years. *Twenty years!* Do you ever think about that?'

He turned away disgustedly, suddenly angry with me. 'No, I don't suppose you do, my selfish eldest son. I don't suppose that crosses your tiny mind when you're busy getting sacked every five minutes. Tell me, because I'd like to know – because I really would like to know – does anybody's life ever impinge on yours?'

He was calm again, but had a sly half-smile on his face as if it was something indisputable, something he had hard evidence about, which I couldn't possibly deny. 'Come on, old son – I'm yer father, you can tell me, you'd tell yer mother – do you ever think of anybody but yourself? Or anything but your bloody book?'

I felt exhilarated with anger. I'd been trying to under-stand, I'd tried to hug him, I hadn't mentioned anything about Charlie, but here he was having a go at me again. I felt my face redden. 'No,' I said, staring into his eyes, 'I'm a fucking gorilla, remember?'

Dad blinked with surprise, then disinterest, and looked away. Nobody said anything for a second, then he tilted his head menacingly at my face as if he was trying to look up into my brain through my nostrils. 'Go on, go inside you little—' he said.

I hate Dad at the moment. We're supposed to sit there and listen to him talking about Mum when he's arse-holed on Cointreau. But as soon as anybody else says anything he doesn't want to know. I haven't said one word to him about Mum in almost eleven months because he just changes the subject and says, 'We've done all that,' or turns it around to himself and how much worse it is for him, or uses Mum against you and says she wouldn't have approved of something or another when it's actually him who doesn't approve of it. It's no wonder Charlie's fucked up. He's a kid – he cries when he gets a fucking blister, and yet he's not supposed to cry and act up a bit when his mum dies!

It would serve Dad right if he had to go to my funeral after I got killed fighting in a war. But, then again, maybe it wouldn't. He would probably wear his rainbow jumper. God knows what Sarah would do – she'd probably be more concerned about the tincture of the funeral ('I think it should have a sable feel, Dad').

Monday, 22 March

Dad's not allowing his secretary to type up my new CV. He says he doesn't want to be implicated in my lies. What does he expect me to do? If I left on all the places I've been sacked from, I could market it as a rival to the Yellow Pages.

I asked whether he was just getting me back for last night, and he said he was educating me about principles. He's turning into *Viz*'s Victorian Dad. He'll be covering up the legs of the piano stool next. He's got to make up his mind whether he wants an upright loafer or a high-flying liar for a son – it's gone too far for anything else.

Had an interview at the Amersham Careers Advisory Centre. The lady there told me I needed to smarten up my appearance and that I wasn't goal-orientated enough. I told her yes I was, I wanted to be a famous writer. She just laughed as if I'd made a joke and had me fill out a Cascade form. There were hundreds of questions on the form about yourself. Your replies get fed into a computer and it comes out with your ideal occupation based on the answers. Mine came out as Admin. Admin work is for people with limited horizons, slow wit and an interest in brands of tea. She handed me some application forms for office jobs in insurance companies, but I threw them in the bin outside.

I signed on for Income Support, visited the Jobcentre and was interviewed to be a sales assistant at Chesham Currys. It's sad but there's a woman at the Jobcentre called Chloe who knows my name. It's gratifying when this happens in a pub, but disrespectful at the Jobcentre. 'Jaaay,' she shouts the moment I walk in the door, 'didn't it work at the

Video Plus/Unwins Wine Shop/McDonald's/the Plough Inn/ Big Al's Golden Delicious Doner Kebabs?' It can be embarrassing, especially if there are people in there from school. (Which reminds me, if *Omnibus* do ever produce a documentary about me and track down Big Al, all I'll say on the matter is Big Al is a fucking liar – he never told me how dangerous it was to serve shish kebabs with the skewers still in the meat. I'm not a mind-reader. It was up to him to tell me not to do this.)

I've decided to become a lawnmower salesman. Chloe's fixed me up with an interview at the Ley Hill Mower Shop tomorrow. What I'll do is learn the mower business and use the grounding to set up a franchised, homogeneous chain of internationally renowned garden-machinery outlets, a bit like McDonald's, but with strimmers. That is my plan. I'll then retire as a millionaire at thirty-five to concentrate on more worthwhile pastimes, such as breaking the land-speed record and sitting around a kidney-bean-shaped pool sucking vermouth through a crooked straw.

Charlie needn't worry about this scheme of things. He needn't work in Dolcis then. He could come and live with me: the two Golden brothers, the Ben and Jerry of horticulture. We'll pad around our ocean-front Seychelles apartment in monogrammed silk pyjamas, getting off with peroxided women called Fifi and Trixie and be contacted only in business emergencies, like, say, if the bottom suddenly fell out of the gardening-glove industry. 'People say to me, Jay, you earn a lodda money. I say to them: "Mister, I spend a lodda money."'

I've also sent a form to join an NCTJ pre-entry journalist course. Dad hates journalists, lots of famous writers have started off as reporters, and the course is in Sheffield, which will be good if Gemma gets her place there.

Sean wouldn't come out for a drink tonight. He was busy reading about the caribou.

'You're not doing this because of the gay thing, are you?' I asked him. 'You're not staying in your room for two years because of the gay thing? Because you're worried about that? Come on, let me take you to see someone.'

Sean said he wasn't doing this because of the gay thing and gave me a lecture on doing something constructive with my own life instead of wasting my time with fantastical dreams, which would never come off. He doesn't think I'll ever make it in mowers. He's wrong. I'll make it big in mowers. I've read five brochures and already I know what type of Qualcast is best in dry weather.

Tuesday, 23 March

'It says here you've spent the last twelve months travelling,' said the bloke at the mower shop.

I said I'd spent the last year skippering a yacht sailing in the BT Global Challenge round-the-world boat race to disguise my recent past and to make me sound go-getting.

'Um, and how do you think you'll settle down into a routine after this excitement?' he said.

As if it was the most natural thing in the world, I said I'd given it a lot of thought and had decided to channel my travel bug into selling garden machinery.

'We don't want to take somebody straight from school, we want somebody rounded, who *has* seen a bit of the world,' he said, obligingly.

I'd read a couple of mower brochures while I waited. 'Yes, I imagine it helps when you're selling,' I said, 'being that much more rounded. By having seen a bit of the world, I'd have the confidence to communicate with a greater range of people, and so perhaps be more successful at bumping them up from a query about a Mountfield 16HP, say, into buying a Honda 450, with an alloy grass bucket.'

I found out I'd got the job when I arrived home. 'Congratulations,' said Ossie, the boss, over the phone, 'it's an exciting time to be entering the lawnmower business,' which made me laugh.

Gemma wasn't too impressed with the new job. 'Oh, lawnmowers,' she said, as if she expected me to be selling something more glamorous from a store named the Mower Shop.

'I've got another job,' I told Dad triumphantly, while he scrubbed the driveway outside.

'Good,' he said, 'you'll be able to pay to have this drive water-jetted. Your van's leaking oil. Park it on the common until you get it sorted. And, here, you can finish this off. I'm tired of clearing up after you.' Where does he get it from? *Boring-Fucking-Parent* magazine.

Rob chipped in as well. He pretended he was phoning about the arrangements for picking up the morning suits from Moss Bros, but really it was an excuse to give me the benefit of his wisdom. I hate it when he gets all big-brotherly. He's only a couple of years older than me.

'You're not going to go back to working in kebab shops, are you?' he asked. 'Why don't you listen to yer dad and give that friend of his a ring? It'll be great, move out of home, have your own place, get Gemma round, parties – you'll have an ace time, man.'

They make it sound so plausible, these people with responsibility. People bent double with it want everybody else to be the same. It lightens their load. It seems fairer. A problem shared is a problem halved; a responsibility shared is not. It just means there's someone else in slacks with a shoulder to cry on over the rising price of toddler footwear. I'll never have responsibility. I'd sooner drown in a pool of my own vomit than own a trouser press.

Before I went to bed Dad really made my night. He showed me the preliminary guest list for the memorial party (something his secretary *had* been allowed to type up, I noticed), and boasted there would be more MPs in our garden that night than at Prime Minister's Question Time, and more celebrities than at a BAFTA dinner. He said he was thinking of hiring caterers because Sarah wouldn't be able to manage everything. He talked about an outside Portaloo to stop people treading mud into the carpets, writing to Roxburgh to make sure Charlie could make it, and he even mentioned hiring a BBC orchestra. By April it'll probably be an outside-fucking-broadcast.

Wednesday, 24 March

First day at the Mower Shop. It's a good job I didn't enter the lawnmower business at an unexciting time, that's all I can say. I swept the showroom floor, lifted a three-stone fascia sign, dusted ten ride-on mowers and was forced to fit a tractor battery. It said '1000 volts' on the side. Concerned about the danger of electrocution, I asked Ossie which way round positive and negative were.

'Oh, just get stuck in, will you?' he said.

When I tentatively connected the first lead Ossie shouted, '*Bang!*' I jumped halfway across the showroom and landed on a shelf of strimmers, and everybody laughed. Apparently, this is a trick played on all new members of staff, which is something I imagine the Health and Safety Executive would be interested to hear.

Later Ossie explained about job cards and invoice processing. I nodded a lot, but my mind had wandered. Immediately afterwards he said, 'OK, now you go through it.' I asked if he could whip through it again and Ossie said, 'Listen this time.' I hate Ossie. He's thick and his eyes are so close together he looks like a Venn diagram.

The guy from Currys phoned when I got home and wanted to know where I'd been. I forgot I was supposed to start with them that morning as well. I told him I'd changed my mind about channelling my travel bug into flogging electrical appliances.

'That's very unprofessional,' he said.

'Thank you,' I replied and hung up.

10 p.m.

I went round to Sean's again tonight. The house was full of boxes – they've started to move some of their stuff to Scotland already.

'He's in his room,' said Mrs F, 'but I wouldn't go in there – it stinks. It smells so much the removal men wouldn't go in there, would they, Geoff?'

Sean's dad didn't look up from his paper. 'It really does smell, Jay. Try to get him to open a window. It's like something died in there,' he said.

Sean was in his bed reading about the Dardanelles. I sat on the end of the bed, leafing through one of his printouts. He'd highlighted certain passages to reread, sections he wasn't absolutely sure about. He wasn't absolutely sure about Clothes Moths and Central American Logging.

'Why am I like I am?' he said in a sing-song voice, putting down D. He must have been reading quite a lot because his eyes were bloodshot. He looked pretty tired, too. 'Why do I find it impossible to engage with life? Why do *you* find it impossible to engage with life?' Sean looked at me and I shrugged my shoulders. 'Exactly,' he said. 'Exactly my reaction when my dad asked me that this morning. What a cunt he is! I suppose he went on about the smell.'

'Yeah, he reckons something died in here.'

'Yeah, my respect for him,' said Sean, shouting through the thin ceiling so his dad could hear.

'The funny thing is, when I'm in the Cabinet,' said Sean, looking at me wildly, 'he's going to be all over me. *All fucking over me!*' He started imitating how his dad would react 'Ooh Sean, can I please come with you to the CBI dinner tonight? Ooh Sean, do you mind if your mother and I are guests at the reception for the Israeli ambassador?' Sean had his face right down on the floor and was actually shouting now to make absolutely sure his dad heard in the living room.

'The thing is, if he thinks he's getting any kickbacks when I'm in the government he can think a-fucking-gain. Maybe I'll even ask for the transport brief so I can build a fucking great bypass right through his stinking precious home,' he said.

'It's only stinking because *you're* in it,' came the muffled reply from his dad downstairs.

'Sean, why don't you see someone?' I said, when he'd calmed down. 'Some expert of the mind.' (I didn't want to say 'psychiatrist'.)

'What, you mean an academic?'

'No, somebody medical. I'd fix it up. What do you reckon?'

'Are you totally happy with Gemma, then?' he said, changing the subject.

'Lots of people see experts, Sean. It'll help you get your mind sorted. You might get a job then, and you could stay round here. You don't want to move to fucking Scotland, do you?' The thought of him going to Scotland was depressing me.

'You don't feel the need to chat up other girls any more. If Gemma gets into Sheffield what about staying in our bedrooms for the next six months, me and you, reading the *Encyclopaedia Britannica*? We could have a race.'

'Sean, you're not going to be around much longer and you've been in your bedroom the *last* six months.'

'Your dad would let me have Charlie's old room, wouldn't he?'

'Sean, he hasn't even gone yet, and what's he going to think when he gets back and you're in his fucking room? Listen, I know lots of people who just talk to these people.'

'Come on, let's have a race. I'll give you a head start. You can start at C.'

'Sean, you need to get a fucking job. You need to sort yourself out. I'm worried about you. I think—'

'What?'

'I think you're fucking losing it.'

Sean looked away and scratched his face. 'All right then. You can start at D.'

Thursday, 25 March

I've noticed Ossie always kicks the mowers while he talks about them. It's as if to say, 'Look how familiar I am with this mower, see how I know how to be just so rough with it.' I tried it when Ossie was in the office checking invoices, and nobody else was about. But I slipped on the floor I'd just polished and left a boot mark in the grass bucket of a top-of-the-range Qualcast.

Attachments-selling course in Chalfont in the afternoon. Ossie and I represented the Mower Shop. Everyone wore gumboots and wax jackets, and the conversation was pitiful: 'The Westland vibrates itself to death. They've put a new AV in it but it don't do no good.' 'What it'll be's yer pipes. Give yer pipes a good blow, start first time, it will.' 'Have you tried the Club Cadet 750? Lovely machine.' 'We carry the Echo – it's got the horsepower. The 548's got the variegated gearbox, but with the weak front axle, no good to no one.' I'm dreading the product-awareness weekend. How much more fucking aware do I have to be?

I felt very weary when I got home and was annoyed with Dad for trying to fob me off with yet another chicken curry. I'm a manual labourer – I need sustenance, not unappetising dietary-deficient meals that couldn't feed a sparrow. Perhaps he'd like me to grow weak and slip under the blades of a 200-horsepower ride-on. Dad told me to shut up when I mentioned this, he'd been up four hours longer than me, and then reminded me for the hundredth time not to plan anything for Mum's memorial party on 24

April. It depressed me so much when Sarah phoned that I asked her whether she thought it would be OK if I didn't go.

'They're his friends, Jay,' she said. 'For God's sake – these are the people he mixes with. You can't ask him not to invite them.' I said that the whole memorial party was just another excuse for Dad to get pictures of himself with his arm around celebrities.

Sarah said I was being unfair. 'You make me laugh,' she said. 'You spend your whole time slagging off Dad's famous friends when all the time all you want to be is famous yourself. That's why you want to be a writer, isn't it? Come on, isn't it?'

I told Sarah she was talking bollocks, but what if she's right? Maybe I only want to be a writer so I get my own montage down the baulk end of the snooker room. Fame is the only measure of worth Dad respects. I certainly wouldn't get chicken curry for tea if I had my own entry in Debrett's *People of Today*.

10 p.m.

Gemma's not bothering to look for a job. She doesn't think it's worth it – she got her letter from Sheffield this morning – she's been fucking accepted. I said that's great news when she told me and tried to sound happy, but my voice was hollow and disembodied. Gemma suggested we go interrailing during her next summer to cheer me up. But we had a stupid row because Rod, her ex-course friend, phoned again to congratulate her. I heard her laughing and chatting with him on the phone: 'Really, you're going to work on a kibbutz this summer? That's sounds great. I'd love to do that.'

It isn't that Gemma used to fancy him, it's that Gemma knows I know she used to fancy him that bothers me. Whenever his name crops up, she gives me a sidelong glance. I haven't deciphered this look yet. It either means 'Go on, let's hear your joke Jay,' or, 'Ha, ha, I'm making you jealous.'

'Travel the world with lanky fucking Rod,' I said, before I stormed off (for some reason I've convinced myself Rod's lanky). 'Get beanpole to carry your rucksack.'

When I got home the back door was open, and I could hear the tell-tale clink and shuffle of Dad drinking in the rose bushes again. I was pissed off enough as it was and couldn't bear another bone-chilling night arguing with Dad about my resemblance to primates, so I tried to sneak off to bed before he noticed I was back. But he must have seen my headlights through the hedge because he came inside and caught me in the bathroom surreptitiously doing my teeth. 'Washyou-doin' inere with the light off, old son?' he said in a drunken slur.

He virtually frog-marched me into the garden. He seemed to have completely forgotten the other night, though, and was quite nice for a while. 'If you get on the ladder, you can always jump off,' he said, thinking it was my first day that was getting me down, rather than Gemma. 'My good friend Alan Price wrote songs for the Animals. He worked in a tax office for five years to finance his writing. That's what writers do when they start – they work to write. They don't write to work.'

It cheered me up slightly. I liked the way Dad said *his* writing. He said *his* writing as if there was *my* writing as well.

He patted me on the back, said, 'Give my friend in the City a ring for yer mother,' and walked inside to answer the timer that was bleeping on the oven.

I was taken aback as I followed him indoors. I wasn't going to ring his friend from the City, but I did start feeling guilty about the way I'd been treating him. That was until I realised what the oven bleeper was for. Because laid on the kitchen table were fifteen foil containers. Dad was standing over them, and, like he was filling champagne glasses at a wedding, was pouring into each of them, with a sweep of the pan, more and more individual portions of his fucking chicken curry.

I read a story once about a man who grew breasts because he ate too much chicken. I do not want breasts.

11 p.m.

Gemma's just phoned to ask if I am OK. I said I was fine, and she said it didn't mean anything; nothing was going to change between us. 'I've been thinking about you all night,' she said. I said I'd been thinking about her too, and said I was sorry – it *was* good news. As I said it I had a vision of my face looking like a ridiculous clown's, I was trying so hard to smile.

I can't remember the last time I was proud of myself. This is unnerving. I'd like to do something with my life, I'm not a waster, but what? Maybe journalism is the answer. But I want to be a novelist immediately so I can't help thinking there's no point in having a stepping stone, and, anyway, who says I ever will be a writer? My funny article about bathing has even been rejected by the Bellingdon Parish Magazine.

The trouble is I just can't care about where I work, unlike Dad and the BBC. A baby is born hungry for knowledge, it learns the most complex language in the world, how to co-ordinate its limbs, communicate coherently. It grows up, goes to school, learns about history, literature, philosophy, the complications of economics, geography and science. Then suddenly, this huge number–crunching computer in our cranium presses the buzzer and tells us it's got the answer. The meaning of life is . . . to renew the ten-year BBC Public Broadcasting Charter. The meaning of life is . . . to have the tidiest, most productive Montons branch in the whole of the Midlands and South East. The meaning of life is . . . to sell a hundred ride-on mowers. It's bollocks. We either need bigger brains to understand the whole picture or smaller ones like animals so we don't go around asking why, only 'where's my food? What's that in the bushes over there? I think I'll bark at it.'

Friday, 26 March

Quiet morning. Sold a Mountfield M1336 blade and three air filters, found a Honda part on the microfiche and then drove to Stow-on-the-Wold for the product awareness course, checked into my hotel, but was almost immediately whisked away to a farm and shown a 512 power-cutter and tilling attachment. Mick, the Wheelhorse rep, said I'd fall in love with the 512. Annoyed by his presumptive arrogance, I told him I'd have to wait and see and that in my experience love burned on a slow fuse.

Had a go tilling some soil, which was a bit dull, although everyone else seemed to enjoy it, and soon began to realise I didn't fit in.

To alleviate this, back at the hotel during the light buffet, I darted about snatching Rich Tea biscuits from different plates so that in the blur of movement nobody'd notice I wasn't talking to anyone about chopping back vegetation.

The final straw came when Mick stood on a chair and told everyone to get an early night because we were getting up at 7 a.m. to watch a demonstration of the new Ridel reversible plough, which was apparently 'a right little beauty'.

I cancelled my evening meal, made myself a toasted-cheese sandwich in the trouser press with some leftover bread and Cheddar from the buffet and spent the rest of the night in my hotel room playing the big-shot impresario, swigging back miniatures from the courtesy fridge, getting the receptionist to put me through to celebrities. 'Yes, I'd like you to connect me to Alec Baldwin. *The* Alec Baldwin. Then can you get me Rowan? Rowan Atkinson, on this number, please.'

I phoned Gemma drunkenly before I went to bed to apologise for last night and to tell her I thought we should be hunter-gatherers instead of drop-outs, because I'd just watched a programme on them. Hunter-gatherers had a great life. No berry-picking-awareness courses. No one telling them what to do. Just spear a caribou on Monday, pick a couple of crab apples on Tuesday, then take the rest of the week off. Who knows what hunter-gatherers actually do the rest of the time? Maybe they just have sex and play leapfrog. But at least they don't get excited about new fucking Peugeots, reversible ploughs and all the other things everybody's obsessed with nowadays.

To make me less jealous, Gemma said, if it made me feel any better, Rod was only five foot three and had a pointed Adam's apple.

'How pointed?' I said.

'Very pointed,' she said.

'Can't he wear scarves because of it?'

'No, he can't.'

We both laughed and called each other Hedge and Gem Gem before hanging up.

I think the whole world should take a hundred-year holiday. It'd be nothing in terms of all the years since the Big Bang. One hundred years of catching up with all the good books we haven't read, all the good films we haven't seen. One hundred years of plonking. We could survive on all the frozen food at Bejam's and Iceland. We wouldn't starve. No more economic growth, no more manufacturing, no more Hotpoint washing-machines and new Fords more aerodynamic than the last ones. We need a hundred-year holiday to realise that self-regulating kettles, smaller and smaller computers, electric car windows, personal fucking organisers and Peugeot 206s aren't all there is.

18 November: Mum was very down today. She said she dreamed she was sharing out the fridge contents between Sarah, Charlie and me – one Tupperware pot of stew for you, one for you, one for you. She said she didn't like the idea of Dad sharing the house with someone else. What do you say to this? I just gave her a hug.

She was aspirated again yesterday. They took seven pints of fluid from her this time. The trouble is, swelling always returns after a few days. Later Dad and I ate steak and chips at the Full Moon, while Mum took advantage of her brief mobility to deliver ironing with Charlie. Dad had a lot of practical things he wanted me to be clear about, he said. We'd probably have to hire a live-in nurse at the end because Mum wouldn't want to go into a hospice. Dad said there might come a time when the house would have to be sold if Mum's mobility deteriorated too much as well. 'And I'll have to transfer everything back from her name to mine,' he said. For tax reasons, and because he thought he would die first, he had put everything into her name.

When we came home we watched *The Guns of Navarone*. Probably to take his mind off everything and to stop me asking questions about Mum, Dad kept up a running commentary throughout – highlighting technically good elements of each scene and revolutionary film techniques, such as showing what the image was really like through binoculars. Sometimes I just wish he'd break down in tears, though; I'd be able to as well then.

Saturday, 27 March

I had a very strange, enlightening dream last night. It was great. In the dream fame was rotated around all the various professions, instead of always being concerned with music, sport and film. One week it was binmen who were famous, then it was pest-control workers, then another profession and so on. In my dream it was lawn-mower salesmen who were famous. It was fantastic. I earned exorbitant wages for assembling Webb lawnmower handle-bars and was on *Parkinson* being asked obsequiously how the new Mountfield coped in wet grass. Dad even had a picture of me in the snooker room behind an electric Hammond 360. I felt very low when I woke up and realised I was still a nobody.

It is how the world should be run, though, the way it was in my dream. Arriving at the Mower Shop in a smoked-glass Porsche, being greeted by a wall of screaming mower groupies throwing their knickers at me, having me sign their grass buckets, chanting my catch-phrase: 'If you bring in your Flymo TH1, I'll trade you up to a Honda 345 and throw in a complimentary set of secateurs.'

Teenage hopefuls anxious for notoriety meeting after their day jobs to form lawnmower sales teams with their friends; putting on ad hoc amateur garden-machinery sales at small local venues in the hope of being spotted by scouts from top lawnmower marketing concerns and being catapulted to stardom. This is the way it should be.

MICHAEL BARRYMORE So when did you first want to be a
   lawnmower salesman, Jay?
ME Well, Michael, my father took me to World's End
   Nursery when I was five and was sold a strimmer. It
   made a big impression.

Spent the day in my hotel room ringing up celebrities, trying to stop myself worrying about what a misfit I was and also trying not to think about the rim of burned cheese that's impossible to shift on the trouser press. Maybe I'm deficient in an important work-related gene. Perhaps I lack the entire nine-to-five chromosome. Maybe that explains it. Maybe when I die the pathologist will discover this glaring anomaly and Dad'll feel guilty about having given me such a hard time: '*If only we'd understood his chronic lack of the entire nine-to-five work chromosome. I feel so guilty about trying to make him wash up.*' Sob, sob, sob.

11 *p.m.*

Gemma wants me to meet her old course friends. She mentioned it tonight when I returned from Stow-on-the-Wold. She's trying to re-establish contact with them before she gets back. Some of them are coming to her house in a couple of days. Lanky Rod wouldn't be there, she said cajolingly, but that I'd like Alan, who's written comedy sketches for Russ Abbott.

Whatever she says, I can't help thinking Gemma will run off with someone else. Everyone says long-distance relationships don't work. Will ours be able to stand the strain? When I went on about it tonight Gemma told me I was paranoid. I am paranoid, too. I don't even like the fact that she fancies Rutger Hauer. I keep thinking about that film of his, *The Hitcher*, and imagine ridiculous scenarios where Gemma'll pick him up on her way to Sheffield and get off with him. It makes me feel nauseous: one word from a celebrity in a big flappy coat and I could be jilted.

Sunday, 28 March

Instead of being sacked today, I was promoted. Ossie called me into his office and announced I could have half his desk and three of the harder-to-reach filing-cabinet drawers. 'We want you to feel you've some responsibility here,' he said.

He clearly knew nothing about the product-awareness weekend and I should've felt glad. But I just felt very sad. All I could think was that sooner or later he would find out about it and then the drawers would be taken away. It worried me. Three rusty drawers – not exactly a finger on the nuclear button – but I was starting to want the responsibility. I was starting to want the drawers.

9 p.m.

To avoid Sheffield talk, Gemma and I spent tonight dreaming up an escapist movie scenario in which we were the drop-out heroes. In the movie I was a Burt Reynolds cowboy-type called Ray Doody who said, 'No Sheet!' all the time and Gemma was Suky-Lou, Ray's Sally Field-type girlfriend. The film was based on us playing fireside guitar, eating luncheon meat and driving around America in a motor home called *Old Sis*, which would overheat if we didn't keep patting the dashboard and saying, 'Udda gal, *Sis*.'

It was a corny film – and a bit of an advert for luncheon meat – but it made me feel better and before I left we did something soppy. We swapped jumpers to have a reminder of each other's smell. Gemma's jumper smelled faintly of Sure for Women. Mine still smelled strongly of McRib sauce.

11 p.m.

Dad was up when I got back and taught me the names of all the government ministers to prepare me for my NCTJ journalists' aptitude test next week. Later he extended the lesson to cover the names of other prominent men of the day. I think he quite enjoyed it – a lot of them are friends of his and it gave him an opportunity to point this out.

In fact I bet hunter-gatherers were just as bad, just as goal-orientated, as the Peugeot 206 people of today. They probably didn't play leapfrog at all. I bet a lot of their time was spent bragging about who had the most pointed stick, who was best at picking fucking berries. I bet they even had their own celebrities – the guy who was best at making fire, the guy with the strongest throwing arm. The guy with the best throwing arm probably had his own glad-handers drawing pictures of themselves with their arms around him on their cave walls in Lascaux. It's depressing – human nature and people with their arms around celebrities – you just can't get away from it.

Monday, 29 March

Had a serious reprimand from Ossie about skipping the product-awareness course. Ossie called me a 'fucking prat'. It was weird, but it made me feel close to him in a father–son type-way. I said I was very sorry, and I was, too. I redoubled my work output all afternoon, sold two strimmers and a pair of secateurs, and when I found a Webb clutch-cable on the parts microfiche Mike the parts manager stuck a pencil behind my ear and called me 'Superstores'. 'Yer learnin',' he said and I felt quite proud. On *The High Chaparral* once, the bloke who's too fat to do up his waistcoat, Ben-something, told Blue Boy that wild mustangs were the hardest horses to break but that when they were broken they made the most reliable mounts. Maybe that's what it is. Maybe I'm a wild mustang.

Crap evening with Gemma's old university friends. It wasn't even a proper party. It was a dinner party! Everybody sat around Gemma's house impersonating their parents, saying things like, 'More wine?' . . . 'Ooh, just a dribble,' complimenting Gemma on the crispiness of her potatoes. They all told Gemma it was great she was coming back and about events they had planned like the Great Pyjama Jump on Sheffield city centre and gigs at some place called the Limit. Russ Abbott Alan tried to befriend me during the dessert, and said he'd heard I was 'a bit of a scribbler', and wanted me to come to TV Centre with him some time to meet some of the other writers. But I could tell he was patronising me because later he pretended to be interested in what type of grass-inch cut I'd recommend for a lumpy paddock. In the end I made an excuse and came home early, Gemma accusing me of not making an effort. Scribbling in-*fucking*-deed!

Dad's bought Charlie a big tea chest. He has to have one to take his stuff to Roxburgh at the end of the week. Charlie starred as Captain Hook in his school play last year and keeps filling it up with shiny brass and silver things from the house because he likes to pretend it's a treasure chest.

Tonight Dad had a go at me about it. 'I'm not saying you're behind this. But can't you at least try to be a positive influence for a change. I'm sick of this work-to-rule attitude, of you undermining me at every turn. He's going, I've paid the fees, and that's it. He looks up to you, God knows why. That gives you a responsibility . . . I don't mind the poker and soot brush, but those silver spoons I got from Grandad, they're a hundred and twenty years old.'

I found where Dad had hidden Charlie's bionic arm-panel, and we played *Six Million Dollar Man* penalties in the garden until it was dark.

Tuesday, 30 March

This morning I heard Ossie shout '*What!*' while I was using one of my harder-to-reach filing-cabinet drawers. I instinctively knew it must be about something I'd done and went to the storeroom on the pretext of fetching a set of Webb handlebars to compose myself.

A few moments later, sure enough, he called me into his office. He was holding up a piece of paper. It was the bill from the Unicorn Hotel in Stow-on-the-Wold for £130, which included phone calls and vandalism to a trouser press. He asked what I knew about it and I made up a story that I'd accidentally had some cheese in my trouser pocket when I'd pressed them in preparation for the reversible-plough demonstration.

'I wanted to look smart for the reversible-plough demonstration . . . Someone may have put some cheese in my pocket for a practical joke. You know what lawnmower salesmen are like!' I also told him to remember what cowboys said about the wild mustang.

'And what *do* they say about the wild mustang?' asked Ossie sarcastically. He was writing out a cheque, not even looking at me.

'They say the wild mustang's the hardest horse to train,' I said, 'but once you've broken a wild mustang, he'll always make the most reliable mount.'

Ossie stopped writing and looked up blankly. 'This is a business, not a fucking cattle ranch,' he said, tearing off the cheque for £29.54 (my wages less the £130 bill).

The world is all wrong. Robots should be selling the mower parts. I said this to Dad tonight. 'The technology must be there. If we can have electric car windows, we can surely have Metal-fucking-Mickeys providing the elbow grease at Mower Shops.'

'Have you been sacked again?' asked Dad.

'No, of course not. Why do you always think I've been sacked just because I express a different point of view from yours?'

'You prat – you have been sacked, haven't you?'

'All right, yes, I have.'

I'm now slightly paranoid about the 'scribbling' comment that Gemma's friend made. Is this really all I'm doing? 'One ought only to write when one leaves a piece of oneself in the inkwell each time one dips one's pen.' Tolstoy's right. When I write this doesn't happen at all. I dug out the start of my novel tonight. It's chronically stifled by Wiggie's total inability to get off his arse and *do* something. It's infuriating – all he does is mooch about swearing. I feel towards Wiggie the way Dad feels towards me: 'For fuck's sake – you're three pages in, isn't it time you sorted out your life?'

Dad thinks everything I do is done purposefully for inclusion in my book. He told me this later. He thinks this might be why I keep getting sacked. 'You put us all in positions to see which way we'll jump,' he said. 'Don't tell me you don't, because I've read some of your diary.'

I told him it was obviously sour grapes: 'What you really mean is that you are unhappy about how badly you come out of it vis-à-vis the bath.'

But maybe he's right – it's appalling, but maybe I am a prat. The golden age of my life was seven years ago at Hawridge and Cholesbury School. That was the last time I was doing really well. I was on *Beta Maths Book 7*, I was captain of the school football team, going out with the only girl in school who looked like a girl and I had a full set of All Stars World Cup football stickers. That's the thing, in those days it was easy to tell how well you were doing because everyone did the same things. Basically, if you could kick a ball straight, weren't in any lower streams and had French-kissed a girl outside the library, you could be confident you were a success. Then you get older and it becomes complicated. The rules change – suddenly footy isn't the only hobby; horse-riding, stamp-collecting, musical interests, all sorts of other pastimes enter into the equation. And how do you compare these? Two goals struck with the outside of your left foot against Ley Hill, with an Oboe Grade 5 certificate. It's impossible.

Then, when you leave school and work it's even harder. You're an architect, or a plumber, or you're a bond dealer, an estate agent, a shopkeeper. The only way to assess your relative worth becomes money. But even that's too unreliable because different professions and companies pay differently, and some jobs are more interesting and cool and sought after. And, anyway, there are hundreds of other variables to consider as well by then. Are you charming, funny, tall, slim, attractive, bald, wise, fit, healthy, interesting? Do your feet smell? Are you bitter, entertaining, sociable, religious? I wonder whether I will end up a tramp, like Dad warned. If I do I will be a gentle one with a twinkle in his eye and a white mouse in his inside pocket.

Another nervy night with Gemma, both of us trying to avoid Sheffield, padding out the Ray Doody and Suky-Lou script. Gemma reckons we ought to have some super-loyal mongrel dog as well. She said in this type of American film there was always a super-loyal mongrel dog.

'Yeah,' I said, 'but wouldn't *Old Sis* get jealous if we had a super-loyal mongrel dog?'

'Not if every time we said, "Udda gal, *Sis*," and patted the dashboard the dog barked,' said Gemma

'Sort of to imply it was saying "Udda gal, *Sis*," as well?' I said

'That's it,' said Gemma. She also wants medallion steaks instead of luncheon meat. She's less keen than me on luncheon meat.

When I kissed her goodbye this evening in the van she had a confession to make, which cheered me up. She said she'd been spooning my jumper in bed as if it was me. When I told her I'd been doing the same with hers she leaned over and said, 'I felt another whoosh then!' in such a sexy voice I was forced to hide my erection with a road atlas.

I need to be stranded on a desert island with Gemma, that's the answer. We're fine until other things get in the way. Spearing small fish, drinking coconut juice, battling for supremacy in the relationship under pendulous trees. I wouldn't be the one to signal to the rescue helicopter.

Wednesday, 31 March

Drove to Sheffield and completed the aptitude test for the NCTJ. Not only did I know the name of every famous person in the general knowledge section, I wrote in brackets that three of them were coming to our house for Dad's fucking party.

I went for a drink with one of the other candidates afterwards. He seemed OK initially, then got cuntish when I mentioned journalism was a means to an end and that what I really wanted to do was write a great novel.

'What? The garret room thing? Yeah, that's what I always told myself I was going to do,' he said dismissively, as if I should really have grown out of this by now.

I made a last-ditch effort to save Charlie later while Dad and I were watching *Morse*. I promised to phone Dad's friend from the City, then said I'd do anything he wanted, even leave home, if he changed his mind about Roxburgh. Dad said it was a tempting offer, but he was sorry it didn't work like that and just laid into me: 'Never mind your brother, you should be worried about yourself. We all are. Another job, Jay. *Another one.*' Then, more restrained, 'Everyone can theoretically win the race on the starting line, my son. I realise how you see it. But it's not really like that any more, is it? The starting pistol's already been fired. It was fired a long time ago. Everybody else is already in their stride. Look at your friends, Mark, Kate, and now even Gemma. It's time you got into *your* stride. The perfect job is never going to *come along*. You've got to work your way up, like I did. We've all got to do it. That's the way it works. Do you think I liked running around after junior producers when I could have been out enjoying myself? You've got to start somewhere. What are you going to be – unemployed, doing a dossy job for the rest of your life? You'll end up very unhappy, bitter. I've seen it happen. Get on the first rung. The first rung of a good ladder, old son. Apart from anything else, I can't go on supporting you. It's not fair – if your mother were alive . . . Well, we both know what she'd have said about it.'

It made me angry he'd brought up Mum like that. 'I told Mum I was going to be a writer and that's what I'm going to be,' I shouted. 'She said I should hold out until I was a writer.'

'Now that's a lie. Stop it, Jay. I don't want to hear you

take your mother's name in vain. She wanted what I want – what's best for you.'

'What's *best* for me is you leaving me alone so I can watch *Morse*,' I said. 'That's another thing Mum said to me, actually. She said, "Tell Dad to fuck off and let you watch *Morse*."' I regretted saying it immediately. I only said it because I was tired of his nagging and didn't want him to remind me he was five foot two again. There's something depressing about being constantly reminded your father's a fucking dwarf.

'What did you say?' he said. He'd got up from his seat. He was bearing down on me.

'I didn't say anything,' I said, and peered round him to watch the telly. I thought he might think he'd misheard me if I appeared relaxed enough to be rude enough to peer round him to watch the telly.

'You've got two weeks to find a job, or' – he pointed outside into the garden with tears in his eyes – 'you're out. Do you hear me? *You. Are. Out.*'

He walked into the kitchen and then came back menacingly. 'And I've got David Dimbleby coming over for dinner tomorrow, so make sure your room's tidy. And I don't mean chuck everything under the bed.'

'What, and David Dimbleby's going to look under my bed, is he?' I said. 'What are you playing after the coffees, fucking sardines?'

I got quite into the pitiful homeless waif role later at Gemma's. I exaggerated to her parents and told them I actually had been thrown out. Gemma's mum made me some tea and I wrapped both hands round the mug, stared listlessly into space, and said, 'I suppose I could check into the Amersham night shelter. I think they've got beds at the Amersham night shelter.' Gemma's mum let me sleep in the spare room in the end.

The white mouse in my pocket would be called Cuddles. I'd teach it to crawl round the back of my neck, talk to it earnestly about where we were going to spend the night and

other incidental facts about the day. And I'd never accidentally squash it, even when I was really drunk on Tennents
Extra.

23 November: One of the worst things is seeing Dad under
Mum's instruction learning how to cook chicken curry and make
meals so he'll be able to look after himself when she's gone. She
taught Dad how to use the microwave and the oven today. It's
heartbreaking to watch. 'No, no, no – the bleeper comes on after
you press the red button and it's only for the main oven.'

It is so calculated, such an acknowledgement of death, that it
seems somehow wrong. It's like the rose bushes Mum's been
planting when she's felt fit enough, in the back garden. They will
not flower until July and by then it's unlikely she'll be alive.

It's slightly weird. I'm almost more concerned about Dad than
Mum at the moment. Like in Dunblane when the head teacher
went from one body to the next, marking the kids who were alive
and a priority with a red slash of felt-tip, I think of him,
emotionally wounded, as the priority. The trouble is he deflects
any concern shown towards him, or changes the subject to
practicalities before he displays any weakness.

APRIL

Thursday, 1 April

Gemma's dad paid for us to visit a friend of Gemma's in Bath. It was a relief to get out of Dad's way. Every time I meet him anywhere in the house now he stops in an exaggerated fashion and waits for me to pass before he moves on. It's like watching a bad driver on a roundabout. He's doing it to emphasise how it's better if we keep out of each other's way and it's annoying. Tomorrow I think I'll shunt him.

On the way to Bath we stopped at a Shire Horse Centre. The guide who showed us round was one of those schmaltzy animal lovers. She petted and molly-coddled each horse as she introduced them. 'This is Dukey – he's my best friend in all the whole world, aren't you, Dukey?' Then, one stable along, 'And this is where Jason lives. Isn't he marvellous? Look at him. Who's a handsome lad, then? Jason's my favourite. I love you so much, don't I, J?' What fickleness. I bet even the horses saw through it. Ironically the horse called J had just been sacked from his job in a military band. Gemma thought this was hilarious.

The best thing about places of interest isn't the place at all, it's reading the letters kids send in thanking the management for their visit. In one at the Shire Horse Centre a kid had said, 'Thank you very much. I think I would like to come back one day. I felt a bit sorry for the horse pulling the cart, which looked very heavy because of the people in it. I tried to sit up in the cart so I didn't weigh so much. I also saw a rabbit, which was the same age as mine. I took a picture of it to show my rabbit. You probably think I live on a farm, but surprisingly I don't. Yours sincerely, Tom Smote (7).'

What really got me was that bit about Tom Smote believing the Shire Horse Centre people might find it surprising that he didn't live on a farm. It was just the sort of thing Charlie would say. The letter saddened me too because 'Yours faithfully' had been changed to 'Yours sincerely'. It was the same on all the letters they'd pinned up. Some stupid teacher had altered them with a red pen. Why can't people leave kids alone to write their own letters? If you get a letter from a kid who's seven and likes your Shire Horse Centre, you don't look to see if he's signed himself off properly. Charlie goes in five days.

In the afternoon we visited the Roman baths. One quarter of a million gallons of piping-hot water spring from the earth's crust every day at this spot. If I lived here I could probably read the whole of *War and Peace* before Dad complained about hot-water top-ups in the bath. I'm a victim of geography.

11 p.m.

I got quite drunk at the pub later and told Gemma's friend I was planning to die trouser-pressless in a pool of my own vomit. Gemma's friend said, 'One day you will get a job, though, won't you? You'll have to – you can't go on sponging for ever.' When I laughed and shook my head comically, Gemma's friend laughed, and said, 'I suppose that means it's my round *again* then,' and went up to the bar.

As she did this, I glanced over and noticed Gemma looking at me in a way I hadn't seen before. Then she held me by my chin and there were tears in her eyes. 'I love you, Jay Golden,' she said. 'I really *do*, but—' Then she wouldn't complete the sentence, even when I called her Gem Gem and tried to tickle it out of her.

The stupid thing is half of me deep down wants Gemma to go. It might just give me the impetus to do something. I'm waking up with panic attacks about going nowhere, but while she's out there with her backgammon board and dimpled smile it never seems to matter much during the day.

Friday, 2 April

As I pulled into our drive first thing this morning I saw everything strewn all over the garden. My books, tapes, CDs, clothes – all my stuff was soaked with dew. Dad was reading the paper, eating his breakfast as if nothing was wrong.

'Good night with Dimblebum, was it?' I said.

'I told you to tidy your room. You didn't, so I tidied it for you,' said Dad, not looking up. 'You've got a fortnight. And I thought I told you to park that van on the common until you get that oil leak fixed.' He lowered his voice. 'I mean it – next time it's for real.'

It took me an hour to bring in my stuff. What a drama queen he is. And he's connected a telephone charge meter. I'm in the poverty trap and all he does is stick the boot in! He said it was to monitor his calls to the BBC for expenses, but really it's so he can monitor me. I'm living in a Stalag.

'The phone bill was astronomical last quarter and they were mostly London numbers, so they can't have been you, can they?' said Dad. 'Can they?' he said more menacingly.

11 p.m.

I've decided to turn Gemma's dad into a twentieth-century hate figure by slagging him off in my Wiggie novel. I went round to Gemma's and asked him if I could spend the night there again, but the petty bastard refused. Apparently he put blotting paper under my oil tank the other night and knows it's my van that's been leaking over his drive. So I had to come home, swallow my pride, say sorry to Dad and agree to attend the fucking interview with his banking friend from Cunts and Co., or whatever it is. I'll do the job for a couple of months, save up, then leave to join a revolution or go to live in a mud hut or look up J. D Salinger in his reclusive bunker and become his protégé or something.

Dad was very pleased, said it had been a long time coming, but that I'd finally made my first grown-up decision. He poured us a drink and we clinked glasses. He said, 'Truce,' I said, 'Truce,' and then he said, 'Follow me,' and took me up to his bedroom, where he took great pleasure in choosing me a work tie from his wardrobe. He gave me sixty pounds to buy some new work shoes and got me to try on one of his old suits. When I had the whole oufit on, he said, 'My God, you actually look smart. Is this possible? Is this my son?' and kept straightening the tie, telling me it was one given to him by his good friend the late, great Russell-fucking-Harty.

My seeming change of heart and new appearance must have moved him strangely because later he went to pour himself a drink looking quite sombre, and when he came back, after much more time than it would have taken to pour the drink, he looked overburdened. He walked slowly back to his seat with his head back, dangling the drink in his hand as if he didn't know it was there. In the middle of the room he looked at the beamed ceiling and touched the rim of his glasses. His eyes looked red and damp. 'All right,' he said. 'All right, I can see you're trying. If the little lad—' He started blinking. He took off his glasses and pinched his nose. 'If the little lad doesn't like it after the first term . . . we'll have a think about it.'

He put his glasses back on and I got up and hugged his head. I still had my reading glasses on and our two pairs clashed like antlers. Dad tensed and made out he was more bothered about straightening his glasses than hugging me, but I could tell he was pleased. 'Is that fair?' he said, straightening my tie again. I said it was. 'Right, now go and get your big bad dad another drink and let's watch a film and start getting on for a change.' I got him a huge Cointreau and when I came back with it he told me to choose what we watched.

'You're not to go putting ideas in his head,' he said, half laughing, half serious, when I came back with

Spartacus. 'Give him a chance to like it, that's all I ask. I know what you're like. And you're to do your best when you meet my friend, do you hear me? He's a very important man and he's doing me and you a very big favour. Remember that.'

I was hoping we'd get to the line in the film – 'Sulla – to the infamy of his name' – so Dad and I could practise it again, but he was snoring in his armchair after about ten minutes so I put up the fireguard and went to bed. As I walked past, I kissed him on the forehead like I used to when I was a kid.

He woke up woozily and clasped my head on both sides in a fit of emotion as if he was a goalkeeper and my head was a football he was about to punt upfield. 'You're impossible, but I do love you, my son,' he said, staring into my eyes. 'You know that, don't you?'

I asked him to prove it by dismantling the telephone charge meter, but he refused.

Saturday, 3 April

Sarah came round to cook a roast this afternoon and to show off her wedding dress. She gave me a kiss when she came through the door and told me in a fit of emotion, 'Well *done*, Jay. You've finally grown up . . . ah. I knew you had it in you.'

For a change, everyone spoke to me during the meal, and Dad was full of how great it was working in the City, and how he'd always known that's where I'd end up. Sarah and I also got on quite well for a change and after Dad left the room we had a long chat about Mum. Sarah told me she talked to Mum about mundane wedding preparations: 'Where should we seat Uncle Roger?' . . . 'Would you have a string quartet, Mum?' She said she imagined Mum in heaven when she felt down: Mum doing Mum things up there like gardening, ironing, getting people to eat tomatoes and talking to Hazel, a friend of hers who died a few years ago.

I told her whenever I thought about Mum, I only had bad memories, and I mentioned the nightmare I keep having.

Sarah was very upset after this and started telling me how much Dad loved me and how pleased she was about my decision to punch buttons on a boring console in the City for a living. 'Dad does love you, you know? He'd be so upset if he thought you didn't know that. Jay, he's always going on about how clever and funny you are. He's just got a strange way of showing it, that's all. You wind him up so much.' She started laughing about some of the things I'd done over the years and how she used to hear Mum through her bedroom wall placating Dad at night. 'You remember that time you dropped his laptop in the bath?' she said. 'He made you weed the garden to pay for it. And on the first day you dug up all Mum's mint plants. It must be harder for you than anyone,' she said, suddenly serious and nodding her head. 'She never said so, but you were Mum's favourite. I know you were.'

I modestly said I wasn't.

'She talked to you about everything. She was always telling me things you'd told her. She was so proud you told her things. She loved that, you know? Dad knows that, too. *And* you've got her blond hair and blue eyes. I didn't mind, I don't mind – I suppose, if anything, I'm Dad's favourite.'

After this, Sarah really surprised me. It was totally out of the blue because Dad and Rob's friend were doing one already. She wanted to know if I'd do a reading at the wedding. I felt honoured she'd asked me. She showed me the sonnet she wanted me to read from Dad's *Complete Works of Shakespeare* in the bookcase and I had a go at reading it. Then she said, 'You will do it properly, won't you, Jay? It was my idea, but Rob's worried you'll do something stupid – read it in a funny accent or something. Promise me you won't.'

I am getting a bit sick of being treated like some sort of lunatic. Of course, I'll do it *properly*. What does she expect me to do? Just because I'm a sharp-clawed animal glaring into the stockade of society, doesn't mean I'll ruin my sister's big day. I felt quite hurt. The drip-drip-drip of disdain's beginning to wear me down.

2 p.m.

After lunch I asked Charlie if there was one thing he'd like to do before he went away. He plumped for seeing the giant turtle at the Tring Zoological Museum. I tried to give him a few words of brotherly advice to prepare him for Tuesday, when he goes to Roxburgh, but I could tell he wasn't really listening so we just played more bionic penalties until Dad accused me of turning the garden into a ploughed field.

I promised Mum I'd look after Charlie. We took it in turns to go in and see her that last day. I went in first and Mum could barely talk and her hair had been straightened out by the nurses and she didn't look like Mum any more because her eyes were so far back in her head and her bottom teeth were jutting out like a wild animal's. Every now and again she'd wake up from the morphine, look disorientated and say something. I don't even think *then* she knew what was happening to her, because she said trivial things like, 'You've got to eat those bananas before they go off, darling' . . . 'Darling, don't forget to tell Dad there's a spare box of washing powder in the utility room.' She didn't mention Charlie; I did. I felt I had to say something significant. She had a few hours to live and there she was talking about washing powder. I said I'd make sure he was all right. Mum was asleep at the time, but I squeezed her hand tight as I said it and I thumped my heart dramatically with my fist. I didn't feel any pressure back on my hand, but apparently your hearing's the last thing to go, so maybe she was listening.

Sunday, 4 April

Sarah phoned today, asking all of us to try on our morning suits to check they fitted and to ask Dad whether Uncle Roger could stay over after the wedding because he couldn't find a hotel. She said she was so nervous about tomorrow her left eye had swollen up. I told her I hoped she'd get better in time, but if she didn't I'd use her misfortune to make a joke after my sonnet reading. 'I'll say, "You've heard of the Hunchback of Notre Dame, well now we've got the Puffed Eye of Westminster Abbey." Then I'll say, "Sarah, you're a great sister," and sit down.'

Sarah didn't realise I was joking and started having a go at me because she'd hoped I'd changed, but obviously I hadn't. 'Jay, it's April. Charlie's going on Tuesday, Gemma'll be at university soon. What are you going to do then? You'll have no money. How are you going to sustain the relationship? Dad'll throw you out, you'll be living in some bedsit. Gemma's not going to want that. Not when she's made new friends. I like Gemma, but how long's she going to put up with somebody who never has a job, and is going nowhere?

'She might not want security now, but she will. She's bound to. It'll wear you both down eventually. It wore me down with Greg' – the ex-boyfriend she dumped who's now a dispatch rider. 'I love you so much, my little brother, but *argh*! . . . you make me so mad I could hit you. You can't muck up that interview next week. You can't. I won't let you. I won't. You can't.'

I told her to calm down, I was only joking. Of course, I wasn't going to say that in the church, and she changed her tone, said, 'God – I really am stressed, aren't I?' and then burst into tears because Mum wouldn't be there on her big day.

7 p.m.

Dad and I practised our readings for tomorrow. We had lunch with Uncle Roger, who's staying over, and in the afternoon I took Charlie to the Tring Zoological Museum. Gemma came, too. Charlie was very funny, and made Gemma laugh by rushing ahead, trying to be first to find the sewn-up bullet holes in the stuffed mammals ('There in his neck! Baby lion – bullet in the tummy! Daddy lion – in the head! Polar bear – head! Gazelle – head! Gorilla – can't see, too much fur'). They got on even better this time, and Charlie made her take part in one of his urges, too, something he normally doesn't do with strangers. She had to walk round the giant turtle twice to stop a tragedy in her family he wouldn't discuss.

It all made me feel very emotional. I put Charlie on my shoulders so he could look a stuffed Indian elephant in the eye, and through *The Story of Evolution* I kept letting Gemma get ahead so I could catch up, put my arm around her and, on the pretext of passing on hushed information about finch beak-widths, nuzzle and smell her perfumed neck.

11.30 p.m.

I'm sleeping the night on the top bunk in Charlie's bedroom because Uncle Roger is in mine. It was just like when he was really small, Charlie waking up the moment I came in, putting on the main light and poking me through the mattress because he didn't want to sleep. 'Jay?' he whispered.

'What?'

'Are you a-fluffing-sleep?'

'No.'

'Neither am I.'

There was a pause and then Charlie poked me through the mattress again, looking for some response.

'You're saying "fluffing" a lot these days,' I said.

'Fluffing, fluffing, fluffing,' he said.

'Don't say "fluffing" so much,' I said.

I turned off the main light, put on the little side-light and lay there writing this and reading my old diary. Charlie said, 'Fluffing, fluffing, fluffing,' very softly for a few minutes to provoke me, and just when I thought he'd finally fallen asleep he poked me again.

'What?'

'Nothing.'

'Why did you poke me then?'

'Jaaay,' said Charlie, a few seconds later, 'will there be any scroggs and scriggs in Roxburgh?'

Scroggs and scriggs are invisible creatures that are out to undermine you and make trouble. I used to talk to him about them. If anything went wrong, it was never your fault. It was always the scroggs' and scriggs' fault. And there were scrangies, too, they were the other ones. They co-operated with the scroggs and scriggs, the scrangies did.

'No, but if you come across a scrangie, give me a call,' I said. I was pleased he'd remembered them.

'I fluffing will,' said Charlie. 'If I come across a scrangie I'll fluffing well call the police . . . and the fluffing army.'

30 November: Mum's started chemotherapy. We won't know whether it's helped for two months.

Dad and I built Charlie a sandpit today. I think Dad needs to do something to take his mind off everything. We rigged up the reclining chair for Mum by the living-room window so she could look out while we worked and shout out if she wanted anything. Dad was in his hyper mood. ('I've got to keep my mind busy, old son'). He dug the hole, I banged in the slats and Charlie ferried the bags of sand around in the wheelbarrow.

Dad spoke in the cockneyish voice he only uses when he's upset or serious and trying to hide it: 'Yer mother's a fighter, she ain't gerner die. She'll be planting bulbs out here long after we've both gone, my son . . . Look at her checkin' up on us again, give her a wave. Yer mother's the heart and soul of this family. BBC-Bel beats cancer – that's what I'm telling 'er, and she will, too.'

I eventually put down the old diary and started thinking of Charlie's room being empty, not hearing his flutey voice shouting, 'Heroes in a half-shell,' every five seconds, not knowing what he was up to every day.

'Charlie,' I whispered, suddenly wanting to talk to him. 'Charlie,' I whispered again, but he was already asleep.

Monday, 5 April

Dad drove us up to Westminster Abbey at 1 p.m. I didn't think it would affect me much, but it did. There were a few hymns, Dad did his reading in a heartfelt way and looked tearfully sincere, but instead of feeling nervous at the prospect of mine as I'd expected, I found myself trembling with emotion. I was in a trance when I read the sonnet and as I sat back down next to Charlie, I was choked. Sarah was smiling at me from a seat next to the altar, waiting to take her vows. And when I lip-read her saying to Rob, 'He read it really well,' I was so pleased I'd done it, been a part of it and hadn't let her down I wanted to bawl.

Marriage – it's one of the three most important things that happen to you: you're born, you're married, you die. Yesterday Sarah was serving me miniature tubs of peanut butter from her cardboard shop; today here she was in a wedding dress.

The rest of the ceremony was a blur because, sitting next to Charlie in the pew, I started trying to imagine Mum was in the chapel somewhere looking down, being there like Sarah wanted, and that got me thinking of the funeral: everybody gawping at us as we took our seats in the front pew, expecting us to cry, wanting us to, so they could, too; holding one hymn book between Charlie and me, wiping his nose with my hanky and his tears on the page enlarging the words like one of Grandad's convex reading aids; how I'd been angry with Dad because of the hymns he'd chosen for the funeral service, which all mentioned God, when Mum didn't believe in God; how I'd been angry with God for gate-crashing Mum's funeral through a friend of a friend; how I'd been angry with the vicar for being that friend of a friend; how I'd been angry with Mr Twain the funeral director for commenting on how well the hymns were sung afterwards because I hadn't sung any of them; how I'd been angry with all the relatives and all the friends and Dad because they *had* sung them; and how I'd been angry with myself for not being a part of my own mum's funeral.

'From the dark there shall come light, out of grief there comes understanding,' said the vicar. 'This is a time for sorrow, but also for great joy. A time to thank God for the miracle of life and the mercy of death.'

I wanted to heckle him, shout him down, swear aloud and smack his face in for his formulaic optimism, but instead I just stared hatefully into his eyes over my hymn book in a way I hoped he'd see and understand. The miracle of life that ends in death, anyway. What's that like? Selling someone a car that's built to fall apart and then giving it the *What Car?* 'Car of the Fucking Year' award.

Then, out in the car park afterwards, that horrible hush, those lowered voices and meaningless condolences: 'It went beautifully, Maurice' . . . 'I always think that's such a powerful hymn.' Grandad was helped out of the chapel by Sarah like an old piece of furniture, then sat in the car waiting to be driven back to Brighton, so totally broken by it all, his mind had regressed twenty years so that he asked me, 'So where's she going on her honeymoon?' The slow drive home, with the windows open for air, Charlie wedged on the floor behind the driver's seat still wearing his off-black tie and fiddling with the ladder on his Tonka Toy fire engine: 'When's Mummy coming back from heaven, Dad?'

'I told you, Charlie' – Sarah, not turning round, her eyes

glazed – 'you can't come back from heaven. It's not that Mummy doesn't want to. She just can't.'

'Why, Sarah? Is she tied up?'

The wedding reception was on a barge, which did a three-hour loop finishing at Tower Bridge. On board Dad had a surprise for Sarah – his good friend Zoë Ball was doing the deejaying. Dad was everywhere glad-handing, Sarah and Rob went round like a king and queen, and I spent the night with Charlie and Gemma at the prow of the boat listening to him talk about Beanie Babies and the chances of getting into the school football team at Roxburgh, trying very hard to keep out of the way of all the guests who kept saying, 'What a shame your mother couldn't be here,' and Zoë Ball, in case she recognised my voice.

At 11 p.m. we formed a cheering arch of arms as Rob and Sarah left the boat to start their married life. Charlie and I were the last pair and Sarah stopped to give us the biggest kisses. She picked up Charlie in her arms, wished him good luck for tomorrow and said she was so proud of him for being so grown up. She showed me crossed fingers about my interview with Dad's friend and said, 'Not that you'll need it.'

When we arrived home I took the top bunk in Charlie's room again. His last night here. I feel a bit depressed. I'm drifting aimlessly in the sea of life with only the thoughts of a fiercely loyal white rodent keeping me afloat.

7 December: Mum showed the first major signs of upset today. She was in hospital for her chemo and talking about another cancer cure that an ironing client of hers had read about in the *Daily Mail*. Dr Gold from the Syracuse Cancer Center in New York claimed he'd had success in turning back the development of tumours with a simple tablet made of rocket fuel.

I phoned the centre from her bedside phone (I got the number from International Directory Enquiries), but there was no reply.

A woman quoted in the story had forgone chemotherapy, which supposedly disables the immune system, in favour of taking two of these tablets every day. Mum was worried she'd already had one chemo session. She thought this might prejudice her chances of being cured by the rocket fuel.

In the middle of discussing this, she said, 'I was eating a piece of grapefruit this morning and one of the nurses told me, "That's right, you eat while you can." ' Tears welled in her eyes and she put her hands up to hide them.

I walked around the bed to give her a hug.

'It was as if she was saying, "You eat while you still can, because later you won't be able to." What did she mean by that?'

I held her head in the crook of my arm.

'You wake up and you think you're all right, then you remember you're not. And you think, Oh shit! It happens every day.'

I could feel the outline of her skull when I squeezed her head through her bristly hair. I couldn't think of anything to say, so I held her, and, just like Mum, she apologised and said normally she didn't think about it. 'I'm all right. It's just every now and again it gets to you, you know?'

What's the point? I can't help thinking. She was born, she raised three children, she ironed thousands of shirt cuffs and served fish pie for tea and she loved and was loved in return. Now she's going to die. What does it all add up to?

Tuesday, 6 April

Dad had made us leave ridiculously early to beat the traffic on our way to Roxburgh. When we arrived the place was deserted because everyone was still in bed. It gave the place a gloomy, desolate feel.

I carried the turtle tank up to Charlie's dorm on the second floor. We'd had to empty out half the water in case it sloshed out on to the car seats, but it still weighed a ton. Charlie followed me, holding the thermostat plug so I didn't trip on it. It took us ages because he was having lots of urges:

he kept peering around bends in the staircase, drumming the banister with his fingers and shuffling his feet erratically. My arms were nearly dropping off by the end.

'Touch your head three times with your right hand and stick out your tongue,' he said to me at one point.

'I can't, Charlie – I'm holding this.'

'Touch your head three times with your right hand and stick out your tongue. It's an urge.'

'Charlie, I can't.'

'You've got to.'

I stuck out my tongue. 'There,' I said.

'Do the rest. You have to do the rest,' he said, and whispered the word 'scrangie' into my shoulder, darting his eyes about from side to side. He touched his own head three times and stuck out his tongue.

I put down the tank. 'All right,' I said, 'but this is the *last one*. I've got my scrangie detector on and there are no scrangies here and this thing weighs a ton.'

'Three times, don't do four, and you've got to do your tongue again. It didn't count before,' said Charlie. He was still looking around like he half expected to be mugged by a gang of scrangies.

We finally found Mr Morton, the housemaster, and he asked if we wanted to go on a tour before we left to get some idea of the scale and history of the place. But even though it was still only 10 a.m. Dad said we should really be making tracks.

We stopped off at the Black Horse in Bellingdon on the way back for lunch. I couldn't eat, though. I still felt bad. Dad picked at some basket chips and talked about how great Sarah had looked in her dress and how they'd now be in the Bahamas, but even he seemed subdued and uninterested. It was like we'd committed a crime, and neither of us mentioned Charlie until we got home, when Dad stopped the car, got out and, walking to the house in his flat-footed, put-upon manner, said to me, 'Jeepers-creepers! Who'd have kids? What they put you through!'

9 p.m.

Dad wanted me to have a drink with him tonight to make himself feel better, but I couldn't face it. I still felt very depressed and went round to Gemma's instead. I wanted to have something to look forward to, some light relief. I wanted to discuss interrailing next summer. But her accommodation list had come through and she was busy talking to her dad about driving up to Sheffield to sort out a house. Her mum and dad are going up with her to scout the area. I tried to sound excited for her, but my heart wasn't in it. Gemma noticed and asked what was wrong. I told her I thought it was *us* who were going up to scout out the area, and Gemma laughed.

'What, 'orrible one, so you can make sure I'm not in a shared 'ouse with other men?' she said.

It was meant as a joke, but I couldn't take it as one, for some reason. I said something nasty about how her jumper made her look lumpy and came home.

11 p.m.

I'm slightly worried about my health. My stomach hurts at the moment and has done for a while. Plus, I've noticed my stools have gone all bitty. They look like meatballs and float on top of the water, like Mum's did before she got ill. Rob reckoned it could be stress, although Dad laughed when I mentioned this to him. 'Stress! You do sod all,' he said.

Wednesday, 7 April

It was bizarre and disturbing taking Sean to his GP. It was made worse by Sean's cheerfulness in the waiting room beforehand. One minute he was leafing through back copies of the *Reader's Digest*, telling me about the electric eel he'd been reading about in the encyclopedia, the next he was telling Dr Fitzpatrick, a complete stranger, he was probably gay.

Dr Fitzpatrick did his best to disguise his astonishment, only occasionally giving wide-eyed looks. I sat in the corner trying not to catch anybody's eye, but when Sean said he might be gay, he looked nervously across at me and half smiled. Suddenly, despite the seriousness of the situation, I felt like laughing. It reminded me of the game Sean and I used to play in the Rose 'n' Crown before he failed his A levels, when Mum was alive, when the future seemed a long way off. Both of us would pretend to be mad to wind up Mark and Kate: Sean drunkenly pinned up an empty sleeve and said he was Nelson in another life; I went around telling the locals I was descended from Samuel Kingston, the inventor of trouser pockets.

And now here we were in a Chesham surgery with Sean playing the game for real. I half wanted to nod to Sean, laugh at the absurdity and tell the doctor something equally ridiculous ('And I'm really a lollipop lady named Vera who looks good in wide belts'). I wanted to do anything but take it seriously. But instead I furrowed my brow and looked on earnestly, which seemed a sad and strange way to betray a friend.

Dr Fitzpatrick began probing: 'Sean, do you ever feel like the television is talking to you?'

'No, the television doesn't talk to me,' said Sean, 'but I think what people say on the television does relate to me. They talk about me.'

Had Sean ever felt like killing himself? Yes, he might kill himself one day. 'Although, strictly speaking,' said Sean, 'in the Bible, like being gay' – he looked at me for so long that the doctor eventually glanced over, too – 'it's a big no–no.'

At the end Dr Fitzpatrick asked when Sean was moving to Dumfries and wanted to know if he'd see a colleague of his – on his own next time. Sean said he'd prefer I was there, too. Dr Fitzpatrick asked, 'Is there any reason you want your' –

he said the next word as if it was in inverted commas – 'friend . . . to be there? Have you anything important you especially want to say to your . . . friend?'

The doctor obviously thought I was gay, too, and I didn't know what to say. I suddenly felt very embarrassed I'd come. Sean said no, he hadn't anything important he wanted to tell me, and there was a strained silence on the way home in the van.

7 p.m.

Charlie phoned up in tears tonight. 'Jay,' he said, out of breath from crying, 'is Mum a monkey?'

He'd got the story of evolution in the Tring Zoological Museum mixed up with heaven somehow, and had got it into his head that you started off as a monkey, got sent down to earth by God and became a human. He thought Mum was now a monkey again and was worried she might be shot and displayed in a museum.

I tried to calm him – Mum was still Mum, she was just above the clouds where we couldn't see her – but Charlie was still in tears and said grumpily, 'Why doesn't she stick a foot out of the sky, then?'

I didn't know what to say to that, so I changed the subject and asked how Greeny-Slowy was enjoying his new home, but that made matters even worse. Mr Scrangie Stratton, the biology master, had dropped the turtle tank while he had been carrying it to the lab because pets weren't allowed in the dorms and Greeny-Slowy had weed himself, and wasn't moving, and didn't retract his head even when you poked him near the eye with a pencil. Charlie thought Greeny-Slowy was now going to die, and wanted to know if turtles went to heaven. I told him they did, and then he wanted to know if Mum would look after Greeny-Slowy in heaven, and how she'd know how much Reptavite to feed him, because Mum hadn't got a *PetSmart Get Smart Know Your Pet* book.

'It'll be all right, Charlie,' I said. 'God will tell her how much Reptavite to feed him.'

Charlie stopped crying briefly, and said he wanted to come home because he missed having Captain Crunch for breakfast and everyone at Roxburgh was a fluffing silly-head.

He was eventually semi-all right, but I felt angry, and when Dad asked how he was, I said, 'He was in fucking tears asking about Mum,' and went upstairs, Dad shouting 'I won't be spoken to like that in my own home.'

He must've been brooding about it, because when I came downstairs later he insisted on telling me about the day he went to boarding school. It annoyed me: here he was talking about himself again. 'I'll never forget it,' he said, staring at the ceiling and shaking his head slowly. 'The sight of that little old Ford reversing down the drive – you wouldn't remember those Fords – knowing I wouldn't see Mum and Dad for three months. It was tough . . . *God*, it was. But it toughens you up. It toughened up me. It'll toughen up Charlie. I know you love your brother, Jay. We all love him. We love him to bits. But it's for the best. It really is. I do believe that . . . At that age, children . . . they're very resilient. And anyway' – he matily slapped my foot, which was resting on the coffee table, as he walked into the kitchen – 'I haven't turned out so bad, have I?'

'Uhm,' I said.

He came back with a sandwich. 'He's a sportsman – sportsmen do well at boarding schools. I had the time of my life and so will he. It will stand him in good stead for the rest of his life. You heard that roll-call – directors, Victoria Crosses, MPs.'

'Uhm,' I said again.

He got up to pour himself a drink. He knew I was angry with him. 'I see, like that, is it?' he said, as he left the room.

He came back a few seconds later with an open bottle of Cointreau and asked if I wanted a drink. I shook my head. 'Come on, have a drink with your old man,' he said. I said I didn't want one. 'We've got everything in this house – whisky, brandy, port, wine, gin, vodka . . . Do you want a beer?'

I shook my head again and he disappeared into the dining room to get a glass, still muttering to himself about who'd be a father. It angered me – he was being the burning martyr again – and I went upstairs because I couldn't bear to be in the same room with him. But I could still hear him. He was pouring himself a drink in the kitchen, talking to himself, for my benefit obviously: he didn't know why he bothered; if he'd treated his father like I treated him . . . he wished he'd never had kids, they were millstones around your bloody neck; sometimes he wished he could be done with the lot of us and retire to a Greek island.

I put the pillow over my head to block it out, but I couldn't stand it any longer and suddenly I was at the foot of the stairs in front of him. He looked slightly alarmed when he saw my face and his weakness encouraged me. We stared at each other for a moment and then he said he was going to bed and edged around me. I said before he went to bed I wanted him to answer one thing. How many times would Charlie have to phone up in tears before he'd admit he was wrong to send him away? My face was stiff with anger. Dad's eyes flickered defensively for a second, then he recovered and told me, 'For God's sake, it was only his first day.' He put his foot on the stairs. I repeated the question: 'How many times?' Dad's hand paused on the banister, but he didn't say anything, so I asked again: 'How many times, Dad? You told me if he didn't like it you'd have another think. He obviously doesn't like it. How many times, Dad?'

Dad slowly started to walk up the stairs, plodding like he was working a treadmill. He looked old and tired in his dressing-gown, and I almost felt sorry for him. 'I've paid for a year,' he said, without turning round.

He'd said one term before. I wanted to chase him up the stairs and hit him, but instead said, 'How many times, Dad?'

I kept shouting over and over again, making myself more and more angry: 'How many times, Dad?'

11 p.m.

I had a strange feeling of disintegration when Gemma and I parked in our lay-by this evening. Gemma tried to cheer me up and told me to think positively. 'Think how nice it will be sleeping together in a proper bed with sheets when you come and visit me, instead of this van.'

Afterwards we played a game where you take it in turns to spell out words on each other's bare back with your finger. Gemma wrote, 'I STILL LOVE YOU' on my back, which I guessed. When it was my turn, the hair on the back of my neck stood up, because for a fleeting moment I thought that I could probably stop Gemma moving to Sheffield if I spelled out, 'WILL YOU MARRY ME?' on hers.

15 December: We'll have news in a few days' time. The stomach swelling hasn't diminished. This indicates the chemo hasn't worked, which means Mum is within the bottom range of six months.

In my daydreams I've always imagined Mum witnessing my writing success, standing beside me at my book launch. But now she'll never meet my children. She'll never know what happens to me.

I wrote a letter to her last night and left it under her pillow with her nightdress. I'd had a bit to drink and writing it made me cry in a way I've not done since I was a kid. I was surprised how blocked up it made my nose. I'd almost forgotten that happened.

Mr Warmly, the painter and decorator, has begun turning the utility room next to mine into another bedroom. He's told Mum it's so that there will be another bedroom for us to use at Christmas when Sarah and Rob come to stay. He's told me it's for the live-in nurse Mum will need towards the end.

Mum seems sombre and withdrawn. Her voice sounds muffled and matter-of-fact and no topic stimulates her. Perhaps she also knows the real reason for the new bedroom.

Thursday, 8 April

How was I to know you're not supposed to put your Sainsbury's bag on an interviewer's desk? The interview at Cunts and Co. was a disaster simply because of this tiny *faux pas*. Dad's not talking to me and Sarah's been on the phone from her honeymoon in the Bahamas nagging.

In a way it was quite funny. Mr Griffiths didn't look me in the eye once. Throughout the interview he just stared at my bag of sandwiches on his desk like they were vermin. It was bizarre, the more he stared at my sandwiches like they were vermin, the more I did, too. By the end it was almost as if he'd been interviewing the sandwiches rather than me, and I'd been interviewed by the sandwiches rather than him.

I told Mr Griffiths – or rather I told the sandwiches – all the usual crap about being self-motivated, goal-orientated. I might as well not have bothered, though, because he just said he'd keep my name on file.

'It could've been worse,' I told Dad when I got home. 'I mean, I nearly took a Kwik Save bag.'

But Dad didn't laugh, and accused me of deliberately sabotaging my chances. 'I suppose this is my fault because of last night. Is that why you did it? Hurt yourself to hurt your father? My son, I can see I'm losing this battle with you. I can see I am going to have to be more draconian. I have tried to be patient. I have tried to understand. But maybe something more old-fashioned is called for. Maybe that's all you understand.' For a moment I thought he was going to belt me one, but he was just walking past me to the desk to get out a pen and some of his 'Maurice Golden, Head of the Fucking World' stationery.

Later, when I came back from Gemma's I realised what he'd needed the stationery for because he gave me a document to sign. It was entitled 'Conditions of Stay Under My Roof'. If I didn't sign it he said I'd have to leave home immediately. It was six pages long and like a legal document. I had to promise to keep my bedroom tidy, spend less time in the bath, get a good job within two weeks, start treating him with respect, stop undermining him, fan him with fucking ostrich feathers . . .

'Haven't you got a bottom copy for my reference?' I said, for a joke, but he just stared at me.

'If you can't take it in verbally, it'll have to be written down,' he said. 'And I warn you, I am serious. Things are going to change around here. Things *are* going to change around here,' he said again, more quietly.

The stupid thing is this time I wasn't deliberately sabotaging my chances with Mr Griffiths – I wanted the job. I'm not a total loser. It was his secretary's fault. She made me all flustered by making out Mr Griffiths was some sort of minotaur who was going to devour me just because I arrived ten minutes late. I tried to tell Dad this later, but he didn't listen, and wouldn't believe me. All he said, in his mock-patient voice that's even worse than him shouting, was 'Please don't call it Cunts and Co. It's the company of a good friend of mine. Have more respect.'

5 p.m.

Dr Kelly is referring me to Stoke Mandeville for an ultrasound. I had to work for it. When I told him about the pain in my stomach he just took off his glasses wearily and asked whether I was worried it was anything specific. I knew he wanted me to say cancer, so he could say it was all psychological because of Mum, so I said I had no idea what it was, although I can feel a small, hard lump when I lie down.

I called out Dr Hill in the middle of the night a few days after Mum died when I thought I was having a mini-stroke and I've never been forgiven at the Tring surgery. Dr Hill must have put a big 'H' for 'hypochondriac' in my patient notes because everyone down there automatically assumes all my problems are psychological now. They have a way of looking at you, too. The look says: 'You're a hypochondriac. You know I know you're a hypochondriac and you know I can't say you're a hypochondriac.'

Friday, 9 April

Dr Kelly has sent me a letter that I'm to give to Dr Goodman, who's carrying out my ultrasound at Stoke Mandeville. I've scrutinised it for hidden doctors' code, implying I'm a hypochondriac, but I couldn't find anything concrete. The problem is that it's all so subtle. It's probably against the Hippocratic oath to call somebody a hypochondriac, so they must do it with sly squiggles understandable only to other doctors. I asked my cousin David what the letters 'FR' with a circle around them meant – I saw this through the envelope – but he claimed not to know. He's a medical student, he *must* know.

Gemma signed on two hours before me at the Jobcentre in Chesham today. While she was there she heard the staff discussing me. When Gemma asked what they were laughing at, they said, 'We've got Jay Golden in again at twelve – he's in and out of here like a yo-yo. Does two weeks' work, then has two weeks off.'

Gemma said it made her think afterwards just what sort of person she was going out with. She half laughed when she said it, but it's still depressing.

Chloe said she might have something special for me next week. I can hardly wait. I wonder what it is? Advanced wood-turning? A delivery driver for Bottoms Up?

We spent the afternoon in a lay-by off the M40. It ended in a row again, though, because I told Gemma she was like a Magic Eye picture, which you had to work at to like. I was trying to be nice, and explain why it took so long for us to get together, and how much she'd grown on me, and how I was going to miss her when she went away, but Gemma misunderstood me.

'At first you see nothing extraordinary and then you scrunch up your eyes and see the three-D. After that the picture's always beautifully three-dimensional, and you can't understand why you first saw nothing at all,' I said.

Gemma burst into tears and said I was calling her a heffalump. It took me over half an hour of dropping my 'h's to bring her round.

'Shall I compare thee to a summer's day?' Shakespeare asked Anne Hathaway, who probably broke down sobbing and said, 'What do you mean by that? Are you saying I'm fat?'

Gemma's my fire blanket. She stops me flaring out of control. You wouldn't catch Camus on the Chesham ring-road getting excited about throwing a double six at backgammon. He ran a tubercular fever, ate snails and hot sauce and discussed sexual immorality with French beauties in the cafés of Montmartre. I want to live in a mud hut, take part in a coup, outrun the flow of an erupting volcano, but she stops me. She's also a comfort blanket. I need her there when things go wrong. Her theory is that things will improve between Dad and me if I move out. She told me yesterday there were people who just couldn't live under the same roof. It was the same with her and her sister Jenny, she said. It wasn't anyone's fault and maybe it would be better if I moved out.

6 p.m.

I asked Dad about Mum's ironing money today. I'm not supposed to get it until I'm twenty-one, but I asked if he'd lend me £2000 of it to go on an Operation Raleigh scheme to Botswana if I don't get on the journalism course. I read about it the other day. You get to hump grain sacks off aid lorries and dig wells. I'm sure Mum would be pleased if I spent her ironing money doing something as constructive as working for Operation Raleigh. I told Dad if he was throwing me out I might as well do something useful. I could use the experience as plot for my book, too. I thought he'd be pleased to get rid of me.

'Nice try. I'm not paying for you to get a suntan. Thirteen days left, then you're out,' he said.

I got so bored later that I told Dad I'd had the jabs for Africa. 'I know you're just trying to provoke a reaction, but I'm afraid I'm tired of giving one,' he said, and walked out of the room. I thought about puncturing my upper arm with a compass to convince him I'd had them, but decided it wasn't worth it. It's a worrying sign – I'm no longer going that extra mile to annoy Dad.

Maybe I will be buried in Westminster Abbey, after all. Perhaps instead of the Tomb of the Unknown Soldier they should have a memorial to the Unknown Failure: an epitaph marking the plight of the silent millions who die unfulfilled after mop jobs. Drop-outs, delinquents, failed writers and people smelling of gherkins dodging tube fares to flock to my candlelit tomb that they'd leave feeling better about their personal circumstances.

Saturday, 10 April

Had my ultrasound at Stoke Mandeville. I didn't give Dr Kelly's letter to Dr Goodman in case it prejudiced his judgement, but it didn't make any difference. Dr Goodman said nothing had come up on the imager and refused to do it again when I suggested he'd missed a bit down my left side that hadn't been smeared properly with jelly.

'What age are you?' he asked. I said I was eighteen. 'Go on with you, a fit young man of eighteen – it's highly unlikely, *highly unlikely*, you have anything seriously wrong with you.'

At least that's some good news. I even shook Dr Goodman's hand on the way out.

Another two run-ins with Gemma (I seem to be arguing with everyone at the moment), first about going to Botswana. She couldn't take it seriously and said I couldn't manage in a civilised society, so how was I going to cope in an uncivilised one? Her attitude annoyed me. And when I went on about it she accused me of starting to sound like Sean.

Second, about my notebook: she asked why I kept getting it out while we were sitting in the living room with her dad watching telly. I didn't tell her I was turning her dad into a twentieth-century hate figure and said I was making a 'To Do' list. But after going through my jacket pocket, she confronted me. 'My dad', she said with eyes blazing, 'does not have' – I hung my head in the manner of the misunderstood as she read aloud from my notebook – ' "a face so uniformly lined with wrinkles the observer could be forgiven for thinking they were staring at the seat of a pair of corduroy pants".'

Since her dad gave her a car she's got all protective over him and completely overreacted, threatening to tell him about the comment unless I crossed it out. 'And I hope you haven't been writing anything about me in there,' she said.

'I like your dad's face,' I said. 'That's why I wrote it down. He's got a lovely lived-in face.'

But Gemma didn't believe me, said she knew I hated her dad, told me it was time I grew up and stopped taking people for granted, and refused to kiss me goodnight.

One thing I don't like about Gemma is her telephone manner. Although her parents are middle class and her dad's chairman of a confectionery multinational, she sounds like Pat from *EastEnders*. She says, ''Ello, darlin'!' when she answers and, 'See yers,' in a high-pitched voice when she hangs up. I'm not a snob, but this vocal slumming annoys me. I told her this on the doorstep and said that was why I wasn't going to ring up and apologise like I normally did. She overreacted again, though, and said although my hair was receding like the gallop tide at Mont St Michel, *she* never mentioned this. Battling to be the boss is one thing, being rude's quite another. Gemma said she was getting tired of me getting at her, why couldn't I just be nice for once? Couldn't I at least try to get a job so I'd have some money to come up and visit her? I said she sounded like my dad and she said, 'I'm starting to feel like your bloody dad.'

Dad said, 'Twelve,' matter-of-factly before he went to bed tonight, indicating the days I have left, and I heard him earlier on the phone talking loudly to Sarah about turning my bedroom into another guest room when I've gone.

Sunday, 11 April

Tamil Tigers are terrorists from Sri Lanka who are trying to create their own independent province in Jaffna. They wear cyanide capsules around their necks in case of capture and the most fanatical, the Black Tiger Suicide Killers, strap explosives to their waists and blow themselves up inside government army barracks. Anyone can join the Tamil Tigers, apparently. All you have to do is train for three months in one of their camps. It would be great. I could write a tremendous book about it entitled *The Struggle for Freedom*. A camouflage jacket from Dad for Christmas, a grenade belt from Sarah, and Grandad could buy me a Kalashnikov, with a few rounds thrown in for my next birthday. Imagine the Christmas photos: Charlie and Dad in Marks and Spencers woollens, alongside ones of me in combat fatigues, assault rifle slung casually over my shoulder, the faraway look of the idealist in my eye. I mentioned this to Dad tonight.

'They have a cause they feel strongly enough to die for, Dad. I wish I did.'

Dad said he knew I was only trying to blackmail him and said threatening to blow myself up inside army barracks wasn't going to make him give me the money for Operation Raleigh. 'You'll just have to earn it like everyone else,' he said.

This wasn't enough for him, of course, so he stormed into my room later when I was listening to some music, yanked off my headphones and dramatically waved a handful of bills in my face to emphasise the point. 'Four thousand – that's for the decorating,' he said, throwing the first one on my bed. 'Five thousand – Sarah's wedding reception. Four thousand – Charlie's fees. And one thousand – the memorial party. That's fourteen thousand I've forked out on you lot in six months. More money than you've earned in your life, my son. And probably ever will.'

Dad doesn't understand that it's the duty of every true artist to seek out, experience and record the dramas of our age. If Tolstoy had worked in a Baker's Oven he'd hardly have written *War and Peace*. He's also got even more anal since Charlie left. Or maybe it's guerrilla tactics to get me to leave. He's reorganised the noticeboard, devised a new system for storing the pans, cleared away all Charlie's downstairs toys and anything left in the living room overnight he throws on to the lawn when he goes to work in the morning. So far he's ruined one suede jacket and two tapes of mine, and made my Dockers boots unwearable.

6.30 p.m.

Huge atrocity! Convene the fucking Hague. I forgot his edict on the new way of putting table mats away tonight. From now on, they're supposed to go back in their box before being put in the drawer. I put them in the drawer loose. 'If the table mats are in the box their edges don't get damaged,' said Dad, dragging me to the drawer to show me what I'd done like he was litter-training a pup.

Charlie called in a totally different mood later as well, which pleased Dad. 'So everything's fine,' said Dad pointedly for me to hear. 'Good, good – I am so pleased, my son. I knew you'd like it in the end. We'll see you at the party, then. Yes, I'll tell Jay Greeny-Slowy says hello. He's standing right beside me. And that you're in the football team. Yes, I'll tell him that, too. Jay,' he said, looking at me with unfriendly eyes, 'Greeny-Slowy says hello, Charlie's in the under-eights first eleven and you've now got' – he looked at his watch – 'eleven days left.'

11 p.m.

Now I'm worried about that bit down my left side that Dr Goodman missed with the ultrasound equipment. That really is where the pain mainly originates. I'm also bothered that Dr Goodman was called away by the nurse to attend to something halfway through carrying out the procedure. I know it sounds far fetched, but I wonder whether this was a ruse. Forgetting to bring the letter from your GP must be standard hypochondriac practice and Dr Goodman probably got the nurse to interrupt him deliberately so he could look me up on some national register of hypochondriacs. It would explain why he didn't bother to carry out a thorough examination and missed that bit down the left side.

20 December: Mum's been admitted to hospital again. Eleven pints of fluid were drained from her this time. The most so far. The doctors don't like aspirating her any more – she loses proteins, which help her immune system. But she was so uncomfortable that they agreed.

When I went to visit she told me how strange it was that in her dreams she never had cancer. She was always doing things like athletic sports instead. One night, she said, she ran in the New York marathon and had come third behind two Finns. Another night she was doing step-aerobics. It's the opposite with me. I'm always dreaming of her suffering. The other night I had my nightmare again.

Apart from on a day-to-day level, Mum never discusses the disease. She talks about the state of the swelling. She'll say if the diuretic tablets are working. She'll say how tired she feels from the chemo. But the actual disease is never mentioned.

The compartmentalisation of feelings is a strange thing. You shut them off in watertight areas of the brain like the bulkhead-protected bays of a submarine. It must be this that wards off depression. A leak in one compartment leads to its being sealed off, the brain moving to other areas to carry on as normal. I suppose eventually all the areas of your life can become water-logged and that is when you sink to the bottom and drown.

Monday, 12 April

I had a haircut at Roy's to smarten up my appearance today. Roy's an old-style barber who doesn't just cut your hair – he talks to you and always seems to know exactly what you'd like him to say. It isn't servile yes-sir-ing, but agreement that backs up everything you think. The man who was having his hair cut before mine told Roy his business was in trouble, so Roy came out with a tale of another customer in an even worse financial position, and the man left feeling better. When it was my turn he cheered me up about a famous short-story writer he'd known in Singapore during his army days, who'd been rejected for ten years before he made it.

He doesn't cut hair very well, but it's reassuring going to Roy's. In fact, I think he should have his own chat show. A chop-show, it could be called. He could invite on celebrities with unkempt hair and chat to them while he cut it.

Nothing at the Jobcentre, though. (Trainee gilder – fuck off. Trainee tachograph analyst – fuck off. Delivery driver for Pizza Hut – fuck off.)

How the mighty fall. Went for a media sales interview at Gorder and Board. Bored, more like; I couldn't have been more bored. I had to stay an hour afterwards, sitting next to the photocopier to see 'how they did things'. It wasn't even an interview – that's tomorrow. There were about five of them in this office. 'How they did things' was to sit around a big table in suits with stupid gonks Blu-tacked to the tops of their computer monitors, having hard-ons every time they sold an ad. It was the typical mournful office atmosphere, with everyone going on about needing a coffee, everyone thriving on team spirit and talking about each other's earrings, babies and chicken tikka-flavoured crisps, making out James from Ilford was mad because he'd accidentally forgotten to sugar his fucking tea.

It's insane, but I've also started to empathise with criminals. I read about a kidnap the other day. An estate agent, who'd been released after the payment of a £175,000 ransom, was telling the *Sun* her story. It was full of words like 'twisted', 'sick' and 'cowardly'. All I thought was – how exciting! I kept imagining myself giggling beneath a balaclava, saying, 'If you want to see so and so again, listen very clearly to what I have to say.' I wouldn't be able to keep a straight face – it'd be so funny. I think I might be a sociopath, because I also can't see the harm in it. The kidnapper gets the ransom, the person kidnapped gets to sell their story. Nobody loses. Everybody comes together and realises how much they love each other – it's a chance to be emotional, let off steam, feel human and morally superior. It's something out of the ordinary, a memory, a tingle down the spine.

Spent the afternoon in the van with Gemma, stroking her head, talking excitedly and trying to make something go whoosh in my heart. But we ended up having another row. I think Gemma's distancing herself from me. She wouldn't have sex again and slapped me down when I said I thought I might be a sociopath. 'Don't be a prat – you've a Banana-man duvet,' she said.

Later I told her I was thinking of doing Voluntary Service Overseas if my journalism application was unsuccessful. You don't need money like with Operation Raleigh – VSO is free. They're looking for volunteers to help dig wells in the Sudan, according to a leaflet at the Job Centre.

I was half hoping Gemma would try to stop me so we could come to a mutually irresponsible settlement in which she'd dump Sheffield in return, and we could then laugh fecklessly at ourselves and get back to normal. She just made an insulting joke, though: 'I see, it wouldn't be Comic Relief – it would be sort of Waster Relief,' she said, laughing. 'Instead of Red Nose Day, you could have Fucks Knows Day.' Gemma is definitely losing respect for me.

10 p.m.

Felt very embarrassed today when I saw Dr Kelly. First the Jobcentre, now the doctor's surgery. I'm making a name for myself in all the wrong places. The two receptionists were on the phone when I went up to the desk, so I waited to say, 'Jay Golden, six o'clock, here to see Dr Kelly,' but the one with the glasses just waved me towards the waiting area. 'Jay Golden,' I mouthed at her. 'I know,' she mouthed back, closing her eyes contemptuously.

I told Dr Kelly I'd lost his letter to Dr Goodman – I thought I'd mention it before he did. Then I told him the pain still hadn't gone and if anything had worsened. Sometimes the lymph glands in my neck are swollen – they're another symptom of cancer I remember from Mum – so I mentioned those as well.

But Dr Kelly didn't even check them. 'The ultrasound was normal,' he said sceptically, glancing at my notes and giving me that look.

I said I knew that, but Dr Goodman may have accidentally missed a bit down my left side. Dr Kelly leaned back in his chair and said quite petulantly that if I wanted to see a specialist privately that was up to me, he could refer me, but that the specialist would only tell me what he'd said anyway and I'd be eighty pounds worse off. I told him to arrange it. Dr Goodman will probably get struck off when they do eventually find the tumour.

'Is it worth writing another letter for you to give to him?' asked Dr Kelly.

I gave a nonplussed look and pretended not to know what he was talking about.

29 December: The family all spent Christmas together. Sarah came over with Rob, even though it was her turn to stay at Rob's parents. It's probably the last Christmas we'll spend together, which made every moment poignant. Sarah videoed a lot of it.

Mum became ill on Christmas Eve and never got better. The diuretic tablets made her dizzy and she couldn't get out of bed on Christmas Day. She was forced to shout instructions through the floor to Sarah for the meal preparations. The floor's quite thin between the bedroom and the kitchen, though, so she was able to follow conversations. She joined in when she could offer advice. For example, Charlie'd ask Dad whether there was any ice cream. Dad would say he thought it was in the bottom freezer drawer and down would waft Mum's voice: 'In the utility room on top of the washing-machine. It's in the Waitrose bag. Don't touch the walnuts – they're for Boxing Day.'

Mum finally came downstairs later on Christmas Day, but needed help from room to room because of wobbliness. She didn't change out of her yellow dressing-gown all day. I stayed in my pyjamas as well to make her feel better, although Dad said it was probably an excuse to get out of bringing in the coal.

On the 27th she caught flu from Rob, we think, and was laid even lower, requiring a twenty-minute sleep after meals and any activity. Dad forced her to ring up all her ironing people in the end, even though Mum didn't want to, and say they'd have to find someone else. Deep down Mum knows she can't do it any more, but she was still very upset about admitting it to herself.

It's weird, but everybody on the telly seems to have cancer, too – Rebecca in Daphne du Maurier's period drama, Barbara Windsor on *EastEnders*, somebody else in a film. It creates an atmosphere in the living room because it's what we're all secretly thinking about but not discussing, and although we all want to turn off these programmes, none of us does, because it would then acknowledge that that's what we are thinking about.

Tuesday, 13 April

Maybe it'd go to Roy's head, the limelight and fame from his chop show. He'd probably become a self-important phoney like Dad and start threatening to go to ITV unless he got more money, tungsten scissors and all his hair-care accessories from Laboratoires Garnier ('I can't do Tamara Beckwith with Boots' own-brand!'). He'd employ researchers rather than doing the work himself, he'd name-drop, come out with rehearsed material and begin twinkling his eyes theatrically into Camera One like Parkinson does (and Dad does when he thinks he's made a good point on *Newsnight*).

Second interview at Gorder and Board. A woman in a power-suit asked, 'Why tele-sales, Jay?'

'Because I'm a fucking waster and I can't get a job anywhere better,' I wanted to tell her. 'Because I'd be good at it,' I said.

'What makes you think you'd be good at it?'

'I'm self-motivated, self-disciplined, a team player, competitive, resourceful, results-orientated, an Aquarius . . . a tit and bum man, a good shag.' I can't remember what I told her exactly.

The ad director Chris Henderson was there, too, and couldn't wait to give me the company-origin bollocks. A fucking hare out of the stalls with the company-origin bollocks, he was. You know the stuff – in 1967 Tom

Tranche took a rib from Gleco and breathed life into Bleco and saw that it was good and had adequate gearing and opened a head office in Swanage. Real edge-of-your-seat stuff!

My eyes glazed over and when it came for me to ask questions I couldn't think of anything interesting to say, so I asked how many branches they had, where they were, how they were staffed and whether they planned to open any more. I probably overplayed it on the branches. Henderson's letting me know, but the truth is, I don't want to know.

Had another bad afternoon with Gemma. We went to the cinema to see an arty Italian film that Adam's-apple Rod had recommended. The cinema is like the elephants' graveyard: relationships instinctively head there to die. We've been five times in the last three weeks. I tried to bring up the Suky-Lou and Ray Doody escapist movie scenario on the way back by suggesting our super-loyal mongrel dog got about on a skateboard strapped to its hindquarters, but Gemma just said, 'Uhm,' without really joining in.

The nearer Gemma's departure gets the less we have to say because the less plans we have to make. I also did the indicator thing. I didn't really want to have sex, but I wanted to see Gemma's reaction. She cancelled it. She said she had to get home and sort out some things, although it was probably because I'd said something sarcastic when she'd stayed behind to watch the film credits. I knew she was only doing this to learn the name of the cinematographer or the art director or the fucking boom-boy or whatever to have something pretentious to say to Rod about it and it pissed me off.

6 p.m.

I saw Professor Jones today at the Cromwell Hospital in Earl's Court. The hospital was full of well-groomed Arabs and I saw Mr Jones in an immaculate, self-contained surgery next to the main reception.

Almost immediately he started asking me a whole series of questions that made me think I was finally being taken seriously. How's your sex life? Is the pain above or below the belly-button? How are your energy levels? Bowel movements normal? Are your stools narrow and ribboned? Do you suffer from headaches? I thought I'd answered them all pretty well and was half expecting to be whisked off to theatre there and then for a biopsy, when I discovered it'd all been a trap. 'I think I can say without a shadow of a doubt that from what you've described to me, it's ninety-nine per cent certain it's stress you're suffering from,' he said with a big smile.

I told him I wasn't stressed at all.

'I've been a doctor for thirty-one years and I can honestly say if there's anything seriously wrong with you I'd be astounded. In fact, I'd be tempted to jack in medi-cine.'

I told him again I wasn't stressed, and he started firing more questions at me: 'How's work? No pressure there? Home life? All right, is it? Nothing on your mind at all? What about your girlfriend? Things going well there? Mum and Dad, they all right?'

In the end I had to tell him Mum was dead. It was like watching a slip catcher diving to his right the way he latched on to it: 'There you are. You'd have to be a remarkably self-contained young man if something like that hadn't affected you.'

I maintained that I wasn't stressed.

'You're stressed,' said Dr Jones, shaking his head at me. 'I believe in being honest about these things. Ask your girl-friend or your father. We internalise things. Stress shows itself in many ways. I could put you down for a cystoscopy, a barium meal, a hundred different things, but I don't want to waste your money. Have you thought of bereavement counselling?'

20 February: Mum's not recovered from the flu. She weighs less than six stones, her appetite's gone and she has to be

helped upstairs. Her arms are covered in bruises and sores that've failed to heal from doctors' needles and her vitality's left her totally.

She's frightened, puzzled and desperate, and is trying not to show it. We keep trying to reassure her that once she's shaken off the flu she'll be better, and Dad goes around chanting his mantra: BBC-Bel beats cancer. But it's obviously more than flu now and everyone knows it, but nobody admits it.

Dad's close to breaking point as well. He said he was low on reserves of enthusiasm tonight. He was 'singing the wrong tune in the wrong hall'. His words of encouragement were beginning to sound hollow, even to him, he said: 'She's heard me beating out the same message for so long she doesn't hear it any more.'

And when Sarah told off Charlie for making a noise playing with the sponge ball in the kitchen this evening, Dad said, 'No, let him make noise. Let the little lad do whatever he wants. This place is like a morgue most of the time.'

I wanted to stay with him and talk and get drunk this evening, but I went to the pub with Kate and Mark instead and afterwards regretted it because my heart felt baggy and soggy, full of un-released emotion.

Wednesday, 14 April

Watched *Dances with Wolves* with Gemma. The video was three and a half hours long and quite moving, and I tried to make Gemma cry in the pub afterwards by repeating the parting words of Kicking Bird: 'Can you see I will always be your friend, Dances with Wolves, can you see that? Can you see that I will always be your friend?' I told Gemma it was me saying goodbye to her at the airport before leaving for the Sudan. She didn't cry, though, and we just ended up having a row.

'What's happening with us, Jay?'

'What do you mean?'

'Us, it's different.'

'What was it before?'

'It was different.'

'How was it different?'

'You were different. You weren't obsessed with yourself, Jay. We didn't talk about you the whole time. We did things. You weren't so jealous. We had fun.'

'I'm not jealous and we still have fun. I'm not obsessed with myself.'

'You are, Jay. I'm going away and we're talking about you again!'

'No, we're not.'

'Yes, we are, we're talking about you being obsessed with yourself.'

'Only because you brought it up.'

'It doesn't matter who brought it up. It's your novel. Your illnesses. Your dad. You being a sociopath. It's been getting worse for about a month.'

'Me being a sociopath has been getting worse for a month? You *do* think I'm a sociopath.'

'Stop it!'

Pause.

'I don't know, Gem. I just think everything's wrong.'

'What, *us*? We're wrong?'

'No – *everything*. Everything *apart* from us. I don't know, everyone wants all these things. Hundreds of things. Fuel-economic cars, midi-systems, DVDs. And even though you don't yourself, after a while you start to, because everybody else does. They force you to. Because if you don't, you end up fucked up about it. And the worst bit is nobody realises you are fucked up about it. They think you're fucked up because you haven't got as good a midi-system as they have. They think you're jealous of their midi-systems.'

Pause.

'I think you *are* a bit jealous, Jay. All your friends have good jobs and you *are* jealous. It's natural. What's so

183

wrong with wanting nice things: a nice car. I've got a nice car.'

'I don't mean your car. I'm not talking about *your* car. When you're young you have dreams, Gem. It's corny and shit but I wanted to be a professional footballer once upon a time. Charlie still does. Then, as you get older and you get jobs in mower shops the dreams shrink. They shrink with age and mower shops. As an adult it's just *things* – a new midi-system. A new car. And what do elderly people dream of? A sunny fucking day? A cup of tea with exactly the right amount of milk in it?'

Pause.

'This sounds like Holden Caulfield to me, Jay. "Everybody's a phoney, blah, blah, blah."'

'I never said that.'

'It's what you mean, though, and I'm getting tired of it. My dad's a phoney because he cares about his drive. Mark's a phoney because he owns a Peugeot 206. I'm probably a phoney because . . . I don't know, because I'm arguing with you now. The only one who isn't is Sean. And look where that's got him.'

Pause.

'Your dad's right, Jay. You've got to grow up.'

'That's the problem, Gem – I fucking am. I don't fucking want to, but I am. I can see what I'm heading towards and it scares me. A brain-dead life in tele-sales looking forward to what's good on telly after the news, making out all my friends are mad because they get drunk and miss trains. Gem, I want more than that. I really want to do something, something drastic.'

'Jay, just get a proper job. Never mind becoming a Tamil Tiger. Never mind living in a mud hut. For you, getting a proper job would be drastic.'

I went round to Sean's afterwards. The house was full of boxes. They're moving in a few days.

'Thanks for doing what you did. He's in his room,' said Mrs F.

I asked Sean if he'd been back to the doctor. Sean said no, but he'd been referred on to someone in Dumfries, who he was due to meet in a couple of weeks.

'So you're definitely moving to Scotland,' I said.

He shrugged his shoulders. Hadn't he even applied for a job? I asked. I was at least applying for jobs. I felt annoyed with him for giving in. Just for the sake of his bone idleness, I was going to be friendless pretty soon. He said he hadn't got time to work. He was up to E but he wasn't kidding himself – most of the really big letters, your Ms, Ps, Ss and Ts, were still to come.

It went quiet at one point because we were both thinking about what had happened in the doctor's surgery. Neither of us wanted to mention it.

'Sean,' I said, 'why don't you retake your A levels and stick around here and get a job? I'm serious – no fucking around – instead of mugging up on fucking eels, why don't you study something useful? Why don't you do some retakes? Why don't we both sort ourselves out? Both of us.'

Sean looked at me in astonishment and asked what my problem was. This made me angry, him acting as if he didn't have a bigger problem than me. 'It's not funny any more. You're becoming a fucking waster, Sean,' I said.

'What and *you're not*?' he said, not looking up from his screen. He was chuckling to himself like it was a joke that we were in the same boat, which we weren't at all. His boat was sinking, mine was at least still afloat. He started talking in his pretend-professor voice: 'The thing about the electric eel is . . .'

I started hating Sean. 'Why do you think you couldn't move into our house?'

Sean carried on: 'The electric eel has a characteristic . . .'

I leaned forward and put my hand over the screen. 'It was nothing to do with my dad not wanting to live with you,

Sean.' I let it sink in. I took my hand off the screen. 'I just told you that. It was because you're such a fucking liability. *I* didn't want to live with you. Not because you're gay. Because you're fucking mental.'

Sean clicked off the page so dramatically I thought he'd break the mouse.

'And anyway,' I said, 'maybe the reason I am a fucking waster is because I've spent so much time trying to sort out you. Have you thought about that? Maybe if you got yourself sorted, maybe if you weren't such a mad cunt, I could sort out my own life. I am fucking sick of nurse-maiding you, listening to this shit about fucking robots doing all the work.'

'Nurse-maiding me?' said Sean, in disbelief. 'And you're the one who's always going on about robots . . .'

His voice was cracking, but I couldn't stop. I wasn't even looking at him any more, but at the little mirror above his head. I was shouting at myself. 'And you can stop slagging off Gemma behind her back as well. I know what you've been saying about her leaving me when she goes to Sheffield.'

Sean said he hadn't said anything about Gemma leaving me. His mum came into the room with a box under her arm. She asked what we were rowing about, and Sean said it was nothing: Jay had just lost *another* job, that was all.

When Mrs F left, I turned to go. 'Just retake them, you twat, and stop using being fucking gay as an excuse,' I said.

'Yeah, all right, Jay,' he said, clicking back on to electric eels, 'just as soon as you stop using your mum as *your* fucking excuse.'

11 p.m.

I'm experiencing a strange sensation in my head at the moment. I can't understand it. It's like my skull's full of soup, a tide of soup that slops from side to side when I tilt my head, like soapy water in a bucket stifling my thoughts. Most of the time it's a thin, minestrone-type soup, but other times like today it feels as thick as homemade potage. It makes me feel slightly insane. My guts are odd, too. It's as if there's a huge spring being wound up inside me. It feels like any minute it's going to unwind. It's going to recoil and catapult me into doing something crazy. If I had enough petrol in the van I'd drive to Grandad's and jump off Beachy Head. That's what I feel like doing. Not because I want to die, but because I need a shakeup, something to put everything into perspective.

I've even started hating Napoleon. I kept looking at the picture Gemma's mum gave me and imagined being with him. I bet he'd be all brash and go-getting and we wouldn't get on. He'd order me about, tell me to fetch things, charge somewhere or something. He'd be just like Dad: the sort of person who got upset if you stole his bathwater.

I think today's entry is a first. Every one before has felt like a duty. I've imagined discovering this diary in twenty years, when I'm a famous writer and laughing indulgently at my former self: ho, ho – Dad said this to me and I said this back and look how I got the better of him, aren't I clever? Wasn't it obvious now looking back on it that I was going to be a writer?

This one, though, is born of loneliness. I'm normally a happy person. I have happy relationships with people and conversations that start off, 'Werhey!' and go on to disclose what's happened to me that day in a perky, undulating tone. I can't talk to these people feeling like I do.

14 March: In the early days I could write Mum letters in which I referred to the end, but now it's gone beyond that. It's taboo.

'She'll just go on until the end, whenever that comes,' says Dad, 'and we must take our lead from her.'

More and more he was falling back on his old adage to deal with misery – buying his way out of trouble. 'We went to MFI the other day,' he said. Then, in the voice he'd used to try to stir

Mum: ' "We're going to MFI," I told her. That trip cost me two hundred and fifty pounds. But that's what it's there for. It did some good. She almost forgot her legs – she was up and down those aisles like Colin Jackson.'

Sarah wept on my shoulder before she went to work today. She was crying because she'd washed and curled Mum's hair for her and Mum is a skeleton, half there, half not.

In the evening Dad was lying beside Mum in bed struggling to ladle spoonfuls of Complan soup into her mouth. Mum said it tasted salty and retched at each mouthful. When Dad left the room, frustrated and angry, I sat with Mum and stroked her head, and she said she was worried about what we all already knew, but she's been refusing to accept: that it wasn't flu at all, but that the cancer had now reached her liver.

'Flu doesn't last this long. You lose your appetite when it gets to your liver,' she said. She looked at me – her face now looking older than Grandad's – and her chin wobbled.

Thursday, 15 April

Interview at Moldon Financial Services. Frank Pond asked how I was diddling and I said I was diddling OK, even though I was actually diddling very badly. Then, out of the blue, he said my green Zig Zag jacket worried him. He was as fat as a house, but, of course, I couldn't say how that worried me.

'You see, Jay, it's like this,' he said, 'your dress is your uniform. You have a uniform in the police, you have a uniform in a Wimpy. And if you work in sales you have a uniform, too. Grey's our uniform, Jay. People don't buy from men in bottle green.' He took out a pencil and stabbed at a photo in the company brochure. The photo was full of body-snatched guys in slate-grey suits leaning nonchalantly over computers or standing behind photocopiers looking dim, but busy and serious, with side-partings. 'In your first year you will earn twenty thousand. Thirty thousand in the second. You'll earn that kind of money, because I will *teach you* to earn that kind of money.'

I started to drift off. Life's a bit like moving around a Cluedo board. You begin by haring excitedly into every room looking for the solution. You try everything. Then, suddenly, before you know it, there's only one place to go, one room left. It'll hold the answer to the riddle, or mean a terrible miscalculation. 'Writing with a pen in the study,' I've shouted. But what if it's wrong? What if the answer's really something I've never tried, and never will try because it's too late? Engineering with a spanner in the workshop. Something in a side-parting?

'I like you,' said Frank Pond. 'I don't like your hair, I don't like your jacket, but I like you. And if I like you so will our clients. Let's get you inducted this week. Let's see if you can sell. You're looking distant. Nothing wrong?'

10 p.m.

Sarah is back from honeymoon. John and Sylvia's annual dinner party is coming up and she came round and tried to persuade Dad to go because she thinks he should start meeting women, as it's been almost a year.

'They don't invite singles because Sylvia's a Catholic. That could be a problem,' said Dad, and Sarah started suggesting people he should take: Kelly his secretary, some divorcee from BBC Planning.

I couldn't bear the conversation so I left the room. I thought of Dad sitting with his new partner at the dinner table, laughing at John's jokes – 'The DG said what? Ha, ha, ha' – and it appalled me. It was like Mum's death was just an inconvenience: 'Oh dear, Mum's croaked and upset the fucking seating plan' . . . 'Sorry, no widowers.'

In the end he agreed to take the divorcee. Sarah was very pleased and phoned up when she got home, expecting me to be excited, too. 'I know nothing's going to happen, but Eileen's lovely, Jay. I met her in Dad's office once. I do hope something happens. It'd be so good for him. Have you seen her? She's very glamorous.'

Eileen. How can anyone with a name like that be glamorous? She sounds more like a school dinner lady.

I looked up my soupy-head sensation in *Symptoms: The Comprehensive Guide* tonight and as I suspected it's more than likely a brain tumour.

29 March: We went to the Rose 'n' Crown for lunch today. Before the food arrived Mum said she had an announcement to make. 'For a number of years—' she said, and started to cry. 'Oh God, I knew this would happen.'

I made a joke about how her crying was because she was thinking about the carrots for tonight's stew. She'd forgotten to get them out of the freezer and it'd been overly concerning her all morning.

Dad said, 'Let me do it, darling. Mum's been ironing for a long time, as you all know. Now she has something she wants to give you.'

Mum held her left arm vertically down beneath the table. She was clenching her fist. With her other hand, she withdrew three cheques from her purse. They were folded into tight rectangles. Dad helped her unfold them.

'I just want you three to have these,' said Mum.

Each cheque was for £6000 and when I saw the amount tears sprung in my eyes. It made me think of *Schindler's List* – the piles of hair and gold teeth extracted from Jews at Auschwitz. Three cheques for £6000: £18,000 earned from ironing at £5 an hour; 3600 hours, 150 days, all to give us a head start.

As I helped Mum walk back home from the pub her hand sought out mine and gripped it with surprising strength. I told her I didn't deserve what she'd given me and she said, 'Of course, you do – I don't know what I'd do without you.'

When I hug Mum now I can feel every bone. She weighs five stones. There's hardly any flesh on her and what little there is hangs off like melted vanilla dripping down an ice-cream cone. Her eyes seem to be set further into her head and her temples are so hollow half a thumb could disappear inside them. The only thing that hasn't changed is her hair. And if there's one thing Mum's pleased about it's that she didn't lose it by having radiotherapy.

Friday, 16 April

There were six of us at the induction. We had to learn by rote this mournful presentation for selling life insurance, which started off, 'Let's discuss your financial plans, because you'd like to be financially independent, wouldn't you? OK, first let's see if we can balance your spending, borrowing and saving, to break the save–spend pattern.'

After we'd learned the script Frank Pond waddled in, thanked the trainer, and asked how we were all diddling. We all said we were diddling fine and he asked us to draw up a list of fifty friends and relatives to sell the Money Club life cover to.

The girl next to me rang up someone without hesitation. 'Hi, it's Karen. Remember me? I lived next door to you two years ago. You must remember, I had that big labrador named Kiki.'

I couldn't bring myself to make the call – it seemed wrong. And Frank Pond came over and put his podgy arm around me. It was damp and sweaty. 'Swallow your pride. They're your friends, but you're offering a service. You're a professional. And, anyway, who do you see when you look in the mirror – friends? Acquaintances?' I thought, The fucker probably doesn't even get a reflection in the mirror.

'We're the tenth-largest financial institution in the world. If somebody walked in that door now and said, "I want four million yen to buy a cannery in Kobi," no problem. This is a big, *big* company, Jay. Sometimes you forget how big. You're out there, an appointment's cancelled, it's raining, your car won't start, you snag your jacket on a nail – you forget how big.'

The day before she died I went to see her with Charlie. She still thought she was going to get better. I think she did believe that. Nobody told her otherwise. It was obvious – she had cancer of everything – but she wouldn't acknowledge it. She couldn't face it.

Her head was propped up on three pillows. She was drugged up on diamorphine, her head lolled about and her eyes struggled to keep abreast of movement, like a closed-circuit TV camera. She was pleased, but also annoyed because I'd taken a day off study to be there and she wanted me to try my best at the A levels.

'I've got an intravenous in my arm. The RMO says-it'llworkwonders,' she said in a slur. She smelled of strawberries, the latest meal she'd failed to eat, and all I could think of were all the times I'd lifted my legs so she could vacuum around me.

'Do you know how many bedrooms I have in my house? Eight! I have five reception rooms. You wouldn't believe how much I earn.' Pond was still boasting.

I dialled the first number on my list of friends and acquaintances: Gemma's mum. 'Hello, Mrs Draycote, how yer diddling? It's Jay.'

'I'm sorry, Jay, Gemma's not in. And what do you mean, *diddling*?'

'No, it's you I want to talk to, Mrs Draycote. You'd like to be financially independent, wouldn't you? You would like me to show you how to break the save–spend pattern?'

Mrs Draycote didn't know what the save–spend pattern was and I felt terrible, made an excuse and hung up.

I put on my coat to go and Pond told me he liked me again and could make me a lot of money if I stayed. The worst thing was it was almost worth staying for the rags-to-riches tale: me a millionaire, in one of my five reception rooms remembering how I'd nearly thrown it all in because of Mrs Draycote. 'Mrs Draycote. Ha, ha, ha, dear old Mrs Draycote. Didn't I screw her on an endowment the day after? How yer diddling? Another cognac, Frank, ha, ha, ha. What a naïve fool I was in those days.'

'You've got a real problem, you know that?' said Pond, as I reached the door.

'You're the one with the problem,' I said. But he's right – I do have a problem. I realise that. I have a *real* problem.

When I got home I phoned Gemma's mum to apologise for trying to sell her the Money Club. She told me not to worry about it, but if I wanted Gemma she was still in Sheffield sorting out her accommodation. I said, 'Still?' and Gemma's mum seemed embarrassed, made an excuse about going to some art club and hung up on me.

15 April: I stayed up late with Dad and he talked about Mum this evening. He sat in his armchair and threw his legs over the armrest so we were at right angles and so I couldn't see the red eyes behind his spectacles. Dad's been off work for three weeks now and says he's less of a husband and more of a nurse. Mum finds it a struggle just walking to and from the kitchen. He's ordered a handrail for the stairs to help her drag herself up. 'We have to do everything, bless her,' he said, staring upwards at the ceiling, and rubbing his eyes. 'She just ain't got the strength.'

In the evenings Mum settles down on the sofa with her bone-thin legs propped up and doesn't move for the rest of the night. Dad, Charlie and I fetch her lime juice and her favourite boiled sweets from the metal tin in the cupboard.

Mum was refusing to accept what was happening to her, said Dad. Every day she spoke about her health – how stiff her legs were, how swollen her stomach was, what she could and couldn't taste – but never translated this into her overall condition. 'I said to her, "It's time we knew what sort of cancer we're dealing with here. Four months ago it was cancer of the

stomach. What is it now?'' She said, "No, I don't want to know.''
I said, "Let me ask Maitland,'' but she wouldn't let me. She just
doesn't want to know. As long as she doesn't know she can
believe it's not happening to her,' said Dad.

Saturday, 17 April

My brain's barely ticking over. My what-am-I-doing-with-
my-life? panic attacks have been replaced with look-what-
I'm-doing-with-my-life panic attacks and I'm getting abyss-
like feelings when I wake up.

I went for an Indian with Gemma, Mark and Kate, and
Mark announced he'd proposed to Kate and she'd accepted.
Gemma wished Kate good luck and kissed Mark over the
onion bhajees. When I congratulated them I suddenly
realised I didn't give a shit what sort of luck they had. It
reminded me I was a sociopath and made me sad.

By the end of the meal I didn't care about anyone in the
restaurant. I hated them all. I'm not sure if it was me being a
sociopath or their conversations – AMEX cards, new car,
rental prices in Sheffield, the quickest way to Hemel. When
you're unemployed you want to talk about big things – life,
death and the tomes of wisdom you've learned parrot
fashion from Chesham library that morning. You feel like a
radical artist living in a Paris commune. You want to throw
up barricades, storm winter palaces, redistribute national
wealth. But in reality all there is to do is get out *Starship
Troopers* at Video Plus.

Karl Marx was unemployed for ten years. He spent the
time in the British Library writing *Das Kapital* with a feverish
pen. Pretty constructive, but there weren't the same distrac-
tions then: no daytime TV; no VCR technology. Put Karl
Marx in the 1990s and you'd see a different person. Forget
communism and the Cold War, he'd have been pounding the
Video Plus aisles like the rest of us, asking if *Godfather II* was
back in and looking forward to *Countdown* at 4.30.

Mark took me home in the end. He said he needed an early night, but I suspect it was because of the derogatory things I was saying about the Peugeot 206. Mark rates the car's fuel economy.

Had another row with Gemma. At one point she told me she thought I was always tired and irritable these days and that her sister Jenny was finishing with her boyfriend Steve for precisely this reason. I yawned ostentatiously to show I don't respond to threats and she spent the night ignoring me. She's going to Sheffield again on Monday to sort things out, not with her parents like she said originally, but with two people the Sheffield accommodation office put her in touch with who are starting the same course. She said I'd distract her if I came too, although I think she just really doesn't want me around.

11 p.m.

Scientists are predicting 500,000 deaths from the human equivalent of mad cow disease in the next thirty years. I read it in the *Daily Telegraph*. The symptoms are deterioration in memory, loss of balance, declining intelligence, blindness, insanity and eventually death. The description of what happens to the brain – the tissue's eaten away by proteins leaving gaping sponge-like holes – sounds exactly like what I imagine is happening inside my skull. Soup, sponge – it's the same thing. Dad's throwing me out in five days' time if I haven't found a job.

Rejection from VSO in the post, too – they say I've no relevant skills. Not even qualified to work with river silt!

Sunday, 18 April

I keep having flashbacks of Mum being alive. They're not ordinary memories, either, but exact feelings, whole flashbulb-lit moments. Charlie, a toddler, watching me playing marbles on the hall carpet, staring at the shiny glass. Putting a marble in his mouth when he doesn't think I'm watching, turning it round in his cheeks like a gob-stopper, then accidentally swallowing it in a gulp of surprise. Then putting another in his mouth to hide the accident, thinking I haven't noticed. Then losing concentration and swallowing it too. Me complaining to Mum, Mum saying, '*Charlie!* Stop eating Jay's marbles!' Us all watching his potty, Mum in Marigolds, as the marbles come out the other end, along with, unbelievably, a miniature soldier from my Waffen SS set.

I can't believe it now, but we didn't think it was serious, the lump Mum found. It was the size of a Ferrero Rocher. I remember her lying on the kitchen floor and Charlie chasing it round her belly like it was a game. It would sink, then rise to the surface again like an air bubble. 'There it is, there it is – I've got it,' he said, prodding it down like he was playing splat-the-rat.

Then Mum in hospital when her Ensure Plus arrived, the vanilla-flavoured protein drink she had twice a day because the cancer had got to her liver and she couldn't eat. Us all watching her sipping it, taking quarter-spoonfuls, psyching herself up for each mouthful like a weightlifter going up ten kilos, then finally breaking down in tears because she couldn't eat any more. Leaning over her bed, talking about *EastEnders* among ourselves, doing it in an exaggerated way, coaxing her to eat. 'What do you think about Bianca and Ricky, Dad?' . . . 'I think she's too good for him' . . . 'Mum, what do you think about Bianca and Ricky?' Mum joining in the conversation: 'She's a right one, that Bianca,' and wiping away her tears before picking up her spoon again and us all exchanging relieved glances.

I don't know what's fucking happened. These feelings – Mum, Dad, Sean, work, Gemma – they're all just clicking about my brain like balls on a pocketless snooker table. No matter how hard I try to pot them, they just bounce around the angles. And all the time it feels like new balls are being added: more reds, more blacks. Every shot's a tricky cannon now and pretty soon I won't be able to move the cue ball at all.

10 p.m.

There was more news tonight of the French still refusing to accept British beef, and as usual the report included old footage of cows collapsing in fields with BSE. But when I mentioned to Dad the possibility of CJD, he just blew his top and accused me of getting on another illness bandwagon because I was bored and worried about being thrown out. 'The other week you had stomach cancer, then you read about brain tumours and thought you had one of those. I'm not saying there's nothing wrong with you. But please be sensible about it.'

I told him he obviously didn't care, and, please, not to worry, I'd shut up and keep my serious illnesses to myself so he could watch *Ballykissangel* in peace. 'Because that's what this is about. You just want to watch *Ballykissangel* and you're annoyed I'm distracting you. Perhaps when I lose my eyesight and can't stand up on shiny surfaces we'll have another chat about it.'

4 April: Mum's been admitted to hospital again. She's so frail she can't stand up without help and is a dead weight when you yank her up off the sofa. She's on steroids to stimulate her appetite. For the last two weeks she's eaten the equivalent of a slice of toast a day. Her voice is heartbreaking. She can't say three words without coughing, and each cough takes her about thirty seconds to recover from. Her sole topic of conversation is her illness, especially the state of her legs, which've wasted to the bone. They're a mixture of dull, lifeless reds, greys and whites, like the carcasses in a butcher's shop window.

Occasionally she becomes confidential: her voice lowers to a whisper that even she, it seems, doesn't want to hear, and with a desperation that hits you in the stomach she says, 'Jay, I am just so weak, so weak.'

Her tears are never far away. It's not these that are so bad, but the effort she makes to conceal them: the sucked-in breath, the pause and then the false optimism. 'Listen to me moaning. How are you, anyway? How's school, Jay?'

Her overriding fear is that the cancer's reached her liver, which it obviously has. She only mentions this when Dad's out of the room and she can't say the word without breaking down: 'I'm worried, it's reached . . . the . . . liver.'

I become almost robotic at these times. I wait for her crying to stop and say, 'Mum – you don't know that. It's probably the drugs. When you have the new cocktail, you'll start eating again. If it was the liver, the doctor would've said something. Wait and see what the doctor says. You've just got to try to eat. It's this bloody flu.'

Monday, 19 April

I've been offered the job at Gorder and Board after a third interview. Dad pretended to be upset that he wouldn't be able to turn my room into a guest room, but he was pleased. I should've been pleased, too, but I wasn't. It feels like an artic's backing blindly down a narrow alleyway. I'm standing at the end of it. The lorry's making that beeping warning noise lorries do in reverse, but it doesn't make any difference because there's nowhere for me to escape to. On and on it's coming and I'm watching it, looking for a way out, trying to scale the sheer wall behind me, squeeze into the corners, but I can't. I got the number from Mrs Draycote and called Gemma in her bed and breakfast in Sheffield tonight to tell her the news about Gorder and Board, but she seemed offish after the other night. I wanted her to sympathise. I wanted her to feel sorry for me, and when she said she was pleased for me I was angry.

'I only meant you'll have some money to come up and visit me,' she said.

'What? It's me who has to come up there, is it?' I said.

She said she didn't mean it like that and asked why I was being funny.

'I'm not being funny, I know what you meant,' I said. I wasn't thinking straight. I was thinking about Rod again, imagining her growing apart from me in Sheffield and getting to think his Adam's apple wasn't so pointed after all. I was imagining them laughing at me and Rod's reaction when she told him what a prat she'd met during her year out ('Stop it, Gemma, stop it, my sides. Ha, ha, ha – I can't believe it. Even the parish magazine turned his stuff down, you say?').

'You think I'm a waster,' I said, out of the blue. 'You think I'm a sad waster. You laugh at me with Rod. You don't think I have feelings. You've no idea what it's like wanting to be a writer and getting rejected all the time.'

'I don't know what you mean. I don't laugh at you with Rod,' said Gemma. 'I haven't spoken to Rod. I told you about his Adam's apple. I thought we sorted that, and I don't think you're a waster. I like your article about baths. I think it's funny.'

'And how do I know he's got such a pointed Adam's apple? I've only got your word on that.' I was going off the deep end, but I couldn't stop myself. It was like a game of pick-up sticks: all these overlapping emotions in a heap and I couldn't lift up one without nudging the others. 'He could have a perfectly normal Adam's apple for all I know. And besides, what if you don't care about Adam's apples? Maybe them being pointed doesn't bother you. Maybe you *like* them pointed.'

There was silence and then Gemma burst out laughing. I wanted to laugh, too, I really did. But all the soup in my head drowned it out. I realised how ridiculous it was rowing about Rod's Adam's apple. An Adam's apple I'd never even seen. But I just couldn't laugh. I started imagining her telling

Rod we'd had a row about his Adam's apple, and Rod laughing incredulously and feeling smug about being so much of a threat that we'd had to row about his Adam's apple.

'There you go again,' I said, 'laughing at me. Ha, ha, ha, the failed writer who even got rejected by the parish magazine. I bet Rod loved that. Why not tell him about the *Bucks Star* while you're at it? Give him a real belly laugh.

'You just think I'm a waster like everyone else. Have a good time in Sheffield, Gem. I won't be visiting you. And you won't be visiting me, because it's pretty clear you don't give a shit. Goodbye and give my love to Rod and his amazing fucking protuberance. And, just for the record, you're right – I am a waster.'

6 p.m.

My consultation with Dr Kelly didn't go well this evening, either. Kelly's a quack. I told him about the sound of brain cells dissolving and the liquidy sensation in my head varying in consistency from powder-based Batchelors Cup-a-Soups to thick, homemade chicken potage, and he said there were a number of avenues to pursue.

'First, we can try X-rays of the fractal sinuses. Second' – he paused – 'we can try psychiatry.'

I didn't mention psychiatry when Dad asked how it'd gone when I got back home. 'I'm having X-rays of the fractal sinuses,' I told him. 'They think there's something pretty seriously wrong with my fractal sinuses, but, look, let's wait for the ad break hey, I don't want you to miss your programme.'

The guilt-ridden tears he'll weep when I'm a human vegetable.

22 April: Dad came into my bedroom tonight and was matter-of-fact, the way he always is in a crisis. He said he'd spoken to the sister and there was a choice: Mum could have an intravenous

drip through her nose that would prolong her life or another form of medication that would give her greater comfort, but might speed things up.

Dad said he wanted to talk to Sarah and me about it before a decision was made. I could tell he wanted me to go for the second option, so I did. Sarah had said the same, he said.

'She's in terrible discomfort,' said Dad. 'She's a lot worse than when you saw her yesterday. The struggle is nearly over.'

I asked what time-scale we were talking. I was being matter-of-fact now, too.

He said the first method might give her ten days, but that Mum had expressly told him she didn't want anything up her nose. With the second option, he paused, 'We're talking forty-eight hours. It's the end-game, my son and I just thought you'd better know.'

Half of me wants to take Mum away. Take her to Lake Orta where we used to water-ski as kids on family holidays, so I can spend her last days simply talking to her in a place where we were all happy once and find out everything about her. She used to live in India, for instance, and I know hardly anything about her life there. But why would I be doing that? Not for her, but for me, to make me feel better. Because she refuses to accept she's dying, nobody else is allowed to accept it either, which makes proper conversation impossible.

I wanted to go to the hospital to see her tonight, but Dad said we should go tomorrow. 'The next two days are going to be very tough,' he said. In the end we sat in silence and watched a film together. Dad fell asleep halfway through and I phoned Mum even though it was after eleven. The ward sister put me through.

'Hello, darlingth,' said Mum with a sleepy slur. 'What time is it?'

I said it was quite late and asked how she was.

There was a long pause. 'I can't eat,' she said. She sounded so frightened and vulnerable I had to hold the phone away. 'I'm sorry, darling . . . I just can't.' She sniffed back tears and I felt guilty for pretending it was her not eating, rather than the cause of her not eating, that was the problem. 'How's Dad?' she said, her voice shaking.

I said he was asleep.

'How did Charlie's game go?' she asked. Charlie had just played his first game for the school under-seven football team.

I said fine. I had an overwhelming urge to tell Mum I loved her, but it sounded too final and I didn't want to frighten her. 'Sleep well, Mum,' I said instead.

'Sleep well, darlingth,' she said, and I heard someone take the phone from her.

Tuesday, 20 April

I'm doing everything ineffectively at top revs, straining in first gear, knackering the engine, doing myself no favours. I feel weird and soupy and don't know exactly what I think about anything. I keep having this urge to drive, just to get in the van and take off somewhere: the Sudan, anywhere, somewhere miles away. I have a mental picture of me afterwards talking to Mark and Kate about it. We're in the Ellie. I've recovered and am wise and deep as a result of the experience. I've got a great job that I love and everyone's looking at me, hanging on my every word. 'You think *you're* depressed! That's nothing!' – sip of beer for effect – 'When my mum died and I split up with Gemma' – misty-eyed look at ceiling – 'I was so low one night I drove all the way to the Sudan. I caught the ferry from Italy. I didn't stop once. When I got there it was dawn and the cafés were just opening and I sat in Mustaffa's Bar all day from nine in the morning until midnight. Just drinking. And when I woke up in the gutter the next day, I did the same thing again. And then again. And again. I was drunk for a month. I didn't speak to a soul except to order a drink. Now what was that about "being down" about your car needing a new head gasket?'

First day at Gorder and Board. Our 'phone station' goes

quiet when it looks like one of 'the team' is on the brink of a big ad sale. Everybody's expected to stop what they're doing and look anxiously at the salesman on the phone. If he says, 'Can I have an order number for that?' we all know he's succeeded and are supposed to stop discussing chicken tikka-flavoured crisps for a second and stare at each other in wonderment.

Overcome with adrenalin when he puts down the receiver, the salesman will then shout out his new sales yield, and sometimes, if it's a particularly impressive one, will *chant* it at less productive members of the team. James did this today: 'Seventeen-five, seventeen-five, seventeen-five,' he chanted, pointing at Bernie. A trainee then gets the 'privilege' of jotting up the sale on the sales board, headed 'The Race for Space'. Samantha did it for James. As she wrote it up she smacked the white board with the flat of her hand and shouted, 'James! James! James!'

DIPADA's the name of the sales formula we're learning on our conceptual-selling course. *Definition* of the problem using *Identification* of the ideal solution using open questions, leading to a trial close. *Proof*: demonstrate through FABS (feature, advantage, benefits) that your product provides the ideal solution. *Agreement*: gain agreement using closed questions: 'Do you agree?' Take the prospect up a staircase of consent with the final 'Yes, I agree' reaching a crescendo. Desire's built through enthusiasm, positive language (a half-pint of lager's half full not half empty) and picture-power (our magazine reaches an audience of 35,000 – that's half the capacity of Wembley Stadium). Restate *Definition*. *Action*: make the close using RATAID – rebound, alternatives, trial close, assumptions, indirect and direct methods. For example, rebound closes: 'Have you a large readership?' . . . 'Is it a large readership you're looking for?' The alternative method: 'So shall I book a full page or a half-page?' The assumption method: 'What's your order number?' The indirect method: 'If you could just put me through to your accounts department.' The direct method:

'Are you buying, then?' We've even been taught a joke to get out of the situation when somebody spots the telephone conversation's scripted: 'Ah, you weren't supposed to say that – I've lost my place now.'

Spoke to Gemma and apologised for the other night. She didn't want to meet me at first. I had to agree to take her out or she wouldn't come. She thought we'd only row if we met in the pub. I took her for a night at the Comedy Store off Leicester Square instead.

I tried to have a good time, but I couldn't. There was a warm-up man, who coerced members of the audience to introduce themselves to each other: 'Right, this row up. I said *up*! Now turn around and shake hands with the person behind you – *come on*!'

It felt too much like being at work – people being bossy, overfriendly and overexcited. When I refused to stand up, the man tried to use Gemma to influence me. 'He your boyfriend?' he said, and when she nodded, he added, 'Not for much longer, hey?' and Gemma and I both looked at each other.

We came home in silence on the tube. I gave her a lift from Chesham station where I'd left my van, but she didn't get out when we reached her house. We both sat staring out of the windscreen at the rain. I was about to tell her about the time I'd nearly written 'Will you marry me' on her back with my finger when Gemma said, 'It's not working, is it?'

I said it was and tried to kiss her, but she got out in tears.

On my way home I cried, too, because I knew she was right, but didn't know why. The tears collected under my chin like a liquid helmet strap and when I wiped them away with the back of my palm it freaked me out because it was like I was miming slitting my throat.

24 April: Her breathing had become shallower all day. It grew gurgly, like the sound of water going down a plughole mixed with the *cerrrk* sound of a gas pilot light. I was dampening her head with a flannel and moistening her mouth with a lemon swab,

until Dad said, 'Right, I want to do that now.' It made me angry: it was like he wanted to take over the controls of a video game. I stood at the foot of the bed. Charlie had the day off school and I held his hand tightly.

The muscle in Mum's neck that moved up and down like an elevator rose more weakly. A nurse came in and took her pulse. 'Won't be long now,' she said and smiled at us. We'd been by her bedside for seven hours. We hadn't slept or eaten. But it still seemed wrong for her to say, 'Won't be long now,' as if we were waiting for a table at a restaurant. Or we were in a fucking hurry.

Then one time the elevator-like muscle in her neck didn't make it all the way up. We all looked at each other. In turns we followed Dad's lead and kissed Mum on the forehead. Her face was sallow and sepulchral, her skin was translucent, folds of it hung like wax from the candle of her neck and she had no lips. Her mouth was open, like a frayed sock. But it was still my mum and she looked more beautiful than ever before. As I bent down to kiss her damp brow I felt ashamed of all the times the previous summer when I'd rubbed suntan oil on her back in the garden and felt revulsion because she was so skeletal.

But then the elevator rose one more time, just enough to discharge another lungful of air. Just enough for us all to kiss Mum's forehead one more time. 'She's teasing us,' said Dad. We laughed in an automatic, weird, macabre way and Charlie looked up at me hopefully and repeated the words under his breath in a way that seemed half a question and half a prayer. And down it went again.

Nobody was looking at Mum now; only at the muscle in her neck. We stared at it for over a minute, willing it up. But this time it stayed down. A trickle of yellow bile left the corner of Mum's mouth and dribbled on to the pillow and Charlie and Sarah turned away and burst into tears. Dad went to fetch the nurse, and I tried to sense Mum's soul lingering in the room saying goodbye, but I couldn't sense anything and could only hear Charlie's and Sarah's crying and the birds outside singing as if nothing had happened.

Wednesday, 21 April

You never get a cheetah backing out of an impala hunt because it's having a bad hair day. Confidence is a weird human trait. It affects our behaviour in a way it doesn't seem to with other animals. When I walk along the pavement at the moment it's like my insides are floating freely inside another body – a swimming pool on an ocean liner. I stare at something, but my eyes take a long time to register what's in front of them. The image they retain is of what they looked at before. My legs feel leaden and odd. Walking along the pavement, I feel them getting shorter with every stride – that visual comic trick of descending down a non-existent flight of stairs.

DIPADA's providing a rich source of jokes for new trainees. Everybody goes around asking each other the how, what, why, who, where, when questions of the *Definition* stage, taking replies to the nth degree. For example, Sam asked Bernie today, 'How was your evening last night?' and when Bernie said, 'Good,' Sam asked him, 'And what made it good?'

'It was a good laugh.'

'How important's laughing?'

'Quite important. It's just fun.'

'What else constitutes fun in your eyes?'

'I don't know – being with friends, feeling relaxed.'

'What other times do you feel relaxed?'

'At the pub.'

'If I could design you the ideal pub what would it look like?'

'It'd have John Smith's on tap, a juke-box and it'd be near a tube stop so I could get home.'

'And if I could show you a pub that satisfied all these conditions would you buy it?'

Went out for a drink with Bernie and Sam after work in the company bar down in the basement and everybody talked about work and what they were going to eat for dinner. What people are going to eat is an obsession here.

Bernie told me he didn't think I was a people-person because I didn't really join in the role-playing exercises. He thought I was a 'reflective observer'. In the end I got quite drunk and blabbed that I'd lied to Henderson at the job interview and had got sacked from five of my last seven jobs.

'Really – and you didn't mention that on your CV?' asked Bernie.

I tried to speak to Sam, too. But when she wasn't going on about being a salady person ('Don't get me wrong, Bernie – I like beef and mustard, too, but sometimes I just prefer something small like a salad. Are you a salady person?'), she just kept DIPADA-ing me. It gets on your nerves after a while, so when she started doing one on what I'd done last night I told her I'd got so depressed I'd thought about slitting my throat.

Sam thought it was a joke. 'And what makes you want to slit your throat?' she said, and when I said, 'Working here with you lot of sandwich-obsessed cretins,' she burst out laughing and carried on until it ended on a bad note.

'And what else makes you want to slit your throat?'

'People who are too thick to realise you're being serious, wear too much make-up and have fat legs.'

'I'm sorry, I don't think I like this. Are you talking about me?'

Dad was waiting for me when I got back. He looked angry. I thought it was because I'd told him I'd help him make some fruit salad for the party and was late, but it turned out it wasn't that because when I started to apologise he interrupted me. 'Never mind that,' he said. 'What do you know – about *this*?' He placed an itemised telephone bill in front of me and I got up and walked over to the fridge. 'Don't walk away from me when I'm asking you a question!' said Dad. I was fetching an ice-cube. 'I want an explanation. One, two, three, four' – he was slapping the bill in mid-air – 'five, six, seven, eight calls made after eleven at night to 0171 in January. Three in February. And so it goes on: seven in March, five in April. I never made any of these calls and Charlie certainly didn't.'

I poured hot water over the back of the ice-tray, slipped the biggest cube in my mouth and started sucking it.

'When you're absolutely ready,' he said, sarcastically folding his arms. I was sucking the ice-cube to look nonchalant. I didn't feel too nonchalant, but I wanted at least to *look* nonchalant. I was thinking about Gemma and digging wells in the Sudan. I didn't have to go with VSO, I thought. Gemma and I could go on our own. We could dig freelance.

'Have you', said Dad, suddenly pulling me around by the shoulder to face him, 'been *borrowing* my contacts book again?' He said the word 'borrowing' very sarcastically because he really meant 'stealing'.

'Oi ont ooh onyfing,' I said. I couldn't speak properly because of the ice-cube in my mouth.

'What?' he said.

'Oi ont ooh ot or orking obort.'

'Spit that thing out!' he said. 'And I hope you remembered to fill up the ice-tray this time. I'm sick of chasing around after you. I've got a report to finish and a party to organise.'

He held the back of my head quite firmly and put his other hand under my chin so I'd spit the ice-cube into it. He was working himself up into a temper. But I spat too hard and the ice-cube went over his hand and on to his laptop, which was open at the kitchen table.

'Oh, for God's sake!' he said, making out I'd done it on purpose. 'Don't just stand there, pick it up, put it in the bloody sink before I lose the lot. There are two hours' work on that.'

The more I thought about it, the better an idea it seemed. Gemma and I wouldn't have any problems in the Sudan. There wouldn't be any *things* getting in the way there. It would be our own desert island.

I picked up what was left of the ice-cube and threw it in the sink. Meanwhile – and this made me laugh – Dad was busy switching his laptop on and off, muttering about how I'd broken the last one, and now probably this one, too. I guess he half wanted it to be broken so he could have an even bigger go at me.

But I didn't care any more. He could turn my bedroom into a study if he wanted. He could burn it down or rent it out to fucking cannibals for all I cared. I wasn't going to be around. I was going to the Sudan. Gemma and I were going to the Sudan.

'I phoned Paul Daniels,' I said. I wanted Dad to have a go now. I wanted him to chuck me out.

'Paul Daniels?' he said.

'Yeah, the TV magician.'

'I know who Paul Daniels is.'

'And Edward Heath.'

'Ted Heath . . . You phoned Ted Heath?' He looked quite serious now.

'Very briefly,' I said. 'Only for a second or two.'

'And what did you say to the former Prime Minister of this country?'

'Nothing really. I said I was Denis Healey and I called him an arse.'

'*An arse!*' He swivelled around on the balls of his feet so he had his back to me.

'Um,' I said.

Then, just as rapidly, he swung back to face me again. He was pretty quick on the balls of his feet. He should've been a ballerina.

'So, let's get this straight. You call up a former Prime Minister of this country, the Father of the House, impersonating a political rival of his, and call him an arse – you who *are* an arse.' He let out a mock laugh, a sort of huh-huh-I-might've-known type of laugh, then started pouring himself a large Cointreau to make me feel guilty about how I was driving him to drink. That was when he noticed the ice-tray was half empty. You should've seen him when he noticed the ice-tray was half empty. He stopped dead in his tracks and his shoulders went all loose, incredibly loose. Like he'd no bones in them. It concerned me a bit, the looseness of them.

'I filled it up – it must've leaked. I definitely remember filling it up. I'm *sure* I did,' I said.

Gemma wouldn't take a lot of convincing. She could defer her place at Sheffield. Making our own bread in the Sudan, a few chickens roaming about, I'd even let her be 'the boss'. I felt a bit faint at the thought of it all and sat down on the bench next to Dad's laptop. He came and sat next to me with his drink. He was now super-calm, as if after the ice-tray incident I couldn't possibly say or do anything that could make his life any worse. I thought about telling him about the Sudan.

'I want to know – I *need* to know – how many of these calls you've made,' he said. 'I want the truth, Jay. When these people – and they will – find out that it is my son who's been ringing them up—' His voice trailed off.

For a second I felt a bit sorry for him, having me as a son. I told him I didn't know exactly who I'd called, which was the truth, and so Dad got out his contacts book and we went through it, with me saying yes or no when he called out the names and telling him what I remembered saying.

Nanette Newman? No.

Peter Sissons? No.

Tom Baker? Yes. What? Davros impression . . . No it was a Dalek.

Anthea Turner? Yes. What? Can't remember.

Carol Vorderman? No.

Lord Weymouth? Yes. What? Called him a cunt.

Eammon Holmes? Yes. What? Called him a cunt.

Phillip Schofield? Yes. What? Cunt.

Keith Chegwin? Cunt.

Arnold Palmer? Cunt.

Nicky Campbell? Cunt. But he called me something just as bad back.

Thursday, 22 April

Bernie tried to chat up a girl on the phone using DIPADA today. He let James listen in. James kept shouting instructions ('More probing, Bernie' . . . 'Go back to *Definition*' . . . 'Don't forget the staircase of consent').

Juliet listened in on another spare ear-piece. ('Not enough closing Bernie!' . . . 'Remember your structure').

It was like a game and at the end of the call James and Bernie had a serious discussion about where he'd gone wrong and Bernie's leg twitched from the excitement. 'You had her with your direct close, then you let her slip. You said: "What are you doing on Friday," and when she said, "No, I can't make Friday," you should've asked her when she could make it. Instead you said, "Oh well! See you some time then!" Your language wasn't positive enough. You'd have probably got away with an assumptive close: "I'll see you the Friday after that then!" '

'It'll be just like *Thelma and Louise*,' I said to Gemma tonight, 'except we won't drive off the edge of a cliff at the end, we'll just grow old together, know everything about each other and eat mangoes.'

'I don't like mangoes,' said Gemma.

She was glancing over at Mark and Kate on the other table, which annoyed me. I'd thought about ringing her up last night, but in the end I thought I'd tell her the plan face to face. I hadn't banked on Mark and Kate turning up to see her off on her final night, though.

'So, you can eat coconut or something. The food isn't important. This isn't a joke,' I said. I was getting irritated by her inattention. You ask someone to give up Western society to live in a yurt, you expect some attention. 'I told you I was sorry about the other day and lately. But I've thought about it and this is the answer. Look, I got you a recorder.'

I'd borrowed Charlie's old recorder. He wouldn't miss

it. They didn't play the recorder at Roxburgh – it was way too swanky. He was probably playing the bassoon by now. I thought Gemma could play the recorder while I sang nursery rhymes. The recorder would really knock out the little black kids. I had big plans for the recorder. Digging wells by day, teaching little black kids nursery rhymes at night.

But Gemma was looking at Mark and Kate again. She had her arms half folded and she was smoking. She didn't usually smoke in front of me. 'Jay, I don't want a recorder. Why would I want a recorder? I've got my course. I've paid a month's deposit in Sheffield. And, anyway, I don't think my Dad would be very happy if I just took off to the Sudan. I don't think your dad would be either. What about your job? What if you get on your course? You still haven't heard, there's still a chance—'

'It's all right, you don't have to shout,' I said. 'They can hear you.' Gemma was saying everything just loud enough for Mark and Kate to hear. It was getting on my nerves.

'They can't hear and I'm not shouting,' said Gemma, blowing out a plume of smoke. 'You're the one who's shouting.'

'I'm not shouting.'

'You are, Jay. You're all hyper. Look at your hands, they're shaking. And I thought VSO rejected you. You told me they turned you down. Or was that another lie?'

I looked out of the window to show how disappointed I was about being called a liar.

'See it from my point of view,' said Gemma, folding her half-smoked cigarette into the ashtray and immediately lighting another. She was waving her hands, which made me laugh, and now she was chain smoking. She was the one who was hyper. 'The other day you finished with me. You told me you wouldn't be coming to see me in Sheffield, remember? And now you tell me you want us to live together in a mud hut. Listen to yourself.'

I was still looking out of the window.

'It's ridiculous – we can't just turn up in the Sudan with our bags. Where would we live?'

'We don't have to go with VSO. We'll convert the van into a camper van,' I said, turning back with my wild face on. 'We'll live in the van until we get a mud hut. We'll become part of the tribe, Gem. We'll make our own bread. Even when we've got enough bread we'll make more bread. It'll be great. Just think of how that bread'll taste. The bread we've made ourselves. Gem, think of the bread.' It was weird. I only half believed it last night, but now I believed it totally. I had this great mental picture of us making our own bread: Gemma kneading the dough, me grinding the flour. Half the reason I wanted to go was probably the bread.

Gemma closed her eyes and reached for my hand. 'Can't we just go interrailing next summer?'

I squeezed her hand back and leaned forward. 'Gem, I'm talking about getting away, really getting away. Imagine it. Think of those black kids. Think of their faces. Interrailing – it's just not the same. Eating baguette and cheese under the Eiffel Tower is *not* the same. Let's do something that we'll remember when we're eighty.'

Gemma was squeezing my hand tighter and there was a tear in her eye. I thought it was because she was thinking about the black kids. I thought I was getting somewhere.

'Those black kids'll probably be outside the hut at five in the morning, Gem. They'll never leave us alone. They'll follow us around. From miles around they'll come. We'll be like pied fucking pipers.'

Gemma let go of my hand and wiped away the tear with her sleeve. Her hand was shaking. I looked at the clock on the wall over her shoulder. Its pendulum was swinging. It reminded me of a finger wagging, telling me off.

'Look at me, Jay. *Look at me!*' said Gemma. She was moving her head from side to side to catch my eye. She held my head at both sides. 'Let's go next summer. I get three months off. And if you still want to go away after that we'll go after my course – the Sudan will still be there in three years' time and I'll have a qualification. We need some time to sort things out, too. Some time apart'll do us good. We've been living in each other's pocket for ages—'

I prised my head away from her grasp. 'Look, let me show you the recorder. Just have a look at the recorder.' I don't know why I thought the recorder would swing it. It was one of those extra-long ones with double holes at the end. I got it out of the bag and had this stupid idea I'd start playing 'London's Burning' or something to convince her. But I couldn't remember the tune and I knew she'd only be embarrassed, so I sort of pushed it up to her lips when she withdrew her cigarette.

'Stop it,' she said, pushing away my hand. 'You're hurting me. You're being' – I let go and she banged the recorder on the table – 'totally selfish. You don't really want to go with me at all. You just want to run away from yourself, because you've got nothing. You're in a mess because of a hundred and one things.' Her arms were really waving around now. 'But I'm not any more. I was, but now I'm not. I just don't think it's going to work out. I don't think it's going to work out between us.' She stubbed out her cigarette savagely. But she didn't do it properly. There was a small trail of smoke coming from the end. I finished the job for her. 'No one can understand why I put up with it.' She was shaking like a leaf. It made me want to cuddle her. 'Mum can't understand it. Dad can't either. No one can. No, I'm not coming with you and I don't think' – she started to cry, tears leaked through her fingers – 'we should see each other for a while. I was going to tell you before, but you didn't give me a chance. I didn't want it to come out this way. I know it's not a good time, what with your mum's anniversary.' Her hand was playing with the cigarette I'd snuffed out. 'Jay . . . I've met someone.'

She couldn't look at me. She had her great clumsy spatula hand up to her face and she was staring out of the window. I got up and went to hug her. I wanted to squeeze out everything she was saying. I wanted to make her laugh like a tuning fork. I realised I really did love her. I didn't care she'd met somebody. I wasn't jealous. It didn't matter. She was all I had left. I just wanted us to be together. But she put her hand up to stop me and said, 'No, Jay – don't. *Please!*'

11 p.m.

I was sitting in the living room when Dad came home. I asked him how John and Sylvia's dinner party with Eileen had been.

'Oh, it was all right,' he said.

'All right how?'

'Weird, I suppose.'

'Weird in a good way or a bad way?'

'Weird in a weird way.'

Sarah phoned up later and wanted to know how it'd gone. She sounded all excited for him, and it got on my nerves. Sarah told me I was going to have to get used to Dad seeing other people. 'Don't you want him to be happy? Doesn't him being happy make you happy?' She asked whether I was anywhere nearer getting a proper job and when I said I wasn't she said it was time I moved on. She'd moved on and got married, Charlie had moved on, Dad was now moving on. It was my turn. 'Come on, Jay, the doctor says there's nothing wrong with you.'

What does she know?

Friday, 23 April

Charlie's coming home soon for Mum's party. I phoned up today and asked what he wanted for a present so he'd be excited about being home. He said he wanted the pair of San Marino boots he didn't get for his birthday. He's playing in the under-eights final soon. I said I couldn't afford them, but got them from Chesham Allsports anyway. I'm trying not to think about the memorial party. It's just a date. But the whole of the last year feels like the magician's trick of removing the tablecloth without disturbing the cutlery: the year's been whipped from under me – *voilà!* Everything's the same, only more bare. The soupiness in my head's worse than ever. It was soup with croutons last night. One so thick you could stand your spoon in it. I actually had to put the pillow over my head when I went to bed to drown out the noise of my brain cells dissolving. I could hear them plinking like Solpadeine tablets. I know illness is devouring me slowly, like woodworm. My brain feels honey-combed, disjointed and cluttered. Last night was terrible. The wind roared like a forest fire, there were malformed faces in the curtain pattern, my head ached and my bum was itchy.

Dad and I watched *The Guns of Navarone*. He said he thought it was fitting because it was what we'd watched together the night before Mum died. 'I'm not going to say anything about the phone calls now,' he said. 'It's not the time. But tomorrow, after the party, we are going to have to have a serious chat, you and I. And I don't think you're going to like what I have got to say.'

When he went to bed I tried to ring Gemma in Sheffield, but a girl in her new house answered and said she was out with Rod. When I asked if it was Rod who did classics, the girl in the house asked who was calling and I hung up.

Saturday, 24 April

I finally got hold of Gemma at about 2 a.m.

'So tell me on a rating scale of one to ten how much you still love me, Gem.'

'Jay?'

'Come on, give me five, Gem.'

'Jay, I was asleep. It's the middle of the night.'

'Lanky fucking Rod, then? He's your new boyfriend. What are you going to give him?'

Silence.

'How tall's he? Come on, how tall's lanky Rod?'

Silence.

'Jay, I don't want this conversation.'

'Well, I do. How tall?'

'He's quite tall. Now can I go to bed?'

'You said he was short. Well, that's it then, I suppose.' Pause. 'Come on, Gem. We could buy a flat or something. In Sheffield.'

'I don't want to buy a flat.'

'OK, we'll rent.'

'Jay, it just won't work any more.'

'Why, I've learned my lesson. Look I'm not taking you for granted now, am I? I'm not obsessed with myself any more at all.' Pause. 'I'm coming up to Sheffield.'

'I'll be horrible to you.'

'You won't.'

'I will.'

Pause.

'Have you snogged him, Gem?'

'Why?'

'Have you?'

'Why do you want to know?'

'I just want to see if you're really going out with him.'

'I'm going out with him.'

'So you've snogged him, then?' Pause. 'What about in the summer? You're coming back then, Gem?'

'I don't know.'

'We could go interrailing. I'll carry the tent. I'll carry everything. I'll carry you if you want.'

'No, Jay.'

'All right, you can walk.'

Pause.

'Jay, you haven't changed, but I have. I want to do something. You never do a thing.'

'I do. I do lots of things. What sort of things anyway – what don't I do?'

'*Anything*. Get yourself sorted, Jay.'

'I am sorted.' Pause. 'Gem, I need you before I can get sorted. I can't get sorted without you. Come on, Gem. One to ten: how much do you love me? Come on, give me three?'

'Jay, it won't work. I've made up my mind.'

'Hello, Gem?'

'Hello. Sheila's got in. I've got to go. I've got to be up at—'

'Gem?'

'What?'

'That time when we wrote on each other's back and you wrote, "I love you," and I wrote, "I love you, too." I nearly wrote, "Will you marry me?" Gem?'

'What?'

'Let's get married and have children. Let's have three children named Boris.'

Pause.

'It's too late, Jay. I've got to go.'

'Too late tonight, or *too late* . . . You'll regret it, Gem. When I'm on *Parkinson* you'll regret it. When I've written my novel. You'll be sorry. When you get that postcard from me in the Sudan.'

'Bye, Jay! Oh and—'

'What?'

'What's the time? Shit, it's today. Your mum's anniversary.'

'Oh, fucking hell. Bye, Gem.'

7 p.m.

Went in dog-tired to work after no sleep and was called into the office for a quick word. Chris Henderson was there with his tiny walnut-shaped head. It looked even more walnutty than usual because his face was all creased up to show how disapproving he was.

Bernie was also there, sat in the corner, leaning forward with his hyperactive leg jockeying up and down like a sewing-machine needle. I knew immediately I was going to be sacked, but I didn't know why. I didn't particularly care, but I did want to know why.

'Sit down,' said Juliet. She said it very seriously. For a second the thought occurred to me someone'd seen me at The Comedy Store and I started thinking of an excuse to explain why I hadn't behaved like a people-person. Why I hadn't stood up like the warm-up man wanted me to.

Juliet picked up a piece of A4 paper from her desk. She held it between her thumb and forefinger like it was infectious. I noticed a familiar name at the top of the page: it was mine. It was my CV. I was being sacked because of my . . . I turned instinctively to look at Bernie.

'Yes, that's right. But you needn't blame him,' said Juliet, following my gaze. Bernie's leg was on a twenty-metre-hem machine-stitch mode. It was a concrete floor, but I could feel the vibrations in my chair leg. 'Bernie was only being professional,' she said.

Professional! I made a 'huh' noise and tried to imagine the scene of betrayal: Bernie's yield a bit low, anxious to get in with the boss, unable to contain my secret.

'I must admit,' said Juliet, 'my first thought was that this was a matter for the police.'

'A breach of trust,' added Henderson.

Juliet laid my CV down on the table in front of her proudly, like she'd just won it off me in a skill contest, which made me laugh. I wanted to tell Bernie to stop jockeying his leg. It was getting hard to concentrate because of the vibrations.

'What made you think you'd get away with it?' said Juliet, raising her strawberry-bon-bon face towards the dozens of management diplomas on the wall above her head.

Henderson was tilting his own walnutty head violently to one side, stroking his chin savagely to show how fascinated he was in how I thought I could get away with it.

'What', said Juliet, looking at Henderson, whose whole head was now rocking from side to side because he was kneading his chin so much, 'made you think we were so stupid?'

I noticed that she was starting to *define*. I was being DIPADAed. I stared at my feet, hoping she'd stop DIPA-DAing me. I didn't mind getting sacked, but I couldn't take being fucking DIPADAed as well.

'Did you think we wouldn't check?' she asked.

I looked at Henderson. If he got any more fascinated, he was going to snap a neck vertebra.

'Haven't you anything to say?' said Juliet.

I thought about telling her I was a 'reflective-observer' and that I was still reflecting.

'You can tell me, or you can tell Chris and the police,' she said, shrugging her shoulders as if she didn't care one way or the other. Juliet obviously did care, though, because her face was flushed from the excitement. That was why she looked like a strawberry bon-bon. She picked up my CV again. 'There aren't just a few lies. It's *all* lies,' she said, and threw it back down on to her desk.

'Some of the hobbies', I said, 'are true.'

'Oh,' said Juliet, pressing an open palm to her chest in mock apology. 'Pardon me! Some of the *hobbies* are true!'

I remembered the dream I'd had last night, one of those fitful, edgy dreams. It was about Mum, but Mum was Gemma. She was in the shallow end of the pool at Chesham leisure centre. Only it couldn't be, because it was outdoors not indoors and the sun was shining. I was sitting on a lounger and drinking something through a straw.

'Come on in – the water's lovely,' said Mum. Then a waiter came up to me, except he was Sean, but it wasn't even really him, it was Charlie and he didn't offer me a drink, but presented me with a box of chocolates, only there weren't chocolates in the little slots, but ice-cubes.

'In case it's news to you,' said Juliet, 'we were never that interested in your hobbies. Cybernetics and twentieth-century literature never really played a major role in our hiring you. What did was your' – she mimed some inverted commas in the air – ' "Previous employment".'

I tried to read the labels on the box menu, but I couldn't see them properly. I ate the whole first layer of ice-cubes. I remember feeling really happy. Then I started on the second tier. 'Moreish, aren't they?' said Mum, laughing. I laughed, too, and was really happy she wasn't dead after all. But then she stopped laughing and the box turned into a drugs cabinet and the ice-cubes were pills. I looked at the box menu again and realised they were diamorphine tablets not ice-cubes, then panicked because I'd overdosed. When, I looked up to the pool to ask Mum for help she was floating face down in the water.

Juliet had flipped over a page of my CV and was reading: 'Previous employment – one year at Montons Recruitment Consultancy – *a lie*. Two years at Reed Publishing – *a lie*. And I like this one best: skipper on BT Global Challenge round-the-world yacht race, which', she chuckled derisively and started to read very slowly, emphasising each word, ' "helped me develop my leadership and communication skills in a taxing, often dangerous, high-seas environment, which included the attendant hazards, to name but a few, of the doldrums, the Cape of Good Hope", spelled *hop*, "and" – my favourite bit this – "*scurvy risk from the biscuits and things*".' She put my CV down on her desk and stared at it in wonderment. 'I mean, scurvy from the biscuits *and things*, Jay!'

'They were old biscuits, I don't know. They were past their sell-by date. Maybe I exaggerated. Maybe the biscuits were OK,' I said.

'I have no choice,' said Juliet. 'I'm going to have to let you go. I'm sorry, I have no choice.'

Henderson was nodding regretfully. Bernie's seamstress leg was still working flat out on that big order. I wanted to cry. I felt so tired and so fucking forlorn. But I just nodded.

'Janice has your coat. You didn't have a bag, did you?' She stood up and handed me back my CV. 'You can', she said 'take this with you. It's two hundred pounds, paying you up to today. You're lucky to get it.' She handed me the cash, then pressed a buzzer and two security guards came in and escorted me out of the building, one of them holding the crook of my arm in case I ran amok, breaking office equipment or something.

I couldn't face the tube, I felt too tired, so instead I sat on the steps by the revolving door, pressed my nose up against the glass and annoyed the security guards by mouthing lines from *The Guns of Navarone*. 'Tonight dey burn Mandrakos asee puneeshment,' I said, but the security guards just stared at me.

A guy in a suit walked past, a mobile pressed to his ear. 'When this is all over we'll meet in Simpson's – roast beef, Yorkshire pudding, a nice little red,' I shouted at him, but he just changed his phone to the other ear and carried on walking.

I tried to imagine Mum in her yellow dressing-gown looking down on me sternly because I'd lost another job. I got out her old lighter and started fiddling with the flint. It was quite comforting to have my thumb where hers had been on the flint. But then I started thinking about how her thumb'd looked at the end, when all her fingers had been yellow because of the jaundice, so I pressed my face up to the glass again and mouthed more stuff from *The Guns of Navarone*. It was surprising how much I could remember. 'The party's over,' I shouted. 'Exhibit A – one clockwork fuse' – I held up Mum's lighter – 'contact arm broken. Tick until Christmas and it wouldn't set off a fire-cracker. My time pencil' – I held up the lighter again – 'seventy-five grams of formulated mercury, enough to blow my hand off. Very unstable. Very *delicate*' – I dropped the lighter on the floor to emphasise my point – 'which means only one thing, Captain Mallory – we have a traitor in the camp. Bernie, you cunt.'

'You're *late*, now at least try to be civil,' said Dad when I arrived home. I said I was being civil. We were in the back garden. It was floodlit, the guests had arrived and I had a camera around my neck. I was supposed to take 'lots of pictures'. Dad said he wanted a few poignant memories of the memorial party. Basically, though, he just wanted more pictures in the snooker room of him with his arm around household names.

'You're not being civil – you're being antisocial.' Dad put a tray of wineglasses in my hands. 'Over there,' he said, steering me towards a gaggle of MPs and news people, 'and smile.'

I was starting to wish I hadn't come home. I'd only wanted to give Charlie his boots before I left, but Charlie'd already gone to bed, so I'd have to wait until the morning.

The guests all had a rose cutting in their hands, which made me laugh. Sarah had given them out on the door. Mum's ashes were scattered over the rose bushes, so Dad thought it'd be fitting if everyone got a cutting from them. But it didn't seem at all fitting to me. It's like when you see a lion at the zoo and it isn't as impressive as it should be because of all the lions you've seen in Disney cartoons. Mum was like the cartoon lion. She was being reduced to a few rounded edges and bright colours by the roses.

'You've all met my eldest son, Jay, haven't you?' Dad had followed me. He put his hands on my shoulders and ruffled my hair as they all took drinks from my tray.

'And what stage are you at?' said a woman I recognised from *Late Review*.

I thought about telling her the stage I was at was fucking off to the Sudan with Dad's MasterCard to live in a mud hut, but I told her I'd left school a year or so ago and was trying a few things out.

'Tell her about the kebab shop,' said Dad. 'Tell her what

happened at the kebab shop. This is a lovely story,' he told her. He started laughing falsely in anticipation of it. It made me laugh – he was prepared to joke about Big Al's when other people were around and he wanted to appear the relaxed, liberal father. He hadn't laughed when I'd been sacked, though. 'Tell her how you got sacked from the kebab shop,' he said. He started massaging my neck in a casual way from behind to show how tactile and affectionate he was. 'Jay's . . . What age are you, Jay?' he said, gripping the top of my head and rotating it to face his. He didn't even know how fucking old I was, which also made me laugh.

'I'm eighteen,' I said, staring into his face.

'Jay's eighteen. He's eighteen and already he's had more jobs than I've ever had in my whole career. He gets fired more times than an Olympic starting pistol, don't you, my old son?' He laughed falsely again and sort of cuffed my head, which irritated me because I'd just brushed my hair. The way his fingers were digging into my shoulders was quite painful, too. 'Yer bluddy daft, what are yer?'

'I'm bluddy daft,' I said.

Dad spoke briefly to one of his Old Roxie mates who was asking after Charlie. I heard Dad thank him and say Charlie was in the fast stream for every subject and doing 'very well'.

'So what happened at the kebab shop?' the woman from *Late Review* asked me, cutting over their conversation. She half folded her arms and looked up over the glass she was sipping from. 'I'm intrigued.'

Dad had heard the question and was back. 'We still on the kebab shop?' he said.

The woman from *Late Review* nodded. 'I was just asking . . . Jay, wasn't it? . . . what happened.'

'Oh dear,' said Dad and wiped an imaginary tear from his eye like Bob Monkhouse does. 'Tell her, Jay. And bear in mind this was his fourth job,' he said, laughing again, 'in *three* months!'

I started thinking about just waking up Charlie, giving him the boots, and fucking off. I couldn't take much more. 'I left a skewer in the pitta bread,' I told the women from *Late Review*.

Dad smacked his thigh and laughed again. He did an imitation of me speaking in a moronic voice: 'Nobody told me I had to take the skewers out of the meat.'

'Oooh dear,' said the woman, grimacing. 'That sounds painful.' She looked genuinely concerned.

'Yes, it was – a woman cut her face open eating one,' I said.

Dad stopped laughing. The bit about somebody cutting their face open I'd just made up. The woman from *Late Review* was holding her face, looking horrified. '*Oooh my Lord!*' she said. The atmosphere had changed completely. Dad took hold of my shoulders and gave them an angry squeeze. His fingers bit into me and I could feel his eyes boring into the back of my head.

'Was it . . . ?' She couldn't finish her sentence.

'She needed seventeen stitches,' I said. 'A severed optic nerve.' I traced a line from the corner of my mouth to my eye, indicating where the imaginary stitches had gone.

Dad let go of my shoulder and led the woman away to the buffet, shaking his head and looking sternly back at me. I heard him telling her I'd only been joking. 'It's the occasion,' he said.

Some *Today* programme presenters walked past talking shop.

'Be careful', I shouted, before Dad and the woman had reached the back door, 'of cocktail sticks in the smorgasbord.' They looked around and so did a gaggle of celebrities orbiting around Anna Ford. 'I made the smorgasbord. Nobody told me I had to take the cocktail sticks out of the fucking smorgasbord.'

Dad glowered and I lifted up the camera and took his picture. 'And when you get back, I've got a couple more,' I said, winding on the film. 'My latest one – at Gorder and

Board. Not even Dad's heard that one. Come back and I'll tell it. It's a *lovely* story.'

Dad left the woman at the back door, strode up the garden and bundled me towards the summerhouse, holding the back of my neck in a Mister Spock grip. On the way we passed a few celebrities and I tried to take some snaps, but Dad snatched the camera out of my hand, yanked the strap up over my neck and told me to stop wasting film: if he wasn't in the pictures it was a waste of film, which made me laugh. He closed the door behind him. 'What's the matter with you? And is that true?' he asked.

'Is what true?'

'What you just said.'

'Yes.'

'You've been sacked?'

'Yes.'

Jeremy Paxman walked past and waved through the window. Dad waved back and then slapped my hand when I tried to wave, too. 'We'll deal with this in the morning,' he said, and went to leave. He wanted to join Jeremy Paxman. He'd rather talk to Jeremy Paxman than deal with me.

'No, let's deal with it now,' I said. 'I want to know where I stand, because I'm not going back out there and talking about stupid fucking rose cuttings if you're throwing me out in the morning. I might as well go now if that's going to happen.'

'I can't believe you've done this tonight of *all nights*,' he said.

Sarah opened the door, saw Dad and me eyeball to eyeball, said something about having run out of dessert-spoons, and left, frowning at me.

'And anyway I thought it was all a big joke,' I said. 'I thought it'd make a *lovely* dinner-party story. You thought Big Al's was funny earlier on. What's changed? How come it isn't funny now?'

Dad didn't say anything. He turned his back on me; I was

back to being an eyesore. 'Tonight of all nights,' he said again.

It started to piss me off, all this tonight-of-all-nights crap. He was trying to make out I'd let Mum down, rather than him. Whereas, in reality, if Mum'd been there she'd have hated the party. She didn't like his celebrity parties. She'd have preferred to watch *EastEnders*. He was the one who loved celebrity parties. It was only him I'd let down.

'And stop pretending this is a memorial party for Mum. A few rose cuttings at the door doesn't make it a memorial party,' I said. 'It's just one of your excuses to get a few pictures of yourself with your arms around celebrities to stick up in the snooker room to show everyone what a fucking hero you are. If anybody's let Mum down, it's you organising this load of crap. Why couldn't Charlie, you, Sarah and I have gone out instead? Why can't you have pictures of *us* in the snooker room?'

Dad went all red in the face. I did, too. I could feel myself blushing. He sat down in a wicker chair and held his head. He spoke very quietly: 'You can stay tonight, but in the morning you're going to leave. I won't be spoken to like this in my own home. I just won't.' He opened the door to leave and kind of stumbled into the door frame.

'Fine,' I said, 'but I'm not spending the night, I'm going now. I'm going to say goodbye to Charlie and then I'm leaving. I'm not coming back, either. I'm going to dig wells in the Sudan and I don't care how uncivilised it is and what diseases I get because even if I got a hundred diseases, anything's got to be better than hanging around here getting shouted at for spending too long in the fucking bath.'

'You'll not wake that boy up!' he said. He was pointing at me, but only half-heartedly.

Charlie woke up as soon as I switched on his side-light. He sat bolt upright and, without saying anything, lifted up the covers for me to get in. As I got in the bed I swung the football boots he wanted from behind my back so they were there in front of him on the covers. I thought I'd give him the boots now as I wouldn't be around tomorrow.

'Da-dah!' I said.

'Wow!' Charlie leaped out of the bed. '*San Marinos!*' He put them on and started doing shuttle runs up and down the room. He was dropping his shoulder, doing feints. I was a bit worried he'd turn an ankle over and that Dad would hear, so I made him stop.

'You reckon you'll score in those boots?' I asked.

He was sitting on the bed, just staring at them on his feet. 'I'll score a fluffing hat-trick,' he said.

I had to put my finger to my lips to shush him.

'Did I tell you?' he said in a breathless whisper. He'd got up again and was taking imaginary penalties. 'Did I tell you that I might be captain? Ferraby-Thomas's on holiday and Worstoncroft's got the flu and Mr Howard says I might be captain.'

The names of his posh new mates made me laugh. I could just imagine them all with their Victoria Crosses. 'If you're captain, you don't have to score,' I said, putting my arm around him. 'You just have to inspire somebody else to score through your captaincy.'

He'd taken off the boots and was sitting on the bed, bending them back and forth to loosen the leather.

'You been working on your tackling back?' I said. He had a tendency not to tackle too much.

'Yessss,' he said defensively and leaped up again and started jockeying me in his bare feet. He was making a bit of a row with his jockeying and Dad shouted up: 'Charlie, light out, please – it's eleven o'clock.'

Charlie got back into bed and I pulled his duvet up to his neck. I wanted to tell him I was going away to the Sudan, but I couldn't, there wasn't time. Dad would be up in a minute to check he really had gone to bed for the night.

Then Charlie thought of something and a big smile came over his face. He pulled the covers down in a swoosh, held his fists to his mouth and pointed his elbows at me. I couldn't work out what he was doing, I was in too much of a hurry to get out. Then I realised. 'Your scabs have healed,' I said.

Charlie shrugged his shoulders.

'That's great, Charlie – that *is* great,' I said, checking them. I wanted to stay around, but I heard Dad moving about, so I switched off the light. When I got to the door Charlie called out my name in a whisper.

'What?' I said, whispering back.

'Donatello says hello.'

'What?'

'Donatello, turtle.'

'I thought he was Greeny-Slowy.'

'That's a stupid name.'

I went to close the door but he called my name again

'What?' I said.

He was lying sidelong now, leaning on his elbow. 'I am going to score a fluffing hat-trick,' he said.

Then I heard Dad coming up the stairs so I darted into the spare room opposite, and when he'd gone I crept downstairs. Luckily everyone was in the garden, so I got my passport out of the documents drawer, walked out of the front door and climbed into the van.

THREE
WEEKS
LATER

Monday, 17 May

I lie in bed most of the time in my T-shirt and boxers, sleeping. I wake up sweating. It's either very hot in here or I have a temperature. I think it's a temperature, because occasionally a doctor walks past my bed and says what I think is 'fever'. The reason I'm not sure is that I'm in an Italian hospital. It's up in the mountains, pretty remote, and nobody has a phrase book or speaks any English.

The treatment's a drip. I have it three times a day, along with a drug, which makes me drowsy and weirdly emotional. They've taken blood and urine samples and the only thing I'm given to eat or drink is camomile tea. It comes every hour.

There are two Italians on the ward: one middle aged, one very old. I'm in the middle bed. The old one mutters and eats directly from his knife. He never speaks to anyone and seems almost to take orders from the man to my left, the middle-aged one, whom I've nicknamed Mr Big. I've christened him this because he uses his words sparingly, is stocky and looks as if he's used to commanding respect. Plus, I think he might be in the Mafia.

Tuesday, 18 May

Mr Big's very thoughtful and when I first arrived he plumped my pillows for me because I couldn't move my back. He's the sort of man who's so grown up and manly he makes you feel about ten years old. I constantly say 'grazie' to him for the small favours he does me. He fetches bread rolls, gives me lumps of sugar to sweeten my camomile tea and calls the nurse when my drip runs out.

Every time I say '*grazie*' he waves his hand dismissively. He does everything with dignity and courage – it isn't obsequious in any way. When he fetches a bread roll, for instance, it's not like he's fetching a bread roll, but more as though he were going on a dangerous mission.

At the end of every meal he collects the dishes, then straightens the table and chairs. He cuts up the left-overs into slithers with his penknife and feeds them to the pigeons that congregate on the window ledge. The window over-looks the car park. Beyond that there's a lake – Lake Orta.

Wednesday, 19 May

I helped Mr Big cut up the left-overs today for the pigeons. He came and collected them from my plate because I still can't get out of bed. He nodded emphatically when he picked them up in a way that made me feel inexplicably proud of what I'd done.

When Mr Big isn't doing me small favours, he paces up and down the corridors, talking loudly to the other patients. Even the matron seems to respect Mr Big and he doesn't get reprimanded like everyone else when he walks around without his slippers.

While writing this I saw him having an injection in his bottom. He received even this with dignity. It didn't demean him at all; it enhanced him. He received it like a war hero accepting a medal.

I think Mr Big's been here a long time. He has his own cutlery, sugar and salt.

Thursday, 20 May

I still don't know what's wrong with me. I'm not sure now whether this is because of translation difficulties or because they don't want to tell me. It's so peaceful here, I don't really want to know. It must be something to do with my lungs, that's all I can gather. I was shown a picture of one by Dr Atori this morning. It was in a medical textbook. '*Comprende?*' he asked, pointing at it.

'*Comprende,*' I replied.

'*Bene,*' he said, and walked away.

Friday, 21 May

My back's still very sore and I can't turn over or move it without incredible shooting pains. I just lie here rigid, staring at the white ceiling like a plank of wood. I feel very emotional all the time, because of the drugs, I think. It's a bit embarrassing. The slightest thing seems to make my eyes well up. If anyone does or says anything kind or even when I just think things, I want to cry. It happened when the nurse called Maria opened the curtains this morning. I wanted to kiss her and tell her I loved her. '*Amore, amore,*' I said as she left the room, which I think means 'I love you'.

We had a list for everything the day after she died: Jay's List, Dad called it. I compiled it at 5 a.m., Dad in a matter-of-fact tone telling me things to put on it as we munched through our toast in the kitchen, unable to sleep. 'Ring Mr Twain and tell him all donations to Cancer Research, death certificate from registrar, copy of it to bank, copy of it to Mr Twain, spare copy for the documents drawer, phone stonemason for memorial plaque in the garden, clear away Mum's little things, phone Mum's ironing people and let them know, thank-you letter to the nurses at the hospital, change answerphone message.'

We did them one by one, crossing them off like robots ('Right that one's done, we're getting there. What next?') until we came to the last one: clearing away Mum's 'little things'.

Dad had a try, but just threw everything blindly and manically into bin-liners regardless of what it was and whether he might still need it, so Sarah and I took over and he went for a walk. We threw away the blue jumper she'd half knitted for Charlie; we threw away her ironing baskets, her diuretic pills, her toothbrush and ointments, the duffel coat on the back of the dining-room chair I gave her for Christmas. They all went in the bin-liner. Tiny things so important one day, so insignificant the next. I saved her hairbrush – it still had her hair on it. I saved a thimble where her thumb had been and her old leather wallet with her initials on it. I put them all under my bed.

Then we went through her wardrobes and Sarah held up the clothes she remembered Mum wearing and talked about them and smelled them and looked up at me and sometimes she smiled and sometimes she bit her lip. There was a bag in the corner of the last cupboard. Dad must've put it there. It was full of Mum's things from the hospital. They were all neatly packed as if for a holiday – her toiletries, her magazines, her clothes, the Danielle Steel book she'd been reading with the last page she'd read folded over: page seventy-six. All this went in the bin-liner except for one nightdress: the lacy black-and-white one she'd worn that last day in hospital and that she used to wear when she sat on the sofa. We couldn't throw it away because it was Mum, more Mum than her body in the funeral parlour that none of us went to see. More Mum because when we lifted it out of the bag it was as if she was suddenly still alive – *whack*, it hit you so hard in the stomach it brought tears to your eyes – it smelled so exactly of her for a second it was as if she was there with us.

Dad and I sat in the garden with Mr Twain, the funeral director. 'Lovely to hear those birds,' said Dad, interrupting Mr Twain as he turned the coffin brochure pages.

'Yes, sir,' said Mr Twain, 'they're out in force today.'

Reg, the stonemason: 'Yes, that plaque'll look lovely, Mr

Golden. We'll bevel the edges so it's not so sharp for the young 'un . . . Some of that Italian stone is very pretty.'

Dad stroked the place it was going to go on the wall and looked at me, and I nodded approval before I had to go inside because my feelings were suddenly toughened to everything concerning Mum, like hard skin on the sole of your foot.

Saturday, 22 May

I was thinking about what Charlie said about Mum being tied up in heaven today and in a way he isn't that far off the mark. It is like Mum was kidnapped, by a gang we didn't know the name of, who wouldn't tell us what they'd done or intended to do with her, or what ransom we had to pay to get her back. They wouldn't even give us any sign she was all right. A pretty shit kidnap gang really.

I'm still not allowed to bathe because of the antibiotics and I'm beginning to smell. Mr Big compensated for this today by dousing my bed in eau de Cologne. He did this with a nod, which I acknowledged with a nod. Mr Big himself bathes three times a day and looks immaculate in his vest and purple pyjama bottoms.

Alan Ames phoned from the BBC on Dad's behalf after breakfast. 'I'd like to speak to the doctor,' he said, after introducing himself.

I put him on to Dr Atori. They spoke in Italian for a few minutes, then Dr Atori handed me back to Alan Ames.

'Would you like to know what you've got?' asked Alan Ames from the BBC.

'Yes, I would.'

'You've got bronchial pneumonia,' he said. 'Would you like to know how long they'll be keeping you in?'

'Yes, I would.'

'Two weeks, then you'll be flown back to England. I'll ring your father now.'

Dad phoned later and asked how I was. I said fine. He said I'd given him quite a fright. 'But you're all right now, are you?' he said.

'Yes,' I said and he put Charlie on because he said he was screaming for a word. Charlie said he'd scored two goals with the San Marino boots. He hadn't been captain, but was going to be next season as Worstoncroft was leaving the school because his parents were moving to Saudi Arabia.

'I'm very pleased about your elbows,' I said, 'very proud, Charlie.' My voice must've gone funny at this point because Charlie asked what was the matter and when I said nothing, he asked me what a scrangie was in Italian. I said it was *scrangio*. Then I told him about Mr Big.

'How big's Mr Big?' he asked.

'He's enormous,' I said.

Charlie put Dad back on. I said I was sorry for what I'd said at the party and Dad said if that's what I thought of him he was very sorry, but there was nothing he could do about it. I said it wasn't what I thought and Dad said he knew that.

'It's been a hard year,' he said. 'I love you, my son.'

Mum's ashes came in a plastic tub like creosote. I made a joke at the time about getting money back on the empties, which Sarah hadn't liked. Dad poured them violently on the rose beds in the back garden, like an arsonist in a film with a can of petrol. He did it hurriedly and some of them caught the wind coming up from the bottom field. 'They'll blow away anyway,' he said. I tried to follow him around, treading them into the soil with my foot, and some gusted up into my eye.

It was the day after this that Dad and I started watching all the films in the house. It seems even more special now, just sitting there on the sofa with Dad, us getting along, not fighting, knowing what each other was thinking but without mentioning it, just saying that line over and over again instead.

'It's "Sull-a – to the in-famy of his name", Dad.'

'No, it's "Su-la – to the infam-y of his name." It's more clipped.'

'What about "Sulllla . . . to the *infamy* of his name"?'

'No, the emphasis is on the "la". "Sul-la." '

Sunday, 23 May

I'm a little better and can get out of bed, and we now sit around a table in the ward for dinner like a family, with Mr Big the head of the household handing out salt and bread rolls. He's the Sarah of the ward, asking all the questions. I keep trying to convince them I'm well. '*Sono meglio,*' I keep saying, but apparently it's still too early.

When I'm not staring at the ceiling like a plank, I'm passing the time by pointing at things and saying, '*Che cosa?*' It means 'What is that?' From this I've learned the words for tongue, pigeon, carrot, mashed potato and lake.

On family holidays Sarah and I water-skied across Lake Orta. It seems weird seeing it out of the window every day.

'Tomorrow I'll try to stand up on my skis.'

'The secret's don't be jerky, be smooth.'

'Yes, Dad, smooooth.'

We came five years in a row when we were kids. Dad drove the speedboat. Charlie was very young, when we last came, only a baby. Mum held him in the back by the motor and handed out corned-beef sandwiches. I used to complain about the jelly bits and ask why we couldn't have peanut butter and Mum'd say, 'Oh, get it eaten.' That was one of her phrases, along with 'buggeration' and 'too much pork for a shilling'. That one's an old-fashioned phrase which means too much trouble is made of too small a thing – she said it to me once when I went to visit her in hospital towards the end.

One year here we went on a walk in the hills and Mum fell down a grassy bank. From then on it was nicknamed Mummy's Bottom Walk. She had great long blond plaits in those days; right down to her waist. I remember the day she cut them off. She got a job in the Mr Chips chippie and they were too big for her bonnet. When she met Sarah and me at the school gates I didn't recognise her. She looked so shockingly different and not like my mum that I burst into tears and she had to promise to grow them back before I agreed to get in the car.

Picnics on the banks of Lake Orta, Sarah swimming with Dad in armbands, me rolling my cricket dice on the rug because I was slightly afraid of the water, informing a sunbathing Mum of the progress of my England line-up – Allan Lamb LBW for 25 – that'll affect his Test average. Making sandcastles: Mum used to help us make enormous sandcastles. They were laid out like mini-towns. People used to come and take pictures of them: a huge great mound in the centre surrounded by dozens of upturned buckets of sand, all laid out symmetrically in rows like terraced housing stretching sometimes fifteen feet. The whole conurbation inside a deep moat, always my responsibility, and brightened by seaweed gardens, Sarah's responsibility. *'Mum, shall I use this flat stone for a drawbridge?'*

I had wanted to send everyone a postcard from the Sudan, especially Gemma. That was the idea. Coolly dismissive: 'Dear Gemma, as you can see, I'm in the Sudan' . . . 'Dear Dad, as you can see, I'm in the Sudan.' But I became pretty ill so I took a detour.

Getting to Domodossola used to be the best bit of our holidays; it was twelve miles from our hotel in Pattenasco once we'd passed the sign for Domodossola, and Dad would start the song to acknowledge how good we'd been in the car. 'Well done, Fifi.' Fifi was the name of the car. 'Well done, Fifi, well done, Fifi, well done, Fifi, weeell done, Fifi.' Then it was well done, Dad: 'Well done, Dah-ad, well done, Dah-ad, well done, Dah-ad, weeell done, Dah-ad.' Then Sarah, me, Charlie and finally Mum.

Dad would lean forward and look at our faces in the rearview mirror when it was his turn; Sarah'd raise her chin proudly when we were singing about her; and Mum used to look around at us in the back and grin before starting to worry about whether last year's swimsuits would still fit us or something.

Monday, 24 May

Things I miss about Mum. Sitting at the kitchen table while she ironed and talking to her about my writing, my jobs and who I'm going out with and what I think about them. Mum cutting my hair and concentrating so hard she puts her tongue in her cheek. Mum substituting butter for margarine and hoping I won't notice. Mum sneaking left-over baked beans into her shepherd's pies to use them up. The click of knitting needles on the sofa, the crunch of the roast chickpeas she liked to eat before bed. Lifting her up clean off the floor when I hugged her, and Mum saying, 'Put me down, put me down.' Sitting next to her in the van's passenger seat as she delivered ironing and telling her to slow down because she hasn't got her glasses on. Hearing Mum telling me of the embarrassing things she's done at BBC dinners with Dad, but is too ashamed to admit to him: for example, being sick at the Royal Albert Hall and Fergie having to step over her puke; sitting next to a BBC governor, who's also chairman of Marks and Spencer, and thinking of nothing to say to him except, 'I like your prawn cocktail crisps.'

Last night Mr Big watched television. The set was brought in by what looked like his daughter and son-in-law. The son-in-law was very accommodating and always looked up to Mr Big when he said anything, like an apprehensive dog unsure of whether to expect a pat or a kick.

We watched *Il Commissario de Koestler*, an Italian detective series, and Mr Big made the occasional passing remark seemingly to check that everyone was paying attention. After it'd finished Mr Big and the old man watched a programme about dinosaurs. The old man kept falling asleep but Mr Big would inadvertently wake him up by making a comment. The only comment I could understand was when he said, 'Aren't they big!' (*'Che grande!'*) It made me feel very close to Mr Big that he should watch a programme about dinosaurs yet still be amazed by their size.

Tuesday, 25 May

Today there was a new man on the ward. The old man's been moved. The new man was fascinated when we cut up the remains of our dinner for the pigeons. Because both Mr Big and I did it, he obviously felt compelled to do the same. At the end we put the shredded apple cores, bread rolls and cheese skins on Mr Big's plate. Mr Big always points at the pigeons with a smile and says, *'Pigeone,'* to me. Today when he smiled I also pointed and said, *'Pigeone.'* This made him smile even more.

My letter from Dad was on his Maurice Golden, Controller of BBC2 notepaper. It was very short, saying only, 'Old son, having a successful father's a strain. I realise you'd rather I wasn't who I am, but I can't help that. But know this – I'd love you whatever you did. You've nothing to prove. I mean that. Charlie misses you and sends his love, as am I and as do I.' He signed it, 'Your loving father'. He'd added a joky P.S., about me really having something wrong with me for a change.

I've been accepted by the NCTJ for a place on their course in Sheffield. They have to know by the end of next week whether I'm taking it up. They need my fees. Dad phoned to ask me about it. He said it was up to me what I did, but that he'd sent a cheque anyway, which he could cancel if I changed my mind.

This is Jay Golden reporting from Pattenasco. This is me,

Jay Golden, who has bronchial pneumonia, handing back to the studio. Actually, I quite like the idea of becoming a reporter. And it's true – lots of famous writers *have* started off as reporters.

I spoke to Sean on the phone, too, today. I got the number from Dad. I asked how it was going in Scotland. He said OK. He'd been referred to a psychiatrist who'd given him some tablets called Thorazin and he was going to have a precautionary brain scan in three weeks.

I asked whether he'd move back at any stage and he said his parents were building an annexe on to the cottage for him. 'And Dad's put my name down at Dumfries College, so I don't know.'

I wanted to say something about how it was all right him probably being gay and how I missed him and how strange it would be when I got back not having him down the road, but I couldn't think of the right way to put it and finally it was Sean who brought it up. 'I never wanted to bum you,' he said.

I laughed at his choice of words, which hurt my back, and Sean laughed because he hadn't realised how blunt he'd been. There was a slight pause after we'd both stopped laughing and I said I'd write to him. He said he'd write back, although I knew he wouldn't and I knew I probably wouldn't, either.

Wednesday, 26 May

We have a new custom at mealtimes. Now, just before we start our food, we look towards the window for the pigeons. At this point we exchange knowing looks and Mr Big smiles and makes a remark about the pigeons being greedy. In the evening, feeling confident about the '*pigeone*' comment I made yesterday, I initiated the window glance and said, '*Hanno fame.*' ('They are hungry.') Mr Big looked extremely pleased.

I had my first bath today, too. I was in it so long the nurse called, '*Vive Jay?*' through the keyhole. It made me miss a phone call from Dad who, when he called back, said he'd found it very amusing that I'd been in the bath when he wanted me, just like at home. I said I'd written him a letter and he said, 'I shall look forward to that.'

I told him, 'I've been lying here thinking about it and it's definitely "*Sullla*". It's "*Sulllla* – to the infamy of his name."'

'No, it's "*Sul-la*", the accent's on the "la",' he said, ' "*Sul-la* – to the infamy of his name."'

'I think I'm right,' I said.

'I think *I'm* right,' said Dad.

'Dad,' I said, 'I think it's going to be all right. I've got a feeling it might be all right.'

Dad's voice cracked slightly. 'Do you think so, old son?' he said. 'I hope so, old son.'

This is Jay Golden, exclusively live, accepting a place at Sheffield.

'Mr Golden, it was touch and go there for a minute, wasn't it?'

'Yes.'

'Mr Golden, could you tell us what was going through your mind when you accepted you'd never be a proper writer?'

'No comment.'

'Mr Golden, do you still miss Gemma? Have you any plans to see her again?'

'No comment.'

'Mr Golden, I've heard she's snogged another man who is very tall. Have you any comment to make on this man's height?'

'I'm sorry, gentlemen, I have nothing to say.'

'Mr Golden, he's enormously tall. Almost two metres.'

'And she *has* snogged him. That has been confirmed.'

'Mr Golden, in the past you have had things to say about people's heights.'

'Gentlemen, please, I'm very busy. I'm excited to be taking up this new position. You have your interview, I have no further comment. Thank you. Goodnight.'

Acknowledgements

Thanks to my friend David Thomas for emptying the A4 cart at work so many times printing this out behind his boss's back; to my girlfriend Dinah Robinson for pretending to still laugh at bits on the forty-fifth read and for sneakily posting it to Curtis Brown behind my back. Thanks to Peter Robinson at Curtis Brown for plucking the manuscript out of the slush pile; to Sara Holloway for buying the book and for the fun she made editing it; to Susan Lamb and Anthony Keates and everyone in Orion sales and marketing for publishing and promoting it. And finally, thanks to my old man whose help, advice and kicks up the backside were painful but invaluable.